MARI

THE HONG KONG
GAMBIT

MARINE E: SBS

THE HONG KONG GAMBIT

Doug Armstrong

First published in Great Britain 1995
22 Books, Invicta House, Sir Thomas Longley Road,
Rochester, Kent

A CIP catalogue record for this book is available from the
British Library

ISBN 1 898125 45 7

10 9 8 7 6 5 4 3 2 1

Typeset by Hewer Text Composition Services, Edinburgh
Printed in Great Britain by Cox and Wyman Limited, Reading

1

All morning the limousines had been arriving, so that by midday the corridors and reception rooms of the villa complex were filled with grey-suited men speaking in hushed tones. Perched on the side of a wooded hill comfortably beyond the furthest outskirts of Beijing, the cluster of squat, red-roofed buildings had originally been built more than seventy years earlier by a local warlord. Intended for his sole use as a retreat from the bustling street life of the growing city, it had served him for barely three months before he was ousted in one of the frequent power struggles of those troubled times, beaten through the streets of the nearby village and finally beheaded in front of a crowd of cheering peasant farmers.

During much of the later war with Japan the villa had served first as an officers' mess for the Chinese Nationalist forces and then as a Japanese divisional headquarters. The infamous Kempetai, the Japanese secret police, had also made use of the welcome seclusion, holding their most resilient prisoners there for prolonged interrogation exploiting the full range of their imaginative techniques; few who had undergone such treatment lived to see the villa liberated towards the end of the war.

As he admired the spectacular view from one of the few windows that had been left uncovered by gaudy orange curtains, Yang Zulin reflected that the villa's use since 1949 by members of the ruling Communist elite had done little to enhance its beauty. The original rich furnishings had long since been plundered, replaced by cheap local products. Bamboo chairs and tables, crude little cabinets made from cherry, and deep, fluffy armchairs that had lost whatever shape they had once possessed – much like the current range of bosses themselves, he thought.

He turned sharply at the sound of a door closing at the end of the passage, but there was nothing of importance to see. Only another white-coated nurse scurrying down the hallway towards a ground-floor bathroom. Yang noticed how, as she passed each knot of people, they clamped their hands over mouth and nose, their eyes involuntarily betraying their repugnance at the stench of vomit and faeces wafting from the covered pan in her pale, thin hands.

Refusing to show his own distaste, Yang turned back to the window. Another limousine was pulling up at the front steps and he craned forward to see who had just arrived. His lips creased into a smile as he recognized a senior editor of the official party newspaper. So the news would be released after all. When the great Mao Zedong had died senior government ministers had flapped around for days before breaking the news to the waiting world. Now, it seemed, the party had learned more from the West than just capitalist chicanery. This time the news of the passing of another great statesman and leader of the Chinese nation would not be kept so long under wraps.

Growing tired of the ceaseless murmuring, Yang went on a tour of the villa. Whenever he entered a new room the occupants would look up at his approach, eyes expectant and hungry for the latest developments. When they saw him their reaction was always the same. They would quickly return to their private discussions, unwilling to meet the gaze of such a renowned member of the Security Bureau, let alone include him in their talk of the jockeying for position that would shortly be unleashed.

Noting this response, Yang couldn't help smiling to himself. People were the same the world over. Power was the only thing that mattered, wherever you lived. In his time he had had his full taste of it, so much so that he had been left with a hunger that could only be satisfied by ever more of the same. He had been lucky as well. Even though the political situation had changed and other faithful servants of the state had been put out to graze like unwanted cattle, Yang himself had manoeuvred with the greatest of skill, going from strength to strength. Under Mao he had been a man of the old school. Then, when the Gang of Four had seized control, Yang had become an anti-revisionist, yet never making the mistake of being too vociferous, but rather feeling his way forward through the political minefield with masterly skill.

The fall, trial and imprisonment of the Gang of Four had left him temporarily on the wrong side of the fence, but within weeks of Deng Xiaoping's triumphant winning of the top governmental posts, Yang had managed the impossible. By calling on his many contacts, he had slowly eased himself back into favour until now, more than a dozen years on, he was almost in a position to execute his most daring move to date.

Sick of the furtive glances, Yang made his way to one of the exits and pushed past the brace of immaculately dressed guards, out into the fresh air. It was a fine, sunny morning, with a light but bracing wind sweeping out of the north from the direction of the Great Wall at Badaling. Yang turned his face towards it, feeling its fierce, refreshing tendrils tug at his hair and buffet his skin. Closing his eyes, he imagined the towers and ramparts of the wall that had guarded the frontiers of the great empire for so many centuries. Now they were just another attraction for the thronging tourists, as unwelcome to Yang as the Mongol hordes of the Great Khan. They too threatened to destroy Chinese culture, swamping it with their own brand of barbarism. Already the illuminated signs of hamburger restaurants sprouted over the heart of Beijing like pock-marks.

Western businessmen flocked greedily to survey this wondrous new expanding market, ripe for the picking, among them the Japanese. Having physically raped the country throughout the thirties and forties, the Japanese were doing the same again, but in another guise. Now they clothed their aggression in the slogans of the market-place. It was all simply 'globalization'. But Yang Zulin was no fool. To him it was all the same. Their divisions had merely been replaced by the far more insidious and persistent international corporations which were accomplishing by economic means what their military had failed to achieve.

Gazing at the broad horizon, Yang started at a sudden shout from the depths of the villa behind him. It was followed by the sound of running feet, slamming doors and the steady rise in pitch of voices all speaking at once.

'So this is it,' he said quietly to himself. 'Now it begins.'

With a brisk step he made his way swiftly to his car, parked with the ranks of others at the side of the villa. Time was now of the essence. So was a cool nerve. But he had been waiting for precisely this occurrence to set in motion the train of events that would, if successful, move him from his place on the sidelines to centre stage. Either that or death.

Hu Fat drew back into the shadows fifty yards from the wharf, beckoning his men into cover behind him. He muttered a string of curses under his breath as he watched the police foot patrol amble slowly along the waterfront towards the tethered barges and small boats, bobbing at anchor in the murky waters of Canton harbour.

'A few more yards and the fuckers will see it,' he spat viciously at his subordinate, a wiry ex-fisherman who peered anxiously round the larger bulk of his boss.

'Perhaps not.'

'Idiot. Of course they will. I thought I told you to moor the boat behind one of the barges. If they decide to have a closer look . . .'

'We can deal with them, no problem.'

'You don't get it, do you, arsehole? I don't give a shit about the cops. But the more corpses we leave littering our trail the easier it is to follow.'

Hu Fat watched intently as the police patrol strolled ever closer to his boat. There were four of them, which could prove tricky. Although Hu Fat was confident that he could overpower them with surprise and superior numbers, he would have to think carefully about the disposal of the bodies.

The patrol was now level with the boat. A large motor-powered sailing junk, it had nothing unusual about it. Nothing except its presence in this part of the docks, reserved for either barges or sampans. The larger junks and other fishing vessels were supposed to moor further out, leaving the waterfront free for the barges to disgorge their cargoes of bricks and other building materials for onward dispatch to sites around the burgeoning city. But in order to get his contraband on board, Hu Fat had been forced to come alongside the wharf. It was far too heavy and delicate to ferry out across the turbulent night-time waters.

Frozen to the spot, he watched and waited. The policemen were now almost past the junk, having spared it scarcely a glance. But then one of them, a youngster, stopped. Hu Fat cursed again as the muffled sound of the man's voice carried across to him. Obviously a new boy fresh from the training establishment, he was questioning the others. At first they didn't seem particularly interested. One of them laughed and with a playful swipe knocked the youngster's cap to the ground. But then the eldest one smiled and stopped. Of course the rookie was right: they would be neglecting their duty if they didn't reprimand the owner of the junk. Such a man should know better than to take up valuable space on the waterfront. At first light there would be more barges queuing up to unload at the wharf. Yes, the youngster was right. A fine would have to be imposed.

Hu Fat clenched his teeth. But then, from behind him came the sound of a truck. He scowled at his subordinate.

'I thought I told you that the truck wasn't to come forward until we had got the motor started.'

The man shrugged helplessly as their carefully laid plans for the smuggling operation rapidly fell apart. Cutting through the darkness, the truck's headlights rounded the corner and shone directly on the six men huddled at the side of the warehouse.

'Come on!' Hu Fat said, marching quickly towards the policemen as if nothing was wrong.

The youngster had taken out a notebook and was scribbling down the junk's name and registration number while his three colleagues peered through the portholes, calling for the owner to come up on deck and explain himself.

'Ah! Good evening, gentlemen,' Hu Fat called as he crossed the final yards separating him from the patrol. Behind him his men followed close on his heels, keeping their knives out of sight in the folds of their jackets.

'Can I help you? This is my cousin's boat.'

The senior member of the patrol looked at the newcomer suspiciously, noting the clutch of men and the sound of the truck approaching. He didn't answer Hu Fat's question; instead a look of alarm suddenly spread across his face. Then he fumbled with the flap of his pistol holster and shouted a warning to his comrades. But it was too late. Hu Fat's men had closed in quickly and by the time the policemen reacted they were upon the patrol.

With brutal efficiency they sprang at the startled

policemen and as the truck lurched into sight its headlights caught the savage struggle in their silver glare. Before the welcoming smile had even died on his face, Hu Fat had pulled his knife from the sheath at the back of his belt and, in the same swift circular movement, swung it up into the senior officer's stomach. Pulling it out, he grabbed the man behind the head with one thick fist and yanked him forward, thrusting again and again with the short blade.

The policeman's fingers still clawed at the holster flap, but now more from reflex than any real hope of saving his own life. His eyes bulged in his face and as he opened his mouth, instead of the scream that he had intended, a torrent of blood coursed down his chin and over the drab olive tunic and dark-blue trousers.

Dropping the lifeless body to the floor, Hu Fat turned towards his next target but the business was already done. His men had worked with the speed of fishermen gutting their catch. Beside the other two bodies, the youngster writhed in his death throes. The blade that had been driven into his chest had snapped and three inches of dull, jagged steel protruded from the spreading patch of blood on his tunic.

'Finish him, Yip,' Hu Fat ordered without interest, flicking the stained notebook into the water with the toe of his canvas shoe.

The little former fisherman darted forward and straddled the young man's chest. With a deft cut he sliced through his throat, leaning out of the way of the scarlet jet that spurted from the wound.

As one of his men started to tip the bodies over the side of the wharf, Hu Fat grabbed at his coat.

'What do you think you're doing? They'll float, you idiot.'

'Do you want us to weigh them down?'

Hu Fat thought for a moment. 'No. We'll take them with us and dump them well down-river. We don't want anyone to pursue us. At least not until we've switched to the powerboat.'

When the bodies of the four dead policemen were stowed in the prow of the junk, Yip guided the truck alongside and the little party began to cross-load the merchandise. Standing to one side, Hu Fat watched the delicate operation. Used to the shuttle run between the Chinese coastal ports and the British Crown Colony of Hong Kong, he would normally have been on board by now, checking his navigation charts and warming up the motor. But tonight was special. He wanted to make sure that his men handled the goods with the utmost care. Unlike the usual smuggling runs this would not be just another cargo of stereos, televisions, drugs or firearms.

The crate was surprisingly small and looked almost fragile – not at all what he had expected. Still, that was all the better. It would be easier to cross-load on to the powerboat waiting downstream. He was following the tried-and-tested procedure for smuggling contraband into the capitalist colony. Just before the slow-moving junk left Chinese territorial waters, it would rendezvous with a large powerboat. The Royal Hong Kong Police and the British military kept a close watch on all traffic between the two countries and high-speed chases were common. But in the powerboat the Triad underworld had found a useful ally. With the latest models they could outrun anything the British had, carrying their smuggled goods into the heart of the colony, lying up during daylight hours and then returning the following night with further contraband for sale on the Chinese black market. It was a lucrative trade and as old as the British colony itself, even if the tools of the trade had evolved beyond the sampan, junk and flintlock. Nowadays, as well as powerboats, the Triads were armed with an array of modern weaponry from M16 assault rifles and Kalashnikovs to grenade launchers.

With the cargo stowed and the men on board, Hu Fat finally steered the junk away from the wharf, turning its prow out into the blackness and heading into the swirling Pearl River estuary. He glanced at his watch. Good. The scuffle with the police patrol hadn't delayed their departure. From his position at the wheel he could just make out the heap of bodies in the darkness. He decided he would give it at least an hour before they tied on the weights and tipped them overboard. If he was lucky he might even be able to attract some sharks to help him with the disposal. There weren't as many as in the old days before the industrial sites and chemical plants had sprung up, pouring their untreated waste into the broad dying river. The oyster catchers and fish farmers had mostly been driven out of business by the start of the 1990s, their stock poisoned with lead and their livelihoods ruined. Then men like Yip had been forced to find a new living. Hu Fat smiled. It was lucky for Yip that he was good with a knife.

As if reading his thoughts, Yip sauntered up to him and pointed at the bodies.

'Shall we cut them up for the sharks?'

'No. I don't want them bleeding all over my decks. We'll just ditch them.'

'What time do we rendezvous with the boat?'

'When I say so. You know the procedure.'

Hu Fat watched him as he walked back to look under the tarpaulin, checking that the crate was properly lashed down. He wasn't a bad assistant but it was a shame he hadn't got a better brain. Like Hu he'd done the trip dozens of times but he still asked stupid questions. He still hadn't figured out that the time and place of the RV changed every time for security reasons. He seemed to think it happened by chance, as if by magic. But the only magic about tonight would be the pay-off if the run was successful. And why shouldn't it be? The Triads were sending their fastest boat, with extra ones to act as decoys, added to which Hu Fat had laid down a stock of firearms that would make the People's Liberation Army green with envy, just in case the interfering British security forces came too close once they entered Hong Kong waters.

He checked his watch again and smiled. Everything was going according to plan.

Corporal Harry Leach was feeling pissed off. First he'd been saddled with some grizzly old-timer and now the fucker had gone to sleep! A night ambush was hardly the place for a passenger, but the OC had been adamant: Sergeant Cooper had to come along. Apparently he was something in the Royal Marines' Supply Branch visiting Hong Kong to inspect the new accommodation blocks on Stonecutters Island and like every rear-echelon git the world over, he would leap at any excuse for a joyride. Harry could imagine the old fart mouthing off to the boys in the storeroom back in Devon about his risky night patrol when his life had been in danger at every moment.

Harry and the other three marines had stared amazed when the old boy had turned up at the jetty, a bulging bergen over his shoulder.

'We're not going up Everest.'

'Any fool can be uncomfortable,' the old sergeant had replied. So the boys had helped him into the boat and watched him extract an enormous sleeping-bag from his pack and unroll it on the floor.

'Won't be in the way here, will I?' he had asked.

'Be my guest. I'm only the geezer in charge,' Harry had replied.

From then on things had gone from bad to worse. Although Cooper had kept out of the way at the back of the boat, he had shown an annoying interest in everything, asking a constant stream of questions. It wasn't that Harry minded the questions, but for the first time tonight they were using a new boat and so he hadn't been able to answer them all, which pissed him off no end. But on it went. What's that for? Why did you do that? Where are we going? How long will it take? What will we do when we get there?

He had kept his patience as long as he could, noticing the smirks on the lads' faces, and had heaved a huge sigh of relief when they had at last reached the ambush point and shut down the engines to lie up. To Harry's immense relief the supply sergeant had finally curled up in his sleeping-bag and announced without even a hint of shame that he was going to get some kip.

'Good bloody riddance,' Harry muttered under his breath.

Then the waiting had begun. For the first time that night Harry felt himself relaxing. Now at last he was left in peace to do the job he was paid for. He had been in Hong Kong for over a year and had been involved in anti-smuggling operations for the past six months. He loved it. Cooperating with the Royal Hong Kong Police, he and the other marine launches would stake out various areas of the rugged coastline, ready to intercept any suspicious craft. He and the boys had already taken part in several high-speed chases but had always got the worst of it. These days the Triads were using powerboats that could easily outrun the Rigid Raiders of the Royal Marines or the launches of the Marine Police. But if they encountered anything tonight it would be a different story.

For the first time Harry had command of one of the new powerboats that the Hong Kong government had invested in, in an attempt to stem the rising tide of Triad smuggling. He glanced back to the rear of the boat, where a bank of five huge, black outboard motors ran the full width of the vessel, so heavy that the boat sat arse-down in the water. But when it was gunned up to full power they could hurtle the craft through the water like a rocket.

MARPOL, the headquarters of the Marine Police, had tonight allocated him a position in a small bay off the island of Kat O Chau. From here it would be a relatively short ride out into the broad expanse of Mirs Bay, which separated the territory of Hong Kong from mainland China's coastline, a prime hunting ground for smugglers. Other police and Royal Marine craft were strung out in a wide arc around the whole eastern side of the colony. With limited numbers of craft available to the security forces, the deployment was changed every night, switching from area to area in an attempt to keep the smugglers guessing.

Harry eased back in his seat and proudly cast his eyes over the bank of controls in front of him. At his side, Josh Higgs listened into his radio headphones for any message from MARPOL. The water around them was as calm as a millpond, dark and warm. Behind him and on each side Harry could see the black humps of the island's hills, sweeping around, encircling and dwarfing the arrow-shaped boat, whose prow pointed east out of the ambush position into Mirs Bay.

'I'm surprised you can hear anything with that old bugger snoring,' Harry said, stabbing a thumb at the curled figure of the sergeant.

'Ssh.'

'Got something?'

'There's some chatter on the net. They're tracking a boat that's just rounding Sai Kung. It seems to be heading this way.'

Harry sat forward and shaded the beam of his pencil torch as he examined a chart. The northern coast of the rugged Sai Kung peninsula was a favourite drop-off point for smugglers where they would rendezvous with road transport in one of the numerous sheltered bays and cross-load their cargo.

'That's us!' Josh said excitedly, spinning round to shake the others awake. 'They're calling us in.'

'Leave grandad,' Harry snapped. 'He'll probably kip through the whole thing.'

But the moment the five motors coughed and roared

into life, the curled sleeping-bag erupted into spasms of life as its occupant tried to break free.

'What's going on?'

'Hang on, Sarge,' Harry called above the noise of the engines, and opening the throttle, grinned at his mates as the struggling sleeping-bag was sent tumbling to the very back of the boat.

'Let's get at them.'

Behind the front seats the other two marines had already snatched up their SA80 rifles, looping the slings around their wrists to secure them for the rough ride ahead. In helmets and life-jackets, they well knew the perils of a high-speed pursuit.

The moon had now risen and as the boat shot out into the open waters a broad silver wake peeled open behind it.

'Strap yourselves in!' Harry shouted, tightening his own seat belt and fastening his goggles.

Josh leaned his mouth close to shout. 'The police have been seen. They're in pursuit. They say we're to take up the chase north of Port Island.

'Roger to that.'

After easing the boat round, Harry sped towards the designated intercept point. The controls handled beautifully, responding to the lightest touch. When the solitary mass of Port Island reared out of the darkness, he closed the throttle and slowed the boat to an idle. As it drifted through the still waters, the marine behind him scanned the horizon with an image-intensifier night-sight.

'Come on, come on,' Harry mouthed. But he didn't have more than thirty seconds to wait. The marine clapped a hand on his shoulder and gave him the bearing to the suspect vessel.

'There she blows. Jesus, look at her move!'

Taking a quick look through the night-sight, Harry saw the smugglers' boat through the sight's greenish glow.

'Have I got a surprise for you,' he said, and settling back into his seat, slowly opened the throttle. Responding immediately, the powerboat lurched forward. Josh gave a loud whoop. 'Bit different from the Gemini.'

The suspect craft was a good kilometre away. Lining up on his quarry, Harry gripped the throttle firmly.

'Let's see what this baby can do.'

As he opened wide the throttle he felt as if a fist was pushing him back into his seat.

'I reckon we just might catch the buggers tonight!' he shouted over his shoulder. 'How's our passenger? Been sick yet?'

'Not on your life, laddie,' a voice rasped in his ear. 'I was born on the fucking water.'

Harry looked round in surprise and saw Cooper's grinning face mere inches away.

As soon as the police launch was spotted Hu Fat himself took the controls of the powerboat. The transfer from the junk had gone smoothly. The bodies of the police patrol had been dumped in the Pearl estuary and thereafter the voyage had gone smoothly. At least until they rounded Hong Kong island and entered Mirs Bay, leaving the relative safety of Chinese territorial waters.

Having ventured out from behind one of the

numerous smaller islands, the police launch had challenged them with a loudhailer. But, ignoring the order to stop and be boarded, Hu Fat had opened the throttle and hooted with laughter as they left the sluggish police vessel standing.

'They don't learn, do they?' he had shrieked across to Yip above the noise of the powerful outboard motors.

Streaking alongside the rugged fringes of the Sai Kung peninsula, where the mountains tumbled down into the foaming sea, he steered the boat north and then gently eased her a little westwards intending to make for the rendezvous on the Tolo peninsula, another vast area of wild and largely uninhabited land.

He was just congratulating himself on another successful infiltration when Yip grasped his arm and pointed to the left, shouting something that Hu Fat couldn't hear. At first he saw nothing, but then, as he searched the horizon, he managed to pick out the object that the fisherman's sharper eyes had detected.

'What is it?'

Yip squinted hard at the object and then placed his mouth close to Hu Fat. 'Speedboat.'

Hu Fat grinned. 'If it's a marine Rigid Raider they might as well not bother.'

But Yip wasn't smiling. Instead he made his way to the rear of the boat and when Hu Fat next turned round he saw Yip and the other members of the gang checking their firearms. Yip was pointing out the target to his comrades, two of whom held Type 56-1 automatic assault rifles, the Chinese variant of the Soviet Kalashnikov AK47 and incorporating a folding stock and spike bayonet. After locking the stocks into place, they crouched down on the port side and steadied themselves ready to fire. Without thinking Hu Fat reached to his waistband and checked his pistol, a Chinese 9mm Type 59.

Glancing again at the approaching vessel, he noticed that it was gaining on them rapidly. It seemed that the British security forces had finally closed the technology gap. But so what? They were unlikely to be carrying comparable fire-power and if it was a fight they wanted, Hu Fat would bloody well give them one.

He closed the throttle a touch and allowed the distance between the two boats to narrow but without making it obvious that he was luring his pursuers into a trap. Waiting until the marines' powerboat had closed to within three hundred metres, Hu Fat suddenly swung his own vessel side on to give them a full broadside. Immediately the Triad soldiers in the back opened up, their weapons on automatic. Those without assault rifles manhandled a Type 67 light machine-gun into position, snapped on a seventy-five-round drum maga- zine and fired a long, continuous burst of 7.62mm rounds at the other powerboat.

Hu Fat watched the thin jets of tracer rounds snake towards the marines and saw their boat veer to the left in an attempt to escape the incoming fire. But no sooner had they done so than the Triad soldiers had corrected their aim, forcing their pursuers to swing right round in a complete arc and withdraw further out of range. Grinning with satisfaction, Hu Fat opened the throttle again and headed once more for the protection of Tolo's narrow bays and inlets.

But he had gone barely half a kilometre when something snapped past his head with a familiar crack.

'They're returning fire!' Yip screamed, ordering his men to shoot back. Within seconds a full-scale fire-fight had developed. Hu Fat noted that the marines were using automatic weapons as well, probably the new British SA80. He knew that it had a far superior sight to the Chinese Type 56-1s and that they were probably also equipped with night viewing devices.

'Damn them,' he growled. He had only expected to encounter police launches or at worst British marines in their usual range of much slower boats. Instead he was locked in a chase with a gang of men in a powerboat equal to his own and with fire-power to match. Normally in a situation like this he would have beached his craft and taken to his heels, accepting the loss of his boat and merchandise as an unavoidable write-off. But tonight of all nights he could not afford to be caught. There was too much at stake.

However, a moment later the decision was made for him. An accurate stream of incoming fire raked across his stern, the bullets creeping ever closer through the foaming water until they found their target. After rupturing the fuel tanks with multiple punctures, the bullets exploded across the deck, splintering the woodwork and cutting down one of the men.

Yip darted to the rear of the boat, checked the damage and then crawled forward to shout in Hu Fat's ear. 'It's no good. We're losing all our fuel. There's no way we'll make the RV and if we lose power out here they'll board us and take us prisoner.'

Hu Fat knew what that would mean. The penalty for smuggling was hardly severe, but that was for audio equipment and televisions. He glanced at the securely tied tarpaulin concealing the crate. No. There was no way he was going to be captured with that.

Searching the coastline for an inlet, he located the dark mouth of a sandy bay and swung the craft round to head straight for it.

'Hang on tight. I'm going in!'

In the back of the boat the wounded man rolled in agony. Yip jumped to his side and checked his wounds. He looked up and met Hu Fat's eyes. They couldn't leave anyone to fall into police hands. The information they might give away would be too harmful. But nor could they make good their escape overland with a casualty. The police would undoubtedly put in cut-offs as well as landing behind them and following up on foot. Whereas healthy men, especially Triad soldiers, could have every chance of slipping through even the tightest cordon in the dark jungle and waste land of Tolo, a casualty was another matter.

Yip glanced quickly at the rest of the men. All of them were busy pouring fire at the pursuing powerboat and no one had seen his quick inspection of the wounded man. Hu Fat nodded once and then turned back to his controls. There were only seconds before impact.

With one more quick check to make sure the others weren't watching, Yip drew his knife, felt for the hollow between the man's collar bone and shoulder muscle where the artery led directly into the neck and brain, positioned his point carefully over the spot and thrust sharply down.

2

The moment Corporal Harry Leach saw the first tracer rounds weaving around his boat and heard the familiar snapping in the air, he spun the wheel hard and took violent evasive action.

'Hold on tight, lads!' he shouted over his shoulder.

Huddling low in the bottom of the boat, Josh Higgs, Cooper and the other two marines gripped anything they could for balance as the powerboat twisted and turned, the air inches above it alive with high-velocity bullets.

'Just like the breakfast cereal, isn't it?' the old sergeant said, grinning at Josh.

'Eh?'

'Snap, crackle, pop.'

Josh looked at the happy face of the old soldier, who seemed to be enjoying their engagement. 'What did you say your name was?'

'Sergeant Cooper to you, lad.'

Josh frowned. 'I thought you were in the Supply Branch?'

The sergeant smiled. 'Got any hardware with you?'

'Just the SA80s,' one of the marines answered.

'Then why the fuck aren't you giving them back some of their own?'

'Rules of engagement, Sarge.'

'Fuck that. Get those butts in your shoulders.'

As the marines fired an opening burst, Harry spun round. 'Who said you could fire back?'

'It's OK, lad. I'll take responsibility. Trust me,' Cooper shouted.

Harry scowled at him. 'Look, I'm in charge here. When you're back in your stores counting blankets you can do what you like.'

'Skip it, lad. I know the rules of engagement better than I know my own granny. We're in a life-threatening situation, so fuck the niceties and put some lead down.'

Before Harry could answer, the Chinese LMG opened up, forcing him to swerve again, a line of scarlet tracer narrowly missing the side of the boat. By now the marines, let off the leash by Cooper, were pouring a deadly accurate fire towards the Chinese powerboat. Tracking the target through one of the night-sights, the sergeant shouted out target indications to the two firers, correcting their aim and bringing their fire to bear directly on the speeding powerboat.

'Bull's-eye!' he suddenly yelled as he detected the impact of a string of rounds lacing the rear of the boat. 'That might just do the trick.'

Sure enough, moments later they watched as the Chinese vessel veered towards the distant shore, searching for the shelter of a bay. Following hard on their heels, Harry closed the distance once again, refusing to risk losing them in the narrowing waterways.

'They're going to beach her and leg it,' he shouted.

'Can you ram them?' Cooper replied.

'Are you daft? It's taken bloody years to get hold of this boat. I'm not going to crash it now. Not for a load of TVs and stereos.'

'Then get as close as you can. We'll take them as soon as they hit the beach.'

Harry turned to the signaller. 'Get on the blower and whistle up a cordon. Where's the police launch?'

Higgs spoke rapidly into his throat mike, listening for the response. 'A good ten minutes behind us. They're coming at best speed. They've already got some backup on land but there aren't any roads near here. By the time they've walked across country the smugglers will be long gone.'

The sergeant thought for a moment. 'It's up to us then, isn't it?'

He moved up beside Harry as the two boats skimmed across the calm surface of the sheltered water. 'When we see where they go ashore, get us on to the beach a hundred metres to one side of them. With luck we might be able to keep them pinned down until the police launch catches up and prevent them from scarpering into the jungle.'

Harry nodded. 'OK. The MARPOL launch has got a mounted heavy machine-gun. That should shut them up.'

In the silver moonlight the smugglers' vessel shone against the backdrop of dark hillsides, its foaming wake making concealment impossible. At last it slowed, swung sideways for a final volley of automatic fire at the marines, then turned towards the shore and drove into the sandy beach. Even above the noise of the firing Harry and Cooper could hear the grating and thud of the boat coming to a violent halt. Almost immediately they saw tiny figures darting over the side and sprinting up the sand and shingle.

'Go, go, go!' the sergeant screamed.

Harry opened the throttle, swung the boat towards a sandy spit of land to one flank of the smugglers and drove it forward, cutting the power at the last moment, so that the boat glided in gently until it grounded on the shore and came to rest. Before it had stopped, the marines were over the side and tearing up the beach. Bullets cracked in the air around them and kicked up the sand at their feet.

Cooper pointed to a line of scrub thirty metres from the water's edge. 'Over there. Move!'

The marines dived into cover and hunted for their targets. Planting himself between the two SA80s, the sergeant scanned the darkness through his night-sight.

'What I'd give for a fucking weapon,' he cursed.

Harry and Josh had hit the ground a few metres away, Josh hugging his precious radio and sending in a contact report to headquarters.

'Bit of a change from blanket stacking, eh?' Harry called across.

'Shut it,' Cooper snarled. He scanned the far end of the beach, waiting for the tell-tale muzzle flash of an assault rifle. But everything had suddenly gone quiet. A hundred metres away they could make out the silhouette of the smugglers' powerboat, but of the men themselves there was no sign.

'Sod it,' Cooper muttered. 'They've bugged out.'

'Like shit off a shovel,' Harry added. 'Well, Sarge? Any more bright ideas?'

The older man swept the hillside until he caught

some movement. 'Got them. Where the hell's that police launch?'

'Unless we do something we'll lose them,' one of the marines piped up, fingering his SA80 and eager to get after the smugglers.

'OK. Here's what we do,' Cooper said after a moment. 'We'll move inland, keeping parallel to them. Try to get behind them and pin them down again.' He turned to face the marines. 'But we're not going to get involved in a close quarter battle. We don't have the fire-power and as the Corp said, it's not fucking worth it for a stack of CD players.'

'What about the boat?'

'Leave it,' Harry answered. 'The police'll be at the mouth of the bay by now. The smugglers won't be doubling back or anything fancy like that. I've been doing this for months. They'll head for the bright lights and lose themselves downtown.'

Keeping a reasonable distance between each man, the marine patrol moved off. Harry took the point with Cooper immediately behind him, stopping every hundred metres to scan the adjacent hillside for the smugglers and ensuring they were not going to clash. Josh and the other two marines brought up the rear. Looking back, Cooper saw the lights of the police launch entering the bay.

'Here comes the cavalry. Have you told them what we're doing?'

'Course I bloody have,' Josh snapped. 'They said they'd passed it on to MARPOL.'

The launch was steaming towards land, but forced by its larger size to keep further out and send in a landing party by inflatable to take possession of the smugglers' boat. A powerful searchlight was combing the shoreline and hung on each boat in turn before sweeping the hillside in a vain search for the smugglers.

'Stupid buggers,' Cooper rasped. 'They'll ruin our night vision. Don't look at the light, lads. They haven't a hope in hell of finding them like that anyway.'

The marines were now climbing steeply, pushing their way through clumps of undergrowth and scrambling over boulders. The night was warm and humid and soon all of them were soaked with sweat. Calling a halt, Cooper used his night-sight to try to locate the smugglers.

'Have we lost them?' Harry asked.

'Temporarily mislaid.'

Harry snorted. 'Nice work, Sarge.'

'Don't worry, lad. We'll pick them up again on the other side of this ridge. The ground opens out and they won't have the benefit of this bloody cover to hide in. They'll have to cross a plain and they'll stick out like a dog's bollocks.'

'How do you know so much about Tolo?' Josh asked. 'I thought you were just out on a visit?'

'That doesn't mean I haven't been here before.'

Cooper took out a compass and got a fix on the beach behind them so that they would be able to find their way back later. Then, having taken another bearing on the prominent hilltop to their front, he led the way upwards, stopping every hundred metres to check the bearing and ensure they were still on course.

The higher they went, the harder the going became. The hill seemed to get ever steeper as they neared the summit, until by the time they were approaching the crest they were almost crawling upwards on their hands and knees.

'Wish I'd brought my crampons,' Josh muttered.

'Don't worry,' Cooper said, not even out of breath. 'Once we're over the top it's all downhill.'

Sure enough, a moment later they crested the ridge and looked down on a bare, moonlit plain stretching into the distance. Far away to the west they could see the orange glow from the first of the outlying urban areas that eventually ended up in the bustle of Kowloon.

'That's where they'll be headed,' Harry said. He glanced across at the sergeant and had to admit that he was impressed with the old blanket stacker. What the hell was a guy like that doing in the Supply Branch? In his younger days he had probably been quite good. In fact he wasn't bad now, Harry thought, smiling to himself.

Cooper got to his feet and set off down the far slope. 'Come on,' he said.

When they had descended from the exposed crest he stopped and checked the lie of the land with the sight. The moon was now high in the sky and the whole landscape was bathed in its silver glow. With the further amplification of the night-sight, Cooper had no trouble in locating the small knot of figures several hundred metres to their right.

'Got them. We're just about level with them now. If we keep on this bearing we'll overtake them and cut them off before they reach the main road on the other side of the next range of hills. We'll take them once they've crossed the valley and just as they start to climb.'

'Good thinking,' Harry said. 'They won't be expecting a follow-up. If they think they've got away with it we might catch them off guard.'

Taking over the lead, Harry set a ferocious pace. Now that they had located the group of smugglers and knew that there was no immediate risk of a clash, he judged that they could afford to trade security for speed. It was essential that they select a good ambush position where they could hit the smugglers and hold them pinned down until the police backup arrived. It was common for smugglers to be armed nowadays, but such a weight of automatic fire-power was unusual to say the least. They were obviously a hardened bunch from one of the main Triad gangs and they couldn't be allowed to get away.

By the time the marines had reached the level plain the thicker clumps of undergrowth had disappeared and the going was easier. Jogging through the shin-high grass, they kept sufficiently close not to lose touch with each other but not so tight that a burst of fire could catch more than one at a time should the smugglers have swung towards them.

Finally, with everyone in the group now panting hard and soaked to the skin, Harry stopped and gathered the men around him.

'What about here, Sarge?'

Cooper looked around at the clearing. All the main tracks crossing the plain seemed to converge at this point, forming a rough junction surrounded by slopes that rose gently away towards the last range of hills before the road and the escape route to the built-up areas.

'Looks fine to me,' he answered, noting the possible

fire positions where the smugglers might dive for cover. 'Where do you want everyone?'

'It's up to me, is it?'

'Your patrol. I wouldn't want to step on your toes. I'm just a blanket stacker, remember?'

'Give me a break.'

Harry studied the ground and decided to split the group in two.

'I'll keep Josh and the radio with me up there. You, Ed and Vince go over to the left, about thirty metres. That'll give us two fire groups each with two SA80s. How's your ammo, lads?'

Each marine did a quick check on his magazines and pouches.

'Not much.'

'Two and a half mags.'

'Same here.'

Cooper looked helplessly at his bare hands. 'I suppose if the going gets rough I can always throw a few insults.'

Harry chuckled. 'Just keep an eye on them and see that no one slinks away.'

After redistributing the ammunition so that all the SA80s had the same amount, Harry sent the men to their positions. Cooper led the way up a slope, hunting until he had found the right spot and then put his two men in position. Across to the flank he caught a last brief glimpse of Harry and Josh before they themselves dropped into cover and were lost from view. Settling down to wait, he checked his watch. Assuming they had chosen correctly and that the smugglers were channelled this way by the lie of the land, he estimated that they wouldn't have more than a few minutes to wait. He was confident that they had overtaken them but they couldn't be far behind. He smiled ruefully to himself. His trip this evening with the marine ambush party was turning out to be anything but routine.

Once on the beach, Hu Fat had shouted orders at his men to lay down a withering fire on the pursuing boat. He had seen it grounding itself off to the side a hundred metres away and realized what they were up to. As soon as he had noted how they had returned to the chase after being fired at rather than backing off and waiting for support, he had understood that they would be British marine commandos instead of police. He knew that he was up against trained professional soldiers and cursed his bad luck. Their use of a powerboat was an unfortunate first as well. All in all the events of the night had put him in an evil temper.

Struggling to control his rage and clear his head for the cool reasoning that they would need to extricate themselves from this contact, Hu Fat guessed that the commandos would not have the fire-power or the numbers to close in for a close quarter skirmish. But if they thought that he was just going to sit there and wait for the police to arrive with their heavy machine-guns they'd got another think coming.

Using the LMG and the Type 56-1 assault rifles, his men raked the far side of the beach with fire, watching with satisfaction as the marines tumbled into cover and hugged the ground. Hu Fat was impressed that they managed to return fire so quickly, but nevertheless his tactic had done its work. By the time the marines had got the range, Hu Fat and his men were into the undergrowth and sprinting for their lives.

They ran for a good three hundred metres until Hu Fat was happy that they were not being followed, and then he closed them up, checked that they all knew the routine and set off at a brisk walk. He realized that there would soon be a police cordon on the north-south road that cut off the Tolo peninsula and separated it from the rest of the colony, but he was confident that they would be able to find some point at which they could slip across it under cover of darkness. The neck of the peninsula was almost six kilometres wide and there was no way the police would be able to cover all of it.

Of course the police would almost certainly use tracker dogs, but Hu Fat had dealt with them before. In a group as large as this it would be impossible to shake them off. For a single man there were always techniques, especially in the early hours and when there was a heavy dew, but the men with him tonight would leave a trail that even an inexperienced dog and handler could track. However, there were more ways of dealing with them than simply evading them.

But for now Hu Fat's main concern was the party of commandos. What would they do when they realized that he and his men had escaped off the beach? The first thing would be a report over the radio to the police launch to guide it into the landing point. Then they would ensure that the cordon knew the approximate direction that the smugglers had taken. But after that? Would they just sit on the beach and wait for help to arrive? Or would they attempt something more heroic, even foolhardy?

As he marched along, leaning into the rising slope and steadying his breath to cope with the climb, Hu Fat remembered the engagement out in Mirs Bay. The British commandos hadn't backed off then so why should they do so now? What would he do in their place?

Thinking himself into the position of the British commander, he ran through the possibilities. He had always had a powerful imagination. It had kept him alive in more than a score of battles. He had risen to become a master of gang warfare, which, when it came down to it, was much the same as any other kind of warfare. Cunning against cunning. Striking at the right moment against the right spot and with maximum available force. It was essential to keep a cool head and it was essential to maintain an aggressive martial spirit at all times. He had made it his one aim in life to be the best in the business and after some twenty years he was nearing his goal.

Of course the commandos wouldn't sit meekly on the beach building sandcastles until help arrived. Their macho male pride would get in the way and cloud their judgement. There was no earthly reason why they should risk their lives but Hu Fat knew that they would. They would probably all be young men in the prime of their strength, virility and physical powers. But that would be the very focal point of their greatest weakness. Even now their bodies would be pumping with adrenalin and the thrill of the chase. Yes, they would follow up. They would probably use their superior fitness to streak ahead. He had often watched the British soldiers and marines out on their runs in various parts of the colony, puffing and panting, enjoying the hard physical effort and sneering at the Chinese locals as if they were inferior human specimens. OK then. He would play it their way.

Once Hu Fat and the others had cleared the crest and dodged the probing searchlight beam from the police launch that now sat in the calm bay far below them, he led the way quickly down to the plain and started across it, taking care to remain in the open instead of seeking the cover that existed here and there. He calculated that the security forces would have night-vision equipment. So let them use it. It would further enhance their false sense of their own superiority.

However, as soon as he saw the first of the slopes on the far side of the valley appearing in the moonlight he called a halt and gathered his men around him.

'OK, boys. Here's what we're going to do.'

As the minutes ticked by, Cooper started to grow uneasy. Could they have miscalculated the time and distance? Had they simply chosen the wrong spot for the ambush? He imagined the smugglers slipping quietly up the hillside at that very moment in some other area.

He was about to risk shifting the position when he heard a shuffling and rustling down on the track junction below him.

'Here come the fuckers,' whispered Vince, tightening the butt of his SA80 into his shoulder and easing off the safety-catch.

'Should we issue a challenge first, Sarge?'

'Fuck that,' Cooper replied quietly. 'We're past that stage.'

'Look!' Ed hissed.

A head suddenly poked out of some bushes bordering the track junction, followed a moment later by the shoulders and then the whole body of one of the smugglers.

'Wait till the whole lot of them are in the clearing,' Cooper cautioned.

'What if the Corp fires first?'

'Don't worry about him. He's all right, your Corp.' Vince grinned. 'He's one of the best.'

'He'd better be. I didn't come on this bloody jaunt for nothing.'

Vince looked at the sergeant but before he could ask him what he meant the far side of the hill erupted with fire.

'Over there!' Cooper screamed, swivelling on his stomach to face the new threat. 'The fuckers have outflanked us!'

'Jesus Christ!'

Bullets tore into the earth all around the little party as the full weight of fire from the smugglers' weapons was brought to bear.

'Where the hell did they come from?' Vince shouted above the noise, jerking himself round and blazing off a return burst of fire. 'Do you think it's the police?'

Cooper hugged the ground. 'Not unless the Hong Kong police have been re-equipped with Chinese army weapons.'

'I'll take your word for it,' Ed called across, before firing off another burst from his SA80.

Cooper raised his head and looked back at the

clearing below. The smuggler who had first come out of the undergrowth was nowhere to be seen. Nice one, he thought. A fucking decoy and I fell for it hook, line and sinker. You arsehole, Cooper. It's time you hung up your boots and retired.

But there was no time to dwell on his error. The enemy fire had shifted and now there were shouts coming from just above Harry's position. Moments before the contact a bank of dense cloud had swept across the moon as the fringes of a mounting storm edged towards the colony from far out in the South China Sea. Robbed of the moonlight, Cooper had found it increasingly difficult to see without the night-sight, but he knew that if he depended on the device too much he would be temporarily blinded every time he put it down; each time it took a good five minutes to regain the night vision of his own eyes. Using it had a similar effect to staring directly into the sun except that the afterglow left by the device was a lucid green.

'What's happened to Josh and the Corp?' Ed shouted, swinging the muzzle of his SA80 in the direction of the smugglers' shouts.

'Don't shoot!' the sergeant ordered, pushing the muzzle down. 'We'll have a blue on blue. The fuckers have got in among us. They must be working their way round.'

An ear-splitting scream shocked the night, followed by a prolonged burst of fire. Tracer bullets were criss-crossing close above their heads and then Ed was hit.

'Ed's down!' Vince shouted.

'Where?'

'In the thigh.'

Cooper wriggled across and fumbled in the dark for Ed's own field-dressing in the top pocket of his combat shirt.

'Here, put this on him,' he said to Vince. 'And give me his rifle and mags.'

Taking the SA80, the sergeant checked the mag and stuffed the spare one in the pocket of his smock.

'I'm going to try and get higher. See if I can sort out this mess. You stay here and keep your heads down.'

'What about the other two?'

'Let me worry about them. From now on only fire if you clearly identify a target as the enemy. I don't want to get shot up the arse by one of my own blokes.'

Scanning to left and right, Cooper crawled away once he was satisfied that the immediate area was clear. The concentration of fire had moved away and from the sound of it he guessed that Harry and Josh had been driven out of their position and were now involved in some kind of running fight. They would have known not to come in his direction because of the risk of a blue on blue. Somehow Cooper had to locate them and see if there was anything he could do to help. The smugglers had obviously pinpointed their locations before opening fire. First they had hosed down his own group, and then they had moved round the top and come down hard on Harry and Josh.

OK, you buggers, he thought. If that's the way you want it. Let's show you what a Royal Marine can do when he gets seriously pissed off.

Moving on his stomach, he leopard-crawled until he reckoned he was in the clear. Then, rising from the ground, he darted away at a crouch, zigzagging to throw off the aim of anyone who might take a bead on him. After about fifty metres he dropped to his knees and listened. The sounds of firing had completely ceased, and the night was as still as if nothing had happened. He took out his scope and scanned the darkness. Nothing.

When his night vision had returned he rose again, and moving very slowly began to patrol forward, heading for the top of the last ridge before the descent to the road. He had barely gone twenty metres when his foot hit something and he stooped to find the body of Josh Higgs, the signaller.

The moment he saw the accuracy of the fire on to the first party of marines, Hu Fat led two of his men further round until they were exactly above the second party. It hadn't been difficult to locate all the enemy. They had done exactly what he had expected them to. They had assumed they were dealing with an ignorant bunch of Chinese thugs and had chosen the most obvious ambush position. Hu Fat had exploited their false assumption by putting one of his men at the track junction. It had worked brilliantly. Then, with half of the force pinned down, he had tackled the second bunch. But this time he decided to teach them a proper lesson. They should learn a little respect for the Triads.

He had crawled as close as he could and had only opened fire when they had been heard by the marines. He had pinpointed them by the hiss from their radio and judged that there were only two of them. The fire of his men was so accurate that the marines had been forced to break from cover and run for their lives.

They had gone ten metres and then split in opposite directions. Hu Fat's men had been about to do the same and divide in order to follow both of the British marines but he had stopped them just in time.

'No. We only need to get one of them to teach them respect.'

After choosing one at random, they tracked him stealthily across the hillside. The sudden cloud worked to their advantage and as they closed on their fleeing victim they got so close they could hear his laboured breathing. He was obviously weighed down with something. Finally they caught him. The marine was trying to wriggle out of the shoulder straps of a cumbersome radio set and as they rushed him he tried to make a grab for his rifle that he had stupidly laid on the ground. But they got to him first.

With a swift front kick Hu Fat sent the man sprawling to the floor, the weapon flying uselessly out of reach. Clamping a hand over his mouth to prevent any scream for help, Yip raised the man's head to face Hu Fat. Yip looked expectantly at his boss, awaiting the go-ahead. But instead of giving him the nod, Hu Fat drew his own knife and closed in.

Feeling the body, Cooper recoiled in horror when he got to the face. Until then he had been unable to detect any wound. When his hands gently touched the skin of the face he realized why. Josh Higgs had been stabbed through both eyes.

It was another hour before Cooper located Harry, narrowly avoiding shooting him in the surprise contact. After breaking the news about Josh he led him back to the body, where they waited until the police landing party arrived. A helicopter was called in to evacuate Ed to the British Military Hospital in Kowloon. The signaller's body was sent with him while the police cordoned off the area and requested a forensic team and a SOCO, a scenes of crime officer. The search for the murderers was taken up by tracker dogs and heavily armed police officers, and when they had done everything they could to help, the three marines made their way back over the hills to the beach and their waiting boat.

They walked in silence, each absorbed by their own thoughts. Vince walked at the back, muttering, 'Bastards. The fucking bastards.' Harry said nothing.

Alone in front, Cooper ran through the events of the chase in his mind. How had he got everything so wrong? How had he misjudged the enemy so badly? Even though he knew that any such ambush operation was fraught with danger, he couldn't help blaming himself for the mess. But who the devil were these men that they had come up against? He had committed the most cardinal of errors. He had underestimated the enemy.

When they reached the beach the news had obviously preceded them. Several police officers from the launch were standing around the marines' powerboat and offered their sympathies when the commandos arrived.

'I can't understand it,' one of them said. 'I've been in the force for years and I've never met any gang with this sort of fire-power.'

The marines were just preparing to start their motors and set off on the return trip to Stonecutters

Island when a police inspector ran across to them from the smugglers' boat.

'One minute. Anyone here know anything about bombs?'

Cooper and Harry looked at each other.

'I do,' the sergeant replied. 'What of it?'

'Can you come and have a look at this?' the inspector asked. 'We've got a specialist bomb-disposal expert coming in by heli but I thought one of you might recognize it before you go.'

With a shrug Cooper jumped out of the boat and followed the inspector back across the sand. I wouldn't be surprised if the smugglers had booby-trapped their boat before leaving it, he thought. If they were professional enough to know how to handle LMGs and anti-ambush tactics it would hardly be surprising if they knew how to knock up a quick improvised explosive device or grenade necklace.

But nothing prepared him for what he saw when he carefully peered over the side of the Chinese powerboat. He froze and slowly waved the police-men away.

'Better get back, gents.'

'What is it?'

One of the policemen who had been first on the scene had done a cursory search of the boat, ripping aside the tarpaulin expecting to see the usual consign-ment of boxed TVs, and audio and video equipment. Puzzled to find only a single large crate, he had used his lock-knife to ease out the nails and remove the lid.

Cooper leaned as far forward as he could without putting any pressure on the side of the boat.

'Anyone got a light?'

One of the policemen handed Cooper a right-angle torch. He flicked it on and swept the narrow beam back and forth until he found what he was looking for.

'Well I'll be buggered,' he stammered, hardly able to believe his eyes.

'What is it, Sarge? Should I move everyone into cover behind the rocks?' Harry asked.

Cooper chuckled. 'You could all take cover in the Blue Tits bar in Wanchai and you'd still be fucked.'

He switched off the light. 'Game's over, lad,' he said seriously. 'I wasn't telling the truth when I said I was from Supply Branch. I'm SBS. And this, unless I've made two fuck-ups in one night, is a nuclear warhead.'

3

Leaning back in his hard bus seat, Matt Harbin screwed up a fistful of cuff and wiped a hole in the mist-covered window. He needn't have bothered. Outside all he could see was the same unending pine forest that they had been driving through since leaving the last village some four hours ago. But it had started even earlier than that, at least another few hours before they had juddered to a halt for lunch in the tiny settlement of Chelyagorsk. A couple of locals had peered suspiciously from their miserable dwellings but had withdrawn the moment they had seen the RVSN uniforms of the guides. Old habits die hard, Matt thought.

Remembering lunch, he reached under his seat and pulled out his cardboard lunch box to see if there was anything left. The curled ends of a cheese sandwich reared forlornly towards him, while next to it a badly bruised apple and half a biscuit were equally uninviting. Matt sighed and closed the box. The Soviet Strategic Rocket Forces might once have been the country's most elite force but they sure as hell didn't march on their stomachs.

Both in front and behind, other members of the monitoring team were smoking heavily, their cigarettes fogging the already stale air.

42

'Hey, Pierre. If you want to kill yourself why don't you just blow your fucking brains out?' Matt said, poking the Belgian major in the back of the head.

Pierre Laval turned round, grinning from ear to ear. 'And deprive the ladies of my winning smile? Did you know that I've been likened to Maurice Chevalier?'

'Yeah, and Roddy the Rat with teeth as yellow as those.'

Pierre threw back his head and laughed. 'Are all Royal Marine officers as charming as you, Matt?'

'Only when they're being buggered around on school outings like this.'

'You mean you're not enjoying the break from slitting throats or whatever it is you get up to?'

'Sure I am,' Matt chuckled. 'There's nothing like a bit of cooperation with our European allies to make me thank God for the English Channel.'

'Stop, you're hurting my feelings. And Klaus here will probably use it as an excuse for starting another world war, won't you, Klaus?'

Klaus Kessner smiled sheepishly. 'Yes, Matt, stop it. You know how weepy I get whenever I visit Russia. It makes me very nostalgic.'

'That's what I like,' Matt said. 'An unrepentant conqueror.'

Matt stood up and yanked open one of the windows, provoking howls of protest as a torrent of icy air rushed the length of the bus. Pierre huddled deeper into his enormous parka.

'And this is summer. God, what a country!'

From the front of the bus the escorting Russian officer announced that they would soon be arriving at their destination and as the fresh air slowly cleared the windows, Matt saw a side road appear out of the green mass of pines and watched as the bus veered on to it and drove up to the first of a series of wire fences and guard posts. The layout of the site appeared similar to those of all the others he had visited over the last two weeks, witnessing and verifying the decommissioning and destruction of nuclear missiles and their associated warheads. It was all part of the last round of arms reduction talks – only now that the new Russia was bent on acquiring Western financial aid, the whole programme had been speeded up.

It never ceased to amaze Matt how quickly the Cold War had come to an end. One moment he was training in the Commando Brigade for operations in Arctic Norway on NATO's inhospitable northern flank and the next he was watching TV news footage of the Berlin Wall being torn down. The pace of change had been little short of incredible. However, the need for vigilance was perhaps now even greater than before. Whereas previously there had been a comfortable stalemate between the two superpowers and their related power blocks, now, with all the pieces of the jigsaw shifting, the number of possible friction points had multiplied.

In the wake of the decommissioning of huge chunks of the old USSR's nuclear arsenal a profusion of missiles and warheads now criss-crossed the country. There was ample opportunity for fraud. Or worse.

One of the great fears that had been mentioned at Matt's Intelligence briefing prior to his secondment to the NATO monitoring team was the possibility not so much of the Russians reneging on their commitments to dismantle missiles, but of the emerging Russian mafia getting hold of weapons-grade plutonium for sale to certain Third World governments. Shipments of plutonium had already been intercepted by the German police and there were rumours that a vibrant market in the stuff was springing up.

Matt wondered what the hell he was supposed to do about it. A few months ago he had been in command of one of the Royal Marines' Special Boat Sections. He had done a double take on receiving news of his attachment to NATO headquarters. His boss had seemed to think it would be a good career move for him and had volunteered him for the job.

'What's wrong with a cabby round Mother Russia?' the boss had said. 'Enjoy the break before you have to get down to some real work in the Ministry of Defence.'

Matt sighed. He had apparently reached the age when active soldiering starts to give way to a succession of dull desk jobs and he wondered if he would ever work in the SBS again. It was a hard blow to take, but if you had to do a desk job then this was one of the least painful. He had travelled all over Russia, monitoring the destruction of missiles, putting ticks in boxes and signing papers to confirm he had witnessed what he was supposed to. Life in the MoD would undoubtedly come as a nasty shock.

The bus had penetrated the last of the defence lines and was now approaching the vast sprawl of buildings, command centres and bunkers that made up the main support base of the 221st Rocket Division.

'Here we are, boys,' Pierre chortled as he eased himself out of his seat. 'Let's hope this lot's a bit more clued up than the last.'

'I sincerely hope so,' Klaus added gravely. They're equipped with SS-18s. The more of them that are destroyed the better.'

Before following the others out of the bus, Matt checked his notes. Pierre was right. Things hadn't exactly gone according to plan on this trip. But what annoyed Matt was that no one had been able to pinpoint what the problem was. There had been constant delays, and the bus with the monitoring team on board had been sent on detours and wild-goose chases, but on every occasion their hosts had always provided cast-iron excuses.

The day before in Breudinsk they had arrived to witness the destruction of another SS-18 only to be told that it had already been transported to another site and destroyed there. What was more, they were told, another monitoring team had witnessed the operation. Sure enough, when they checked the story proved true, but with so many cock-ups it would be no big deal for one or more missiles to be spirited away.

Matt prayed that he was wrong. Especially with the SS-18. The largest missiles in the Soviet nuclear arsenal, the Model Four SS-18s that the team was now concentrating on had a range of some 11,000 kilometres. What was more, each missile was a MIRV, a multiple independently targeted re-entry vehicle. Under the nose cone of each 35-metre-high missile were ten or more smaller nuclear warheads, each of 500 kilotons. As the missile approached its target, the nose cone would jettison and each mini-warhead would peel off and head for its own separate target. In effect you were getting ten missiles for the price of one.

Stepping out of the bus, Matt joined the rest of the team and followed the escorting officer to the briefing room, where they were welcomed by the Russian Divisional Chief of Staff before being led out to the destruction area. When they got there they were shown to a stand and ushered into seats. Two hundred metres in front of them lay the enormous bulk of an SS-18.

'Jesus, what a monster!'

Pierre was scribbling furiously, making notes that would later be typed up as his official report.

'What time are we seeing the warheads?' asked Matt.

'After tea,' Klaus answered.

'Shit, not another break. We could have the job done in half the time if they just got on with it.'

The missile in front of them resembled a vast empty tube of toothpaste. The rocket propellant had been siphoned off and the warheads removed for the more delicate dismantling process. But the body of the missile itself was simply torn to pieces and crushed like the wreckage of an enormous car. As each stage of the rocket's outer casing crumpled, Matt could feel the team heave a sigh of relief. For once the destruction had gone smoothly.

'Thank God for that,' Klaus said as they walked away from the stand. 'I didn't fancy having to chase yet another phantom missile halfway across Russia.'

'You must have more faith in our new friends,' Pierre joked.

'It's not easy after facing them across the Inner German border for nearly half a century.'

'You're too suspicious. You and Matt make a good pair. He's been picking faults ever since the trip began.'

'That's my job,' Matt said, defending himself. 'If you believe everything you're told you might as well stay at home and trust them to do the job themselves like good little boys. Personally I'd rather check and double-check.'

With the team assembled in the officers' mess, the Chief of Staff led in the Divisional Commander to address his visitors and lead them on the next part of the inspection.

'It is a great pleasure, gentlemen, that today we are destroying our missiles rather than firing them. No one could ever have won a strategic nuclear war between NATO and the Warsaw Pact. Let us all be thankful that our countries have at last come to their senses and let us hope that nations will never again be held hostage by such terrible weapons.'

'Amen,' Pierre murmured.

'I will now take any questions that you may have.'

After a pause, Matt put up his hand. 'General, what do you say to the reports in the Western press that the new Russian mafia is anxious to get its hands on decommissioned nuclear warheads.'

The general laughed. 'On complete warheads? That would be impossible. It is true that some small quantities of plutonium have found their way on to the black market, but my government is doing everything in its power to bring a quick halt to the trade. But whole warheads? No, that is impossible.'

'Why?'

The general frowned, taken back by the directness of the question from a junior officer.

'We do not just keep our warheads in a bicycle

shed. There are thorough accounting and security procedures.'

'Yes, sir, but with warheads being transported from the more remote silos in, say, Siberia, do you mean to say that the reports of possible hijack are completely unfounded?'

'Of course I do,' the general protested.

Pierre leaned across and hissed at Matt. 'Steady, my water-borne friend. You're about to put our host into orbit.'

'That's what we're here for. To get answers to hard questions.'

'Fine, but try not to restart the Cold War while you're doing it.'

The Chief of Staff was on his feet. 'Right, gentlemen. If you'll follow me we'll now go and see some of the warheads being dismantled.' He narrowed his eyes at Matt. 'That is, unless they've gone missing.'

Minutes later the team were ushered into one of the laboratories and confronted with the two-metre-long black cone of a warhead. When permission had been given, Matt took out his camera and started to take photos of the process.

'There can't be many people who've seen an SS-18 MIRV this close up,' he said.

'I'm just grateful we're not seeing it under different circumstances,' Pierre sniggered, clapping his hands loudly and startling the technicians.

'Do you really think the Russian underworld could get hold of one?' Klaus asked.

'Sure,' Matt answered. 'Why not? There are enough of them around and as we've seen during the trip, the Russian set-up isn't the most organized of institutions.

For all their protestations of good faith I'd lay a bet they don't know how many they've got themselves, let alone where they all are.'

'That's a very pessimistic point of view,' Pierre said. 'And anyway, how many buyers do you think are out there?'

'Plenty. Iraq, for one. In fact, any little country with an ego problem and no nuclear programme of its own.'

'I think you've been in the commandos too long. You're seeing shadows and spooks where there aren't any.'

Matt loaded a fresh film and looked hard at the dull black cone before him. 'I hope you're right.'

The low, whitewashed cottage was made of solid stone and hugged the bleak hillside as if it had grown out of it along with the wind-blasted trees and the granite boulders. Looking back at it from the end of the narrow unmade road that led away from its front door, Linda Kirkdale felt again the thrill of excitement that had seized her when she had first spotted it barely two years ago. She had known immediately that she would buy it.

There was something about the severity of the place, its wonderful seclusion and austerity that attracted her. It was as if the cottage was saying to all the world, look at me, I dare to live here, I dare to exist in this wild place. Linda had driven straight into Brecon, tracked down the estate agent whose board had been displayed outside the cottage, and had put in her offer. The next week, at her desk in London, the phone had rung and the same bemused agent had told her that she was to be the proud owner of High View. She had gone back to her Putney flat that evening and had barely been able to sleep. Lying in bed, she had thought about the cottage for hours, her own quiet retreat from the city, and from the bustle, clamour and alarms of the Intelligence world.

Now, two years on, the renovations were almost complete. Leaning on the gate at the end of the lane, she cast her eyes over the newly tiled roof, the grey slates shining as they dried in the fresh morning air. The windows and doors had all been replaced and a new kitchen fitted, and the new boiler would have just started to heat the water for a long, hot bath when she returned from her run.

Swinging over the gate, Linda set off at a steady trot. Luckily the lane was flat and level for the first few hundred metres. Stretching her stride gradually, she felt her body ease into the accustomed rhythm. She had given up running in London. The hard pavements and roadways were unforgiving on the knees and even in the parks the cloak of car fumes was ever-present. A run in London was inevitably followed by a fit of coughing. No, when confined to the city on weekdays she preferred to stick to a demanding gym routine, rounding it off with fifty lengths of the pool. But come Friday evening she would be on the motorway, following the M4 all the way across the broad gut of the country to the Severn bridge, then on to Brecon and finally up into the hills and the waiting cottage.

As she turned off the lane, vaulted a stile and started up the first gentle hill she realized that she had come to live for her weekends. It wasn't that she disliked company, but rather that here she could be most truly herself and not what other people expected her to be. There were always plenty of invitations at the weekend. People at work seemed to take pity on a single woman at the start of her thirties, as if her only fulfilment should be in hitching herself to a husband, packing up her own life and putting it on hold until a family had been started, raised and released. Then, at the approach of her twilight years, she would be allowed to retrieve whatever was left and play with the tattered remnants of her once proud and independent self all the way to the grave.

She smiled at the thought. She knew it wasn't really as bleak as that, but there was at least an element of truth in such a stark picture. Of course she hadn't always felt like that. There had been a time, once, when she would have liked nothing more than to settle down, but that was another story. Instinctively she steered her thoughts away from it. And anyway, with him, 'settling down' was hardly the right description for the unorthodox sort of life they would have led together.

The hill had steepened and as she came over the crest she felt a blast of cold air almost lift her off the ground. But, steadying herself on the summit, she stopped momentarily and stood with her hands on her hips, breathing deeply and looking down on the beautiful Llyn Brianne reservoir. At the far end the huge dam curved into the water's blackness, holding it back, harnessing the immense power. Stretching back from it, the expanding depths of the reservoir twisted and forked through what had once been a wooded valley. To one side an old track led down the hillside and disappeared under the gently lapping waves, leading to a long-flooded village. Here and there the tops of ancient walls and buildings could just be glimpsed beneath the surface. Linda always stopped at this point to regain her breath before starting on the downhill stretch. She would stare mesmerized at the submerged village, imagining the lives that had once flourished there and listening for the tolling bell that, it was rumoured, could still be heard coming from the old church when the current was right.

She was just popping her ears to see if she could hear it when she heard instead another sound, a car engine. Hunting it down, she eventually made out the red Volvo estate cruising slowly along the road that came out of Llandovery and led all the way up past the reservoir and on to the little village of Tregaron. Damn them, she thought. Someone was always disturbing her day-dreams.

She started down the hill and made her way straight towards the reservoir, noticing as she did so that the car had pulled into a lay-by several hundred metres away. It was always the way with tourists. They would ruin the peace and calm of a place, sit there staring into space and stuffing their mouths with sandwiches, before moving on, probably dumping their litter in the process.

But at the back of Linda's mind something stirred. She hunted for the memory but it wasn't to be caught so easily. Instead, she reached the bottom of the hill, clambered over a wire fence, dropped on to the road and started on her homewards run. She felt full of energy now. The exercise had cleared her mind and she could feel herself in full control of her life. Only the one worrisome thought struggled for clarity in her brain.

Her new direction was taking her closer and closer to the parked car and she gauged that she would pass within fifty metres of it. Perhaps when she saw it close up she might remember what it reminded her of.

For the first time that morning the leaden clouds parted and a brilliant sun pushed through. Firing its rays off the surface of the reservoir, it sparkled on the dew still clinging to the wire fence bordering the road and dazzled Linda so that she had to shield her eyes against the sudden glare. She was almost level with the red Volvo when she tracked it down in her memory and the moment she did so she instinctively quickened her step. It was the same one that had narrowly avoided colliding with her on the motorway on Friday night. She had not escaped from work until late but had determined to do the long drive to Wales all the same. The M4 at that time of night had been quiet and she had enjoyed the peaceful drive, at least until she noticed a car closing on her at high speed, its headlights blazing, dazzling her in her rear-view mirror. That was what had reminded her, she realized: the flash of light blinding her on the motorway just as the sun did now, both preventing her from getting a clear view of the car and its occupants.

On the motorway Linda had automatically increased her speed, assuming that the driver was dozing and would wake at any second and take evasive action. But the car just kept on coming. At the last moment it had swerved into the middle lane and drawn alongside Linda's Ford Escort. Sitting in it were four men, not the sort of irresponsible youths that she had been expecting but all in their thirties or forties, large and anonymous. She had gesticulated at the driver, telling him to watch where he was going, and to her horror he had swung the car towards her. However, at that moment they had passed a police patrol car tucked in behind a bridge. The other car had seen it first and had sped away. The police had obviously been chatting or listening to the radio for they had remained where they were and although it had crossed Linda's mind to reverse back to them and report the Volvo, she had shrugged it off as just another bunch of arseholes out to prove something.

Now, however, seeing the red Volvo and certain that it was the same one, she felt her blood run cold. For a moment she consoled herself that it was just a coincidence, but when she saw the doors open she realized she was in trouble. Four men swung out of the car and raced back towards the road where Linda was now level with the car. But they still had fifty metres to cover and none of them was built for speed. The fastest of them made straight for her and yelled something unintelligible. Linda lengthened her stride, turning her jog into a sprint and gradually pulled away from the nearest of the men. Even though she had been running for an hour or more the danger of the situation gave her a sudden burst of adrenalin sufficient to carry her beyond the immediate reach of danger. But she knew that it could only be temporary. She could only keep this pace up for two hundred metres at the most and then she would be finished. She would barely have enough breath left for the slowest of jogs, let alone a life-or-death struggle with four burly men.

Glancing over her shoulder she noticed that her pursuers were tumbling back into the Volvo. She saw the reversing lights come on and heard the tyres skidding in the gravel. She was now a good hundred metres beyond them but knew that so long as she remained on the road they would catch her with the car in seconds. From what she had seen she doubted that the men would be able to follow her on foot if she attempted a hill climb, but as she was nearing exhaustion they might just be able to close the gap.

And where would she head to? She would be all the more vulnerable on the bare hillside. At least on the road another car might come along and be able to help her.

As she heard the car squeal on to the tarmac and surge towards her, she looked ahead and saw the fringe of a forestry block another hundred metres away. Extending up the hillside, the densely packed fir trees spread the length of the valley. If she could only reach those she might be able to lose the men there.

Pouring her last ounce of strength into her legs, she powered away, spurting towards the cover of the firs as the car roared closer. Something cracked past her head and in her confusion she thought that a bird had hit her. But when it happened again and she saw a fragment of tarmac splinter at her feet, she realized that one of the men was using a gun.

'Jesus Christ,' she mouthed silently to herself. 'Who the fuck are these guys?'

Then, with only seconds to spare, she was at the first line of trees. Veering off the road she flung herself deep into the cover of the firs, sprinting down the long, straight lines of trunks, swinging right, running down another line, right again, and so on, zigzagging away, ever deeper into the artificial forest, ignoring the lower branches that whipped and snapped at her. Far behind she heard again the squeal of tyres and the slamming of car doors as the Volvo lurched into the roadside ditch and the men leapt out in pursuit.

Pushing herself further and further into the trees, Linda realized that her only hope lay in getting as far into the forest as she could. Anywhere near the edge it would still be possible to be seen from a relatively long distance, the firs having been planted in straight, even rows. But as she penetrated deeper she started to reach the older parts of the plantation, where the lower branches had become entwined and where dead wood had clogged the spaces between the rows, rebelling against the hand of the forester and growing to resemble more closely a real wood. Although it became harder to move, there was ample compensation in the better cover this area afforded.

Finally reaching a dense clutch of thick firs, Linda fell to her hands and knees and crawled underneath. Here the lowest branches were thick and green, and swept down to ground level, interlocking and creating a blanket of cover. Pushing and clawing her way inside, Linda suddenly found herself in a tiny space no bigger than a two-man tent. Turning to face the direction she had come from, she pressed herself flat on the ground and waited. Voices carried to her, but they sounded from the distance and were muffled by the dense trees. The men appeared to have split up and were now combing the wood, heading in her direction, shouting to each other as they went. As she listened Linda was able to distinguish between the four of them, roughly gauging the direction each was moving in. They were doing a sweep, but in cover as good as this they would literally have to tread on her to find her.

Lying as still as she could, Linda fought to control

her breathing. She knew that it was essential for her to regain her strength for whatever lay ahead. As she did so she struggled to order her thoughts. Who the devil were these men? At least they had made their intentions clear. The pistol shots had been too close to be simply for warning. They wanted to kill her. Well, she thought, at least that much is clear.

With a creeping chill of dread she eventually came to the conclusion that it was an IRA active service unit. Of course! How could she have been so stupid? After all, she had been instrumental in putting away the Gibb brothers only last year. Despite the security surrounding her identity at the trial, it would perhaps have been possible for a leak to have occurred. Linda had been one of the first agents to become involved in counter-terrorism following the retasking of the Intelligence Service at the end of the Cold War. Even if she had since moved on to other areas of Intelligence interest, terrorist organizations had long memories. The ceasefire and peace negotiations might prevent the IRA and the Loyalist terror groups from carrying out their more usual acts of murder and savagery, but everyone on the inside knew that, peace or no peace, there would inevitably be a private settling of scores before any of the weapons were truly laid to rest. Blood feuds and revenge attacks would be carried out by both sides, and no one in the Service on the mainland was stupid enough to assume that they would be immune.

So that was it. They had come for Linda. She was to be the first member of the Service to go down. It was not a distinction she wanted.

But something still troubled her. The whole operation had hardly been smooth for her attackers. Was the IRA losing its touch? A bomb under her car would have been a more usual method, but then they would know that all Intelligence and Security personnel were trained to check routinely for such devices and to recognize them. Then why hadn't they simply driven up to her cottage, burst in and shot her? The bungled ramming on the motorway, then the sight of the overweight thugs trying to catch her on the road. There were a number of things that didn't add up.

Linda was brought sharply to her senses by the crack of a twig not ten metres away. She froze on the spot. Then, in the silence that followed, she pressed her face low to the ground and peered under the lowest branches out on to the forest floor. The moss under her nose was soft and springy and its fresh scent added to the fear to hone her senses and clear her head. She had managed to regain her breath and tensed her upper arms and drew up her legs in case she suddenly needed to make a break for it.

She could just make out a pair of legs. The man seemed to be standing, turning this way and that, presumably scanning the forest for his target. Elsewhere Linda could hear the crash and snap of branches and the occasional shout as the other men called to each other to check on their progress. But the man to her front remained silent. To her horror, he took a step towards her, and then another and another, until he was standing right in front of her hiding place. She heard him clear his throat. Another two steps and he would be on top of her. She realized that it was now too late to break from cover and run for it. If he was armed he would be able to cut her down before she had run half a dozen paces.

Desperately searching through her mind for other options, Linda thought about trying to tackle him. In other circumstances it might have been possible. She had been trained to defend herself and was quick and nimble. But before she could close with the man she would have to struggle to her feet through the branches and break through the outer cover of the fir beneath which she was hiding. By the time she got anywhere near him he would have heard her and would be ready and waiting. She had seen that they were all big men so, even without the pistol, he would be a tricky opponent to fell. What was more, he would undoubtedly have time to shout to the others, so that unless her attack was successful in the first flurry of blows, she would be faced with multiple opponents and the game would be up.

The man took another step towards the hiding place and Linda braced herself for action. But instead of pushing his way through the undergrowth and on to her, the man seemed to steady himself as if squaring up to an opponent. Linda's puzzlement was answered a moment later when a jet of yellow liquid cascaded on to the moss inches from her face. In the silence of Linda's hiding place the sound of the man urinating was deafening. Unwilling to draw back for fear of cracking a twig and giving herself away, she remained immobile, keeping her face towards the enemy in case of compromise and steeling herself to ignore the pungent smell and steam that arose from the spreading pool.

His task done, the man sighed with pleasure and

zipped up his flies. He stamped up and down as if loosening muscles stiff from running so soon after confinement in the car. Then, to Linda's relief, he turned and moved away, as silently as he had approached.

'That was too close for comfort, Linda my girl,' she said to herself. 'Time to move.'

Swivelling on her stomach, she turned in the narrow space and sought a back exit from her cover. Nudging quietly out from under the branches, she wriggled into a shallow irrigation ditch; it was just deep enough to keep most of her body below the line of the forest floor. A few minutes later she felt secure enough to peer above the lip and look around at the forest for her pursuers. The shouts were now sounding from far away and it seemed that the men were making their way back towards the Volvo. While they had been searching, Linda had heard the sound of other cars from the road below. One had even slowed down and she had heard the driver call to the men, asking in a broad Welsh accent if they had broken down and needed help. Presumably, Linda thought, the men had decided it was getting too risky. They could ill afford to attract too much attention. Their target had managed to give them the slip and they would have to cut their losses and withdraw.

Sure enough, a few minutes later she heard the sound of slamming car doors and an engine starting. She eased into a position where she could just see the thin black line of tarmac through the mass of trees. The Volvo was easing slowly along the road, all windows down and the four men scanning the forest in a last desperate hope of spotting her. And then they were gone.

Still unable to believe her narrow escape, Linda struggled to her feet. Her knees instantly gave way and she had to grab at a tree trunk for support. The long run, the sprint along the road, the scramble through the forest and then the sudden enforced inactivity had all taken their toll and her muscles had seized up and stiffened. After rubbing her legs until the feeling returned, she waited for a further ten minutes to make completely sure the car had gone and then turned for the top of the hill and set off at a steady pace. As long as she observed the cottage covertly for some time before approaching it directly, she judged that it would probably be safe. As she had decided earlier, if the men had known exactly where she lived they would surely have tackled her there. Yet she didn't have much choice but to return home. She was in the middle of a wood dressed only in her running clothes and track suit. Her wallet, money, car keys, identification – everything was in the cottage.

So, working painfully up through the trees, she headed for home, and tumbling through her mind one overriding note of alarm had started to sound. The attack had not been the work of an IRA active service unit. Of that she was now certain. Not because of the inefficiency with which the hit had been attempted, but because, as the men had finally withdrawn back to the Volvo at the end of their hunt, she had clearly caught a single shouted phrase. It was in Russian.

4

Sergeant Des Cooper was a puzzled man. He was sitting in the Cat's Whiskers bar in Kowloon's Mody Road and had leafed through every page of the *South China Morning Post* without seeing a single mention of the find on Tolo. The death of Josh Higgs was reported briefly but nothing was said of the heavy gun battle that had erupted in Hong Kong's usually peaceful waters.

OK, he thought, so the government wants to keep it under wraps for the moment. He could understand that. The last thing they needed was a mass panic at the idea of the Triads nearly getting hold of a nuclear warhead. Presumably they would have used it for blackmail purposes or something similar. The jails were full of their comrades and they could perhaps have engineered their release as well as an enormous ransom. Whichever Triad had been to blame would also have been able to use the opportunity to clear the streets of every rival gang and end up as top dog.

But what puzzled Des was that, apart from the usual in-depth debrief from his CO and the SIB report by the plain-clothes investigation branch of the Military Police, no one had asked to question him about the bomb. All the interrogations had centred on the killing of Higgs. Barely anyone had so much as mentioned the device. Naturally he had included it in his debrief and patrol report, describing what he had seen in as much detail as possible, but it had been brushed aside and he had assumed that it was being dealt with by the police's own Special Branch and the Intelligence Service. Still, it was strange that he hadn't had a single telephone call.

He folded his paper and finished his beer. After calling across to Mimi for another can of San Mig, he stared absently out of the window. It was a bright, sunny late afternoon and the pavements were crowded with shoppers and tourists. The US fleet was obviously in town, judging by the number of American sailors hanging around the bars or hunting for duty-free cameras in the China Fleet Club. Des loved Hong Kong. It was the liveliest place he had ever been to, a melting-pot of East and West and a few other places that didn't even feature on the compass. Despite the various well-intentioned clean-ups, to his mind it had lost none of its old colour and spice. He had to admit that he regretted never having known it in its heyday during the Vietnam War, when it was one of the major R&R centres for GIs. He had heard from some of the old-timers in the squadron that it had been an even wilder town in those days, when the kids in uniform descended on the place with pockets full of money and not enough time to spend it.

When Mimi brought the beer, Des shoved a chair towards her and invited her to sit down.

'Anything new in the papers?' she asked as she slumped lazily next to him.

'No. They're still full of the news about old Deng. Anyone would think it was unexpected.'

Mimi chuckled. 'Let's drink to Deng.'

'To Deng, God rest him,' Des replied, taking a swig of his beer. 'Do you think it will change anything?'

'What the hell do I know?' Mimi said, grinning.

'You know everything, Mimi. You can't fool me with your simple old *mama-san* act.'

Mimi beamed delightedly, gold teeth jostling with black in her loose-lipped mouth. She wagged a conspiratorial finger at the tall sergeant. 'Know plenty, say little. That way stay alive long time.'

'What have you got to stay alive for, you old buzzard?'

Mimi leaned back in her chair and folded her arms. 'Why, my bar, of course. This is my world. You can take the rest and stuff it.'

'Here's to your bar.'

'And to long life,' Mimi added.

Having drained his San Mig, Des pushed the paper over to Mimi.

'What I want this for?' she asked.

'You can read all about Deng. They say there won't be any power struggle. It was all sorted out before he went.'

Mimi snorted as the sergeant got to his feet. 'If you believe that you believe anything.'

'Why's that?' Des asked, his attention wandering. But Mimi had flicked the paper over and thumbed for the sports page.

Des ambled towards the door. 'Can you put it on my tab?'

'You fuck yourself, Sergeant,' Mimi called pleasantly without looking up from the football results.

'Worth a try.'

He dug deep in the pockets of his jeans and fished out a red hundred-dollar note. 'Got any change?'

'Put it on my tab,' Mimi chuckled, as the barman accepted the note and slammed the till shut.

Out on the pavement Des gasped in the sudden humidity. After the air-conditioned bar the atmosphere in the street came like a damp smack in the face. Turning into the oncoming crowd, he pushed and weaved his way until he came to Hanoi Road, deciding to go to the Joint Services Recreation Club in Gun Club Barracks for a swim. He had just turned the corner when he walked straight into a stocky Chinese man in slacks and short-sleeved white shirt.

'Oops, pardon me,' Des apologized, stepping aside.

The man smiled kindly, but stepped in front of him again. Des laughed and stepped to the left, but again the man confronted him, grinning broadly and shaking his head.

'Look, you go to your right, and I'll go to my right,' Des said, clearly enunciating each syllable, feeling the crowd press tightly about them. But someone was pushing him in the small of the back, shoving him closer to the man.

Something in the man's eyes had alerted Des to danger; it was no more than a flicker but to Des it might as well have been a written declaration of war. Aware that his back was wide open to whoever had pushed him from behind, Des swung himself against the adjacent wall, blocking downwards and sideways with the heel of his palm and bringing his knee up at the

THE HONG KONG GAMBIT

same time into the Chinese man's groin. The man grimaced and doubled and even above the street noise Des heard the tinkle of the blade on the paving stones.

Spinning round, Des hunted for a second opponent but found himself staring instead into the terrified eyes of two schoolgirls and by the time he turned back the man had gone. Des just caught sight of him above the heads of the crowd, hobbling away in pain. He bent down and snatched up the knife from the pavement and barged his way into the crowd in pursuit. Shoving and knocking people aside, he managed to close on the man but when he rounded the next corner he had vanished. He stood up on tiptoe to see as far as he could, but his attacker was nowhere to be seen.

'Enough's enough,' he said to himself, and set off for the nearest police station.

When he got there the duty room was almost empty. A man sat miserably in one corner cradling his head in a blood-soaked bandage, and a drunk lolled against the wall as he was questioned by a young policeman. As he reported the attack to the desk officer, giving as full a description of the man as he could, Des looked up to see an inspector march briskly by, a sheaf of papers under his arm. With a start Des recognized him from the Tolo operation.

'Excuse me,' Des called across. 'I didn't catch your name but we met the other night.'

The inspector stopped and stared at him blankly. 'Do I know you?'

Des was sure now. 'Yes,' he smiled and held out his hand, which the policeman shook uncertainly. 'We met on Tolo. I was the Royal Marine sergeant in the boat chase. One of my men was killed.'

The inspector slowly went scarlet. 'I read about the death. I'm sorry.'

Des looked around to check they couldn't be overheard. 'I was the one who identified the device you found.'

The inspector frowned and looked away. 'I think you must be confusing me with someone else.' He snatched his hand away.

'The hell I am. You came and asked me to have a look at what your boys had found in the Triad powerboat. You gave me a torch and I said it looked to me like a nuclear warhead.'

'Don't be absurd! Are you drunk? I've never seen you before in my life.'

'But . . .'

'I think you'd better leave the station if your business here is finished.'

Des took a step back. The duty officer had come out from behind his desk and stood to one side, his hand on the flap of his holster. The inspector said something to him in Cantonese and the man sniggered.

'The door is over there.'

As Des backed away the inspector called after him, 'You should lay off the booze. It's making you see things.' To the sounds of the two policemen laughing he made his way down the steps and within minutes he had been swallowed up by the crowds coursing along Nathan Road.

Some fifty kilometres west of Beijing, in the Xi Shan hills, Yang Zulin pulled aside the curtain of his bedroom and peered out at the spectacular view. Dressed only in a long bathrobe, he had just lit a

68

cigarette and was debating whether he had time to make love once again to his mistress. Stretched out on the bed, like a cat she curled in a ball as he looked at her, luxuriating in the feel of the fine silk on her naked flesh.

Yang twitched the curtain open and sunlight flooded into the room.

'Why can't I see you more often?' the girl asked. 'I'm sick of these weekly engagements. Why does everything have to be so secretive?'

Yang strolled across to the bed and sat beside her. 'Because life is secretive,' he said coolly, tracing a fingertip the length of her leg. 'At least, the only life worth living is.'

'That's nonsense and you know it. What you mean is your life is secretive. None of the party bosses would mind if we were found out. Don't you think every ordinary minister has his mistress?'

Yang slapped her thigh playfully. 'Don't ever call me ordinary.'

'You know what I mean.'

Tin Li swung her legs away from him and stood up. Yang leaned back and smiled at her, watching the way her breasts moved as she strode angrily to the dressing table.

'You use me just like a whore.'

'And what exactly are you, then?'

Tin Li pouted as she sat to brush her hair. 'Not that.'

'No. I never said you were.'

Yang lay back on the mattress and folded his hands behind his head. Poor Tin Li. She had obviously been his mistress for too long; either that or he had treated her too well. It always ended the same. One mistress after another eventually gathered expectations and ideas way above her station. After pressing a few mattresses with a government minister they started to think of themselves as part of the ruling elite. It was really quite sad. Still, he had to admit that there was something special about Tin Li.

He had met her during the official visit to China of a trade delegation from the United States. Tin Li had been assigned to the group as an interpreter while Yang himself had been shadowing the Americans in the guise of liaison officer. In truth he had been monitoring their communications with their companies back in the States, thereby gaining valuable insight into their appreciation of the potential of the Chinese economy. But the trip had almost been overshadowed by his infatuation for Tin Li.

She had cottoned on to his real work very quickly, demonstrating an insight and intelligence that Yang found as attractive as her body. The relationship had become physical during the first week of the mission and had continued ever since. But with an eye to the future Yang had decided to keep it a secret. Tin Li was right. Far from being to his detriment, there was even a certain amount of admiration to be gained from his peers and superiors for possessing a mistress of such beauty and talents, but Yang wasn't concerned with the opinions of his peers or superiors. No. In the final analysis it would be the opinion of the masses that would count. They would be his ultimate judge and arbiter, and it would be before them that he must expect to have his life laid bare by his opponents in the power struggle to come.

For now, however, there was time to spare and such moments Yang devoted to Tin Li, or, to be more precise, to the pleasure he derived from her.

'Come, my dear. Don't sulk. You know I don't like it.'

'And what about me? Doesn't it matter what I like?'

'We can talk about that later. And besides,' Yang added meaningfully, 'I've got a surprise for you.'

Trying to suppress her curiosity, Tin Li nevertheless looked round.

'Come,' Yang said, crooking his finger.

Tin Li flounced towards the bed, but sank to the floor before reaching it and crossed her legs.

'Well?'

'Is that any way to behave?'

A smile spread reluctantly across the girl's face, starting in her eyes and broadening to her full lips.

'That's better,' Yang pronounced triumphantly, and took the small rectangular box from under the pillow. As quick as a flash Tin Li had snatched it and wrenched it open. She stared in wonderment at the string of pearls.

'Try them on.'

She handed it to Yang. 'You do it.'

He undid the golden clasp, reached behind her neck, refastened the clasp and gently pulled the necklace into place.

'There,' he said. 'Look.'

Tin Li looked in the mirror across the room and smiled, angling this way and that to catch the sunlight on the pearls.

'They're beautiful,' she cried, flinging her arms

around his neck. Yang let her tip him backwards, feeling her hands at his waist, untying the cord of his bathrobe.

'You see,' Tin Li beamed. 'You do love me.'

Yang kissed her passionately, her mouth opening on his as she wriggled across him and pulled open the robe. Yang felt his head swim at the touch of her flesh the full length of his body and the delicate pressure of her hand seeking him out and bringing him into her.

'Now,' she sighed, losing herself in the moment. 'Now I will show you how much you love me.'

Tin Li clutched at his shoulders, her nails digging into the muscles as her thighs pressed downwards on to him, weaving their rhythmic magic with agonizing slowness. Yang grasped her upper arms and drew her down, thrilling at the rub of her breasts against his chest.

He rolled the palms of his hands along her back, his fingers circling her buttocks, clasping and digging at the taut muscles of her hips. He reached under her knees and eased her legs further apart, straightening them and forcing her down on to him, penetrating her ever deeper as he did so. Tin Li gasped, moving slowly on to her side, coaxing Yang with her until she lay beneath him.

'See what your gift has done,' she whispered in his ear as he bent low over her, driving furiously as if the passion consuming him must be spent or else destroy him. But Yang could barely even say her name.

Tenderly, Tin Li enfolded him in her arms, saving her own pleasure until she felt the first break and rush of her lover, and taking more comfort than ever before from his utter surrender and vulnerability.

Afterwards, Yang watched Tin Li while she slept beside him, feeling the sun's warmth magnified on his flesh through the closed windows. He was not so much mystified by the strength of human emotion as amused by it. It was certainly the domain of the female, he reflected. How absurd that she should so misinterpret his enjoyment of passion, misconstruing it as a surrender of his male reasoning power. He reached across to the bedside table and found his Western cigarettes and gold lighter.

Of course he loved Tin Li, but then he strongly suspected that her own meaning of the word was somewhat different to his own. For Yang, the intellect would always rule – cold, pure and isolated from contamination by the heart. And intellect was what he would need most of all when the next meeting in his secret programme took place.

At the last one with the Russian he had barely been able to recall his grasp of the language, learned in his younger days at university in the Soviet Union. But it had sufficed. So much had happened since that meeting. Things had not gone according to plan, but then they never did. He had prepared for that. But the next meeting would be the most crucial. And with this particular foreigner the language was even uglier and more bizarre than Russian.

'The CO wants you, Sarge.'

Des Cooper looked up from the table where he was enjoying a large mug of coffee before going to brief the lads on the real reason for his presence in the Territory. He checked his watch for the time, sighed with annoyance and ambled out of the canteen.

He crossed the compound, skipped up the steps to the single-storey office block and knocked on the CO's door.

'You wanted to see me, sir?'

'Yes, Sergeant Cooper, come in. Have you briefed the men yet?'

'Not yet, sir,' Des answered, trying hard to keep the irritation from his voice. 'I was just on my way to do so.'

'Oh, right. I won't keep you long then. I must admit that I don't agree with this new SBS recruiting drive.'

'It's just a briefing, sir. Telling the lads what the SBS is all about. That's all.'

'Sure it is. And the next thing you know all my best men have vanished!'

'Your best men might not be good enough, sir,' Des replied with mischievous satisfaction.

The CO glared at the sergeant in front of him, standing at ease in the centre of the room, confident to the point of arrogance. Anxious to change the subject, the CO picked up a note from beside his telephone.

'I've had a call from the police.'

Instantly Des was on the alert. So they did want to speak to him after all. He had been right. It had been put under wraps until the facts could be gathered.

'Apparently you've been making a nuisance of yourself . . .' – he squinted at the handwritten note – 'An Inspector Chan has reported that you were drunk and disorderly at Nathan Road police station.'

Des almost exploded. 'That's the biggest load of shit I've ever heard. What the fuck's going on? Something's up, Colonel.'

'All right, all right, keep your hair on.' He picked up

a pink folder. 'I read the patrol report from the Tolo operation and your comments about the contents of the Triad boat. I have to admit that I think you were probably mistaken.'

'I know what I saw, sir.'

'Have you ever seen a nuclear warhead before?'

Des shifted uneasily. 'No, I haven't. But I'm certain that's what it was, sir.'

'Have you any idea how big a thing like that is? It's hardly the kind of device you'd stick on the back of a powerboat.'

'But you could with a MIRV,' Des replied, unwilling to admit defeat.

The CO shuffled through the papers in the file. 'Well, we've had nothing back from the police. I'd say that it's none of our business now. The correct procedures have been followed and it's out of our hands.'

'What about Military Intelligence, sir. Have they been informed?'

'It was a police operation. We were just giving assistance. It's got nothing to do with the Int boys.'

'It has if there's a fucking nuke floating around Hong Kong.'

The CO stared out of the window. After a moment's pause he turned back to Des. 'All right. I'll see your suspicions are passed on. But as far as you're concerned that's the end of it, do you understand?' He flicked the note. 'Another report from the police like this, true or false, and you'll be on the next plane home. With the hand-back of the Colony to China closer every day the last thing we need is a bad press.'

Des slammed to attention. 'Is that all, sir?'

The CO waved him away and he marched out of

the office, fuming. As he strode across to the lecture theatre where the Royal Marines were assembled for his SBS familiarization talk, his mind was buzzing with questions. What were the police trying to cover up, and why? If it was a matter of security then there would hardly have been the need for the call to the CO. Unless, he thought, it was an attempt to discredit him. If they could plant the idea in the CO's mind that Des was hitting the bottle the CO would be less likely to give any real credence to his reports of what he had seen in the boat. And what exactly had he seen? Could he have been mistaken? It was possible, of course, but he didn't think so. He had always had a keen interest in technology and particularly in nuclear weapon systems and strategy. The CO was right. It wouldn't be possible to carry an ordinary nuclear warhead on anything as small as a powerboat. But a MIRV was another matter. Barely two metres long, it would fit easily. And that's exactly what Des was sure he had glimpsed. He wondered if he had been right not to tell the CO about the knife attack. But Inspector Chan's ploy was already causing the CO to doubt him. If he had reported the attack he would probably be listed as paranoid.

When his address to the lads was over he decided to go into town. His trip to Hong Kong only had another week to run and he wanted to make the most of it. Apart from visiting his old haunts like the Cat's Whiskers, he had been asked by some of the boys back in Eastney to hunt around for some cheap cameras and radios. Ted Wilcox had asked him to pick up a fake Rolex from Chungking Mansions, the inappropriately named warren-like building and market in Kowloon where every illegal trade under the sun was conducted.

Having changed into jeans and T-shirt, Des set off for Tsimshatsui, the busiest part of the Kowloon peninsula, crammed with hotels, shops and some of the oldest and seediest built-up areas in the Colony. Hopping on the MTR underground system, he squeezed into a carriage for the short haul into town. He set out at Kowloon Park and emerged into the humidity and bustle on the corner of Haiphong Road. After waiting for a break in the traffic he jogged across Nathan Road, heading for the grubby sprawl of Chungking Mansions. Sure enough, within thirty seconds he was accosted by a man on a street corner who flashed a catalogue at him. Des nodded and the man turned on his heel and disappeared into the building with Des following.

They weaved through the rows of market stalls and climbed several flights of steps until they came to a dark corridor. Looking around, Des could imagine the many shady business deals that the place had witnessed. The man stopped abruptly outside a door and knocked. A hatch slid open and a second later the door opened on a dingy little room. A handful of tourists sat on chairs around the edge, looking at various watches and bargaining over prices. Seated at a desk, another man looked Des up and down, then opened a drawer and took out half a dozen assorted watches.

Des scanned the selection. 'All genuine, of course?' he asked smiling.

The man stared at him, no hint of an answering smile on his hard face. 'What do you think?'

Des shrugged. He thought about Ted and picked up the gaudiest watch on the table. 'How much?'

'Three hundred Hong Kong dollars.'

'Two hundred.'

'Two seventy-five.'

'Two fifty.'

The man glared at him as if he would love nothing more than to slit his throat. Des shrugged again. 'It's a buyer's market, pal.'

'Done.' The man cleared his throat noisily and spat a huge gobbet at Des's feet. Des took the watch and checked it over. The working parts were probably Japanese rip-offs but the best fakes often kept the time almost as well as the originals. But who cared? Two hundred and fifty Hong Kong dollars was a far cry from the price of the most basic genuine Rolex. He could imagine Ted down at his local in Devon, flashing it at the birds and kidding them it was the real thing.

The transaction completed, Des waited for the dealer's backup to check that the coast was clear before showing him out into the corridor. This time, however, there was no escort. He was left to find his own way back out into the street. But one corridor looked much like another and he soon found that his attempt to retrace his steps had gone sadly wrong. Instead he found himself lost in a maze of doorways, corridors and stairwells.

'Brilliant,' he muttered, and turned to try another direction.

He was just passing a stairwell when a door opened on the floor below him and he heard voices speaking rapidly in Cantonese. Out of curiosity he peered over the banister and found himself looking at the back of Inspector Chan. The person he was speaking to was out of Des's field of vision but they were clearly arguing. Des tried to lean over to catch a glimpse of the other man, but it was no use: he was standing well inside the room speaking through the open door. Chan had obviously just been visiting and was about to leave.

With a final shouted exchange of invective the door slammed and the inspector strode off down the hall. Des slipped silently down the stairs and peered round the corner. He dug into his pocket and fished out a bunch of keys, then sought around for an unobtrusive spot on the chipped wall and scored a small cross at ground level a metre from the closed door. Then, following Chan, who had already vanished down another corridor, Des let the policeman lead him out of the building, stopping at every turn or staircase to score further crosses, marking a secret trail that he would be able to follow later if need be.

When he emerged at last into the street, he had to look around to get his bearings. They had come out into a side road that was unfamiliar to him. It seemed to be at the back of a food market and the stench of rotting vegetables was overpowering. As he made one last mark beside the foot of the back exit from Chungking Mansions, Des spotted the retreating back of the inspector. Chan was dressed in a checked shirt and slacks and was walking rapidly towards an MTR station. It took Des a split second to decide to follow him.

Fortunately the Tsimshatsui underground station was crowded with tourists and Des had no trouble in losing himself among the other Westerners, although he knew that the further out of the centre of town Chan travelled, the fewer tourists there would be and the harder it would be for him to remain inconspicuous among the Chinese locals. The inspector was bound to spot him eventually.

Taking cover behind a pillar, Des waited until the policeman had boarded a train before slipping into the next carriage himself. Inside, the train's interior formed one long, open tube. But fortunately the tunnel twisted and turned so much that it was rarely possible for Chan to get a clear long-distance view down the full length of the train. Des pressed himself into a space on one of the bench seats, ignoring the protests of two Chinese women.

'Sorry, love. It's my heart, you know. Have to sit down.'

They scowled at him, not understanding a word he was saying. As the train pulled into the next station Des peered carefully through the passengers until he was able to see Chan. The inspector was standing with his back to Des and appeared to be lost in thought. The doors closed and the train moved on, the process being repeated until eventually they branched westwards, heading for the high-rise suburb of Tsuen Wan, near the end of the line. At each stop more and more of the tourists disembarked and Des sank ever lower in his seat. Then, as the train pulled into Tsuen Wan, Chan moved towards the carriage doors ready to alight.

'This is it,' Des said to himself. 'Time to go.'

He waited until Chan had stepped on to the platform and had gone some way towards the exit before getting out himself. Then, once Chan was halfway up the escalator, Des followed him, keeping his head low and hunching his shoulders, willing himself to become small enough to remain undetected. There was a moment of alarm at the exit barriers when Chan dropped his ticket and turned around to retrieve it, but Des moved even quicker, backing down the escalator through the puzzled locals until he saw that the coast was clear.

With Chan safely out of the MTR station, Des found a place behind a stand selling fishballs and deep-fried beancurd. He watched as his target crossed the main road and headed into the town, and as soon as he passed round the first corner Des followed. Avoiding the corner itself and the risk that he might run straight into Chan if the policeman had decided to backtrack, he swung out in a wide arc while still on the safe side of the road until he could get a clear view along the full length of the street. That way he kept a considerable amount of traffic between himself and Chan. It was harder to keep his target visual but it only needed a couple of glimpses to get a fix.

This cat-and-mouse game went on for half an hour, and Des had to call on every bit of his experience to keep from dropping the contact. Twice he thought he had lost him but in both cases a quick static search eventually produced the desired sighting. At last Chan left the most crowded part of Tsuen Wan and walked towards an area of modestly comfortable housing set on a series of low hills looking out to sea.

'Very nice,' Des said aloud, watching as Chan made his way towards a small but attractive house, unlocked the front door and went inside. Now that he had tracked Chan to ground, Des wondered what the hell he was going to do with this bit of information. There's only one thing to do, he thought. Now that the inspector was on his own Des decided it was time they had a nice little chat.

Checking to see that no one else was watching the house, Des made his way towards the house, again moving in a wide arc to keep out of its direct line of vision and approaching from the side. Bracing himself for a sudden scuffle, he stepped up to the door and rang the bell. As he waited he noticed the small sticks of incense burning at ground level, a Chinese custom intended to ward off evil spirits from the hearth and home. Didn't work with me, he thought grimly.

From inside the depths of the house he heard footsteps, but not the sound of someone coming to answer the door. Instead it was more as if the occupant was running on the spot, or shifting something, or . . .

Des put his shoulder to the door and shoved with all his might. After two more thrusts the lock gave way and he stumbled on to a tiled floor. The house was sparsely decorated. A couple of gaudy wall-hangings and a picture brightened up what would otherwise have been an empty room. The house was silent. Despite the noise of the splintering door, no one came to investigate. Des longed for his Browning pistol but he had hardly seen fit to carry it on what was to have been a simple shopping trip. Instead, he raised his left hand, palm open, thumb towards him, in the knife-hand alert blocking position, and balled his right fist, holding it close to his side, loaded and ready to strike. He sank into an unarmed-combat fighting stance, dropping his centre of gravity and sliding stealthily forward, his balance maintained at every shift of his body, every sense alert to the slightest danger, poised for action.

The next room he came to was the kitchen and beyond that was the dining-room. From his position by the entrance he could just make out the edge of the table. But it was the floor that his eyes were drawn to, and the sight of a body lying immobile on the tiles. He resisted the urge to rush forward, moving even more cautiously than before. Only when he was satisfied that the room was empty did he enter and crouch beside the body, feeling in vain for the pulse that had been stilled moments before by a knife thrust straight into the heart.

From the rear of the house came the sound of a car door slamming. Des raced into the final room, a narrow storeroom that led out into a tiny back garden beyond which a wooden gate gave on to an access road that had been invisible from the front of the house. Des cursed and bolted for the gate, but it was too late. All he could see when he emerged on to the road was the back of a grubby van, the number-plate caked with mud and unreadable. The rear window had been painted over and he could not even see how many men had just committed the murder.

Dispirited and more confused than ever, Des made his way back into the house and the prone, lifeless form of Inspector Chan.

5

Sir Anthony Briggs had been silent for a long time, staring out of his fourth-floor window at the wet gravel expanse of Horse Guards below. He was holding a fine porcelain cup in one hand and in the other a silver spoon with which he rhythmically stirred his strong-smelling coffee, well beyond the needs of his single sugar lump, which had long since disintegrated into oblivion.

'Well, it tells us one thing at least, Linda,' he said at last, his eyes still fixed on the light-brown gravel as if it had the beneficial properties of a Zen rock garden. 'You are obviously getting close to them. You've made them hurt and they had to try and stop you.'

Linda perched on the edge of an armchair, wary of the huge cushions, which threatened to engulf her with a sense of relaxation and informality that would be wholly inappropriate in front of a man such as Sir Anthony. In her first meeting with the head of the Intelligence Service she had thought the chair out of place in the office of such a man, but had later understood its true role. Lulled by its comfort, subordinates and other interviewees would inevitably end up saying more than they had originally intended until, by the time they took their leave, they felt as if they had been hypnotized and drained of their inmost secrets.

'Has there been any news from Special Branch?' she asked.

'Not much. The attempt on your life may have been inept but the gang's escape route was well planned. It bears all the hallmarks of a newcomer to the field, one of the many Russian mafia-type gangs that are diversifying their business. It's a bit like a little boy in the playground getting up the courage to hit someone, darting in and throwing an ineffectual punch and then scooting like a bat out of hell.'

Linda smiled at the analogy. 'It was quite a terrifying punch, for all its ineptitude.'

Sir Anthony turned from the window and looked at her. 'Of course. And that's why I'm having your flat placed under protective close observation. You'd better stay away from the cottage for a while though; we can't spare the men to cover that too. I don't think they'd try again but there's no harm in playing it safe.'

He picked up a folder from his desk and leafed through the loosely fastened pages. 'When was the last find?'

Linda referred to her notes. 'Two weeks ago, sir.'

'Ah yes,' Sir Anthony said, finding the copy of the relevant correspondence. 'That was . . . how much?'

'Nearly two hundred grams of weapons-grade plutonium-239. It was seized at Heathrow.'

'Was it in bar form?'

'No. Pellets. It looked just like lead shot. The find before that was almost a kilogram of enriched uranium-235.'

Sir Anthony shook his head and sat down behind his desk, stretching his long legs and beginning to read a report from one of the department's scientists.

'If it's correct that it takes eight kilos of plutonium or twenty-five of enriched uranium to make a home-made nuclear bomb, then at this rate it won't be long before someone somewhere achieves it. And then God help us.'

Linda nodded. Ever since the break-up of the former Soviet Union an initial trickle of nuclear material had grown into almost a flood. With their economy in dire straits and nuclear scientists and high-ranking army officers suddenly out of work after decades of stability, the Russians had little incentive for tighter controls on their nuclear industry. Given the choice between starvation and dealing with unscrupulous criminals who were after plutonium and uranium, a significant number of the scientists and army officers seemed to be opting for the latter.

Working with the Russian Ministry of Atomic Energy, Minatom, Western government agencies had attempted to stem the growing tide. The smuggling route to the West through Germany had been partially blocked but there were still the routes through the old Soviet Republics of Central Asia and the Caucasus. Here the new micro-states were primarily concerned with the establishment of their fledgeling independence and the development of their economies. The illicit nuclear trade might well be of concern to the West, but it was far from the prime worry of the new republics.

'I've been looking at your latest project,' Sir Anthony continued. 'The report on the Central Asia route. Because of the attack on you I think it would be worth increasing our efforts in that direction. The idiots have given us the surest confirmation yet that we're looking in the right place.'

'Right, sir,' Linda said. But she was puzzled.

Sir Anthony caught the doubt on her face. 'Is anything the matter?'

'Well,' she began, 'I don't mean to be rude, but we've known that's been the main conduit for some time. Have you heard anything new?'

He smiled. 'Frankly, yes.' He leaned back and scratched his head. 'I don't know how to put this. Here, you'd better have a look.'

He passed her a copy of a bulky report. 'Don't bother wading through it. Just skip to the summary of conclusions at the back.'

Linda turned to the relevant pages and skimmed them, her frown deepening with every paragraph.

'I can't believe it,' she stammered. 'If this is true it changes the whole ball game.'

Sir Anthony sipped his coffee. 'Exactly. Until now we've been chasing relatively small amounts of weapons-grade plutonium and uranium smuggled out of old Soviet research establishments and reprocessing plants. But this latest report voices the concern that entire warheads may well be going missing.'

'But it's a bit different from selling old tanks or aircraft, isn't it? Who would have the ability or technological know-how to use them?'

'Sadly, any number of countries. Iraq, Iran, Libya . . . and plenty of others. The warheads could be sold complete with a team of scientists who are willing to make them work.'

'And the delivery system and launch vehicles? Do you mean entire rockets are involved?'

'Why not?'

Linda stared at the document in disbelief. 'I know it's not that difficult for a sophisticated terrorist group or Third World country to produce a home-made nuclear bomb once they've got their hands on suitable amounts of the right ingredients, but if they ever got hold of a complete warhead they wouldn't have to bother. They'd have achieved the lot in one swoop.'

'Exactly.'

She eyed her boss suspiciously. 'OK, so this report expresses some concern. But so far that's all it is, right? Just concern?'

Watching her calmly, Sir Anthony slid a single piece of paper across his desk. Linda leaned forward and caught it.

'That arrived this morning,' he said.

Seeing that it was in signal format, Linda scanned the address group at the top right-hand corner and saw that it was from the Hong Kong office. She read it through once, and then read it again, more slowly, focusing on each word, her scalp tingling as its full significance hit home.

'You see, Linda. I'm afraid it may already have happened.'

In terse signal-speak the message told of the Tolo operation, the suspicions of the Royal Marine sergeant who was involved and the inexplicable silence from the Hong Kong authorities. Linda hardly knew where to begin.

'How can we be sure?' she asked, still numb from the shock. 'Couldn't this sergeant have been mistaken?'

'He could have been, but he wasn't. Apparently he was SBS.'

'Ah.'

'Exactly. He was taking part in the routine anti-smuggling ambush by pure chance.'

'And the Hong Kong government? The date of the operation was ages ago. Why weren't we notified immediately?'

'That's what you're going to chase up. I spoke to our man there earlier this morning. I believe there was some internal police problem. Find out the details and send me a fuller report as soon as you can.'

'I'm going to Hong Kong?'

'I thought that would please you. It'll give you a chance to do some early Christmas shopping.'

Linda grinned. 'I doubt there'll be much chance of that.'

Sir Anthony finished his coffee and poured himself a fresh cup from the *cafetière*, adding milk and the customary single lump of sugar, which he then proceeded to chase round the cup with his silver spoon.

'There's something else. The fellow who wrote that report.'

'He's done a pretty thorough job of it,' Linda said admiringly, leafing through the closely typed pages and examining the maps, charts and diagrams. 'He's certainly done his homework. Is he Foreign Office Nuclear Non-Proliferation or our own Science and Technology Branch?'

'Try again.'

Linda smiled. The boss liked his little games. 'Atomic Energy Agency, Euroatom?'

'No. Funnily enough he's SBS again. An old friend of yours, I believe.'

The smile froze on Linda's face and before she could stop herself she had looked up and met her boss's eyes. Although it was always hard to read what was behind the steely grey of Sir Anthony's measured gaze Linda thought she glimpsed sympathy.

'It's Matt,' he said simply.

She looked away, her reflexes betraying her again.

'It's strange how things go, isn't it,' Sir Anthony continued, his voice kind and understanding. 'Sometimes it seems impossible to get away from certain things.'

'Or people,' Linda added woodenly.

'Yes. Or people. Call it fate or what you will.' He paused a moment to give her time to gather her wits and then continued, his tone returning to its usual business-like manner.

'As you'll appreciate, this whole business is of the utmost importance. Matt produced the report you're holding and I'm afraid I want him to go to Hong Kong with you.'

Linda felt the words drop like bombshells all over her peace of mind.

'You're both going to have to put your private differences to one side. Nothing can be allowed to get in the way of this investigation. I'm sure you understand.'

'Of course,' Linda replied, summoning every ounce of cold professionalism she could muster. 'Besides, that's all in the past.'

Sir Anthony smiled warmly. 'It's one of the drawbacks of our line of business that no one has any secrets. Our personal lives are an open book – at least to our superiors.'

Linda wondered who on earth Sir Anthony's superiors were.

'But it has its advantages too,' he continued. 'Nothing's allowed to fester. We are forced by circumstances to examine our problems in the coldest light of day and come to terms with them. Even the things that hurt us badly.'

'Yes, sir,' Linda replied.

'And it is all behind you, isn't it, Linda?'

'Of course,' she said, a little too harshly. 'I couldn't have put it better myself. It was examined in the cold light of day.'

The words almost stuck in her throat. As she was by nature a private person, the break-up of her relationship with Matt Harbin had been made twice as painful by the whole office knowing about it. Whereas he had been able to lose himself in some other reckless escapade like an overgrown schoolboy, she had had to return to the silent scrutiny and nine-to-five sympathy of her London colleagues. It was part of the reason she so loved to escape to the solitude of the cottage whenever she could. But now that too had been denied her. She was beginning to wonder how much more she could take.

The intercom on Sir Anthony's desk burst into life and his PA announced that he was late for his next appointment.

'Thank you, Celia. I'll be right there.' He passed the complete file to Linda. 'Celia will sign this over to you. Study it thoroughly and Matt's report as well. I've appended a list of the most pressing questions that we need answers to. If you've got any problems, come and see me. OK?'

Sir Anthony stood up, signalling that the meeting was over. Linda rose from the armchair, clutching the bulky file.

'Administration will give you your flight details and so on. Have a good trip.'

She smiled, forcing some warmth into it.

'And be careful,' Sir Anthony called after her as she left the office and closed the door.

Deciding that she was in need of some fresh air, Linda locked the file away in her office and walked out of the building. The rain had stopped and a weak, watery sun was trying to push through sodden clouds scudding away across the London rooftops. For a moment she was torn between walking to St James's Park or down to Westminster Abbey. Then, on an impulse, she turned towards Whitehall and made her way to Trafalgar Square. Whitehall was busy with its usual jam of weekday traffic but Linda was absorbed with her own thoughts and barely noticed where she was until she emerged from a side road and found herself already in the cobbled streets of Covent Garden.

For a while she strolled through the market stalls, looking at the trinkets and half-heartedly watching the jugglers and street musicians who were warming up for the lunchtime crowds. A couple of drunks whistled at her as she went past. Normally she would have ignored them or scowled with indignation, but today she just looked and smiled. How badly had they been burned, she wondered? Life certainly hadn't done them any favours. Who was she to judge them?

Encouraged by her smile, they nudged each other, hooting and winking at her as she walked on. A crowd of pigeons fought savagely for a crushed and sodden bread roll, their necks and beaks like pneumatic drills, ripping into the rotten grey mass that jerked under the frenzied assault as if electrified.

Finding herself at the outer edge of the market with nowhere else to go except a return to the faceless streets beyond, and with only the dull confinement of the office behind her, she stopped, pivoting on the spot as if stuck to the glistening cobbles, suddenly indecisive, trapped between two alternatives neither of which held the slightest allure. She raised her face to the sky and for a moment blocked out the noise and the surrounding drab bleakness. The clouds were moving faster now, whipped up by high-altitude winds that wisped them into frail tendrils that mocked the city's heaviness and its colourless sprawl.

She wanted suddenly to be very far away, somewhere bright and warm. Somewhere, quite simply, different. She smiled to herself. She would shortly have her wish, it seemed. But how ironic that, of all people, it had to be with Matt Harbin.

Fred Turner glared at the heavy nose-to-tail traffic that was clogging Central and fidgeted with his watch strap. His unmarked police car hardly seemed to have made any progress along Connaught Road in the past ten minutes and he was due at Government House by nine-thirty. On top of everything else, the Governor would take a very poor view of things if he was late. He leaned forward and tapped the driver on the shoulder.

'Can't you cut up to Pedder Street?'

The driver shrugged helplessly and nodded at

the rows of cars blocking any quick exit from the jam.

'We'll just have to wait it out, Chief Inspector. I think there's been an accident up ahead.'

Fred knew full well that there hadn't been. The road was always like this, but the driver was attempting to excuse his bad choice of route.

'Well, blow your horn or something.'

The driver obediently gave two short blasts on the horn but produced only a torrent of abuse from the driver in front.

Collapsing back into his seat, Fred looked again at his watch. Whereas the minute hand seemed to have leapt round the face, the car remained obstinately motionless.

'Fuck it.'

In an attempt to distract himself he flipped open his briefcase, took out a file marked 'SECRET' and began thumbing through the various documents inside.

'Jesus Christ,' he sighed, as he reread the contents for the hundredth time. 'What a bloody mess.'

Some time later the car suddenly surged forward and the driver announced triumphantly that they were on their way again.

'Thank God for that,' Fred sighed, replacing the folder and then straightening his tie as the car swept up Albert Road and passed through the impressive gates of Government House. The policeman on duty recognized him and gave a salute, which Fred acknowledged with a regal wave of the hand. The car had hardly drawn to a halt before he was out of the door and striding towards the front entrance. Huge potted plants and palms bordered the steps and once inside he came face to face with the effete and well-manicured figure of the Governor's aide.

'Nice timing, Chief Inspector. You've got . . .' – he consulted his Cartier watch – 'forty-five seconds to spare.'

'Is that right?' Fred grunted as he barged past. 'And does Mickey Mouse also say that I'll punch the next fucker who comments on the time?'

The PA in the outer office pressed a buzzer and announced the arrival of Chief Inspector Turner. As Fred entered the impressive room and the aide withdrew, the Governor got up and moved from behind his desk, showing Fred to a seat and then taking one opposite for himself. Fred noticed that while he was cordial there was a distinct absence of the usual pleasantries, and one glance at the Governor's eyes told him that he was in for a hard time.

'To put it simply, Fred, we're in the shit.'

'Yes, sir.' Fred felt himself cringing, withering under the Governor's close scrutiny.

'I'm being briefed by the Police Commissioner and the Commander of British Forces in an hour but I wanted to hear it from you at first hand. I believe you're Special Branch's man on the job and I want it straight. What the fuck happened, and why wasn't I or anyone else informed immediately?'

Fred opened his file, feeling like a naughty schoolboy being grilled by the headmaster.

'It seems that the Triads managed to turn one of our men.'

'A Special Branch man?'

'No, sir. Marine Police.'

'Which Triad?'

'We think it was the Triple A.'

'Them again?'

Fred leafed through his papers until he found what he was looking for. 'Well, yes and no.'

'What does that mean?'

'Here, look at this.' He handed over a post-operational report from the anti-smuggling ambush. 'According to our evidence the Triple A were behind the smuggling operation but it seems that several different Triad gangs have drawn together on this one.'

'That is bad news. Why's it happened?'

'We don't know yet. Gangs that have been fighting one another for turf are now cooperating like the best of friends. I can only assume there's someone or something else behind it.'

'It would take a pretty powerful force to pull a group like that together. Is there any evidence of involvement from mainland China?'

'No more than usual. Various corrupt officials always have their fingers in the smuggling pie but they're usually just mavericks operating on their own. As far as we can tell the Chinese government knows nothing about this.'

The Governor thought for a while before continuing. 'And what about this policeman? The one they turned? Have you got him?'

'In a manner of speaking, yes.'

'What do you mean?'

Fred passed across a black-and-white photograph. 'He's in the morgue.'

'Good. At least there's some good news.'

Fred smiled. 'I agree, although it would have been useful to have had him to question.'

'What happened to him?'

'He was murdered by a Triad hit squad.'

'Triple A?'

'No, sir. Another one. We think he got greedy. Asked for more money than they were prepared to pay. From what we figure, the Triads only got hold of him after the smuggling raid had gone wrong.'

'What makes you think that?'

'Well, he knew that there was a military powerboat capable of catching the Triads' boat, so if he'd been in their pay all along he wouldn't have alerted the marines. Then, when he and his men were in possession of the captured boat, he apparently asked one of the marine commandos to have a look at the find. He'd hardly have done that if he was being paid to hush things up.'

'No.'

'I believe they got hold of him later and paid him to keep things quiet. At that early stage it was purely his operation. It was no big deal to treat the packing case as if it was just another load of electronic goods and return them to his own base for storage.'

'Wasn't anyone else involved?'

'A police bomb-disposal expert was tasked, but the heli that was supposed to get him there was diverted to a search-and-rescue mission out at sea. By the time the ordnance team was ready to investigate, the Triads had made their move and Inspector Chan was in their pay.'

The Governor shook his head. 'You mentioned a marine?'

'Yes, sir. A sergeant.' Fred dug out Cooper's details from his file and passed them across. 'An interesting fellow. SBS, I believe. He was out there purely by chance. But what's more, it was him who reported the murder of Chan.'

'How the devil did he get involved in that?'

'It seems he smelt a rat, followed Chan to his home and found the body.'

'Enterprising chap.'

'And,' Fred continued awkwardly, 'it was also his report via his CO that found its way to London and alerted Intelligence.'

The Governor stood up and paced the room. 'You can imagine how all this looks from London's perspective, can't you? A third party informs them that a nuclear warhead is floating around somewhere in Hong Kong. Has the Hong Kong government informed them? No. Instead a police inspector in the Triads' pay has secreted it away in a storeroom before he himself has his throat cut.'

'It does rather put egg on our faces,' Fred said sympathetically.

'It puts us slap in the middle of a fucking omelette! The one saving grace is that so far it's been kept out of the press.'

'Yes, sir.'

'And I intend to keep it so until this whole bloody mess is sorted out. The next question, of course, is that if we've found one warhead, who's to say there isn't another one, maybe more than one?'

'I think that would be very unlikely, sir,' Fred replied, far from convinced by his own answer. Indeed, it was one of the things that most concerned him, and his men were at this very moment drawing on every contact they had in the Triad underworld to find out the truth.

'Well, let us hope so. In the meantime London's sending its own team out here to join in the investigations.'

He rounded on the policeman. 'I expect your full cooperation with them. They are to be informed of every development, however small or trivial, and they are to be given every assistance in whatever investigations of their own they want to pursue. Is that understood?'

'We really do have things under control now, sir,' Fred tried.

'Sure you do,' the Governor replied, finding it hard to keep the sarcasm from his voice.

As Fred shuffled his papers back in his briefcase and got up to leave, the Governor gave one last word of warning.

'I want you to have another look at any possible involvement by China itself. But assuming they're innocent, under no circumstances must they be alerted to what has happened. It's the excuse they would love, proving to the world that the British have lost control of the Colony. In the run-up to the 1997 hand-over it would discredit us completely. Is that understood?'

Again Fred nodded solemnly and without another word left the office, the palms of his hands damp with perspiration.

Des Cooper walked briskly along Hennessy Road, every stride taking him deeper into the heart of the Wanchai red-light district. Beside him, Corporal Harry Leach continued his attempts at persuasion.

'Look, Sarge. I know you're up to something. Let me come along. The bastards killed Josh and I want to get even with them.'

'That's why I wish I hadn't bloody brought you.' Against his better judgement, Des had allowed the eager young marine to accompany him on his covert recce, but he knew that if they ran into any trouble he would probably be glad of an extra pair of fists.

After crossing O'Brien Street they turned north towards Lockhart Road. Salesmen heckled them as they passed stores piled high with radios, and girls lolling outside the gaudily lit bars tried in vain to entice them in.

'No thanks, love,' Des replied as one girl draped herself on his arm. 'Not tonight.'

After walking for several more minutes they stopped in front of a bright-red advertising sign hanging over the entrance to an alley. Des peered along the dark, narrow passageway, then dug in his pocket and fished something out.

'What's that?' Harry asked.

Des held the crushed matchbox in his hand and compared the design on it with the overhead advertisement.

'Bingo. I found it in the street behind Chan's house when the van with his murderers drove off. It might mean nothing at all but it's the only lead we've got.'

Harry stared in disbelief. 'Why didn't you give it to the police?'

'I couldn't be sure Chan was the only copper on the Triads' payroll,' Des replied. He grinned at the young corporal. 'Not getting cold feet, are you?'

'Me? Get stuffed.'

'Come on then. Let's join them for a drink.'

Des led the way down the alley, found the stairway at the end and climbed to the first floor, where the entrance to the club was firmly shut. He knocked heavily and a moment later a hatch slid open and an angry face glared out at them.

'I've been told this is a good place for a beer and some company,' Des said evenly.

The hatch slammed shut, a bolt was slid in a rusty lock and the door opened. The guard was dressed in jeans and a T-shirt and behind him another two sat on the bottom step of stairs that disappeared up towards a dimly lit corridor.

'Pay up there,' he said roughly.

'Charming manner,' Des said to Harry and winked as he led the way. The corridor upstairs was lined with numbered doors and at the end was a large room with a bar and an array of battered sofas.

'Nice place,' Harry said. 'I might have guessed you'd hang out in a dump like this.'

'Beats the mess,' Des answered, going to the bar and ordering two San Miguels. A heavily made-up woman in middle age sidled up to them and asked what they wanted.

'Just a drink, dear,' Des replied. 'And some company perhaps.'

The woman smiled through scarlet lips and beckoned two girls over to join them.

'I leave you here, but you be good. If you want go room, you pay first, OK?'

'Sure, love. I'll let you know.'

The girls led the way across to a sofa and started to make small talk, asking the two men how long they were staying in Hong Kong and quickly getting to the subject of paying for further pleasures in a couple of the adjoining rooms. But Des was in no hurry. Instead he talked idly of this and that, pumping the girls for as much information about the brothel as he could.

After a while one of the girls got up and went to order a second round of beers but instead of returning, Des noticed that two of the men from the front door had appeared and were talking to the *mama-san*. She pointed across the room at the Westerners, and seeing the approach of trouble, the second girl got up and moved quickly out of the way. The guards sauntered up and stood over Des and Harry.

'What's up, boys?' Des asked innocently.

'The girls,' the larger of the two men replied. 'They say you ask a lot of questions.'

'I wouldn't bother about it,' Des said genially. 'That's just my way.'

The man's face was stone. 'You want fuck, go fuck. If not, then fuck off.'

Des looked at Harry. 'Well, when he puts it as nicely as that I think we'd better be on our way, don't you?'

They got to their feet and with the guards escorting them, made their way towards the stairs. But as Des passed one of the doors he stumbled on the ripped carpet and went down, grabbing hold of the senior guard for support. The man shook him off and the other guard thrust his hand in his pocket, pulling out a revolver in case the Westerners were about to try anything. In a bound, Harry was between them, his hands in the air.

'Steady, lads, steady. We're just going.'

He hustled Des down the steps and out into the alley, hearing the door slam shut behind them. When they were out in the main street he rounded on Des.

'What the fuck was all that about, Sarge? You almost got us shot! Are you so pissed you can't stand up?'

Des straightened up, a sly grin spreading across his face.

'I don't see what's so funny,' Harry snapped.

Instead of answering, Des led the way around the block. Reluctantly Harry followed him. Des was busy searching for something.

'What the fuck are you looking for now?'

'Shut your gob and help me look.'

'What for?'

'A Honda van all covered in shit.' He held up a bunch a keys. 'Unless I'm mistaken I'd lay a bet that these will fit it, and that bloke was probably one of the slimy yobs who murdered Chan.'

'You've nicked his keys?' Harry said, gaping.

'And not just his keys,' Des said, producing a stuffed wallet. 'Let's see what we can find in here.'

6

As he arrived outside the terminal for his British Airways flight to Hong Kong, Matt was confirmed in his opinion that Heathrow got worse every time he saw it. The number of passengers using the airport had long outstripped its capacity to handle the flow but still the numbers increased. Cars and buses clogged the narrow one-way system, the jams exacerbated by road repairs and lane closures, and when his taxi at last deposited him in front of the terminal his relief was only momentary, as another onslaught awaited him at the check-in.

The news that he would be accompanied by Linda Kirkdale had been as much a shock to him as it had to Linda. As he queued with his suitcase, slowly edging towards the desk, he scanned the crowds for her, a baffling mix of emotions racing through him. He had been delighted that his report had borne fruit and that he was to be closely involved in the investigation into the find of the nuclear device in Hong Kong, but of all the Intelligence agents that had to be assigned to the case, why on earth did it have to be Linda?

His bag was weighed and labelled, then disappeared out of sight on the conveyor belt.

'Smoking or non-smoking?' the girl at the desk asked.

'Non-smoking.'

Then, as an afterthought Matt added, 'Has a Miss Kirkdale checked in yet?'

The girl scrolled through the passenger list on the computer screen.

'Yes. Are you together? There's a free seat next to her.'

Jesus, Matt thought, if this was a fire-fight I'd be able to react without thinking.

'Well?' the girl prompted impatiently, aware of the glaring customers in the seemingly endless queue behind Matt.

'Yes.'

She hammered his details into the keyboard and a moment later the printer spewed out his boarding pass, the seat number emblazoned on it as if written in blood. Matt stared at it as he was elbowed away from the desk by the next passenger.

Now why the hell did you do that? he asked himself. Brilliant. Just fucking brilliant. You spend months burning her out of your system and then you plonk yourself next to her.

But as he stepped on to the escalator that swept him up to the departure gates he became more resigned, regaining the firm control that he always kept over his feelings. No. This was business. They would have to get together soon enough in any event. And anyway, things were different now. Everything that had gone before had happened in another world. On another planet even. They had both been different people. Ireland had changed all that.

All through the duty-free shops he kept an eye out for her without meaning to. He picked up a bottle of whisky and an *Economist*.

Better have some comics as well, he thought, and picked up a *Newsweek* and *Time*.

He cast his eye over the shelves of paperbacks, but it was all the usual airport rubbish. The latest Jeffrey Archer, Tom Clancy and Frederick Forsyth, fat wads of fantasy that seduced the reader away from the real business of living.

The address system called his flight and he made his way to the departure gate. Still there was no sign of Linda. He went down the long, winding tunnel that led to the 747 and ducked into the plane. A smiling stewardess greeted him with the sincerity of a TV game-show host and directed him to his seat. Edging down the long aisle, he finally caught sight of her. She was sitting in a window seat on the right side of the aircraft, looking out at the runway where the last of the baggage was being loaded into the hold. The seat next to her was empty.

Despite all his training and experience he felt his blood run cold. This is stupid, he thought. It's over, over, over.

Feeling the muscles in his stomach clenching, he swung his hand luggage into the overhead locker, stuffed his magazines into the pocket of the seat in front and sat down. He cleared his throat and she turned towards him.

'Hi,' he said simply.

From the expression on her face he might as well have broken wind.

'Hello, Matt.'

Her voice was level, empty of warmth. She was greeting a stranger that she would rather not have been obliged to address.

'I see the office seated us together.'

'Actually, I did,' he confessed, deciding that she had probably guessed the truth anyway. He tried out a smile. She didn't respond.

'This business was going to bring us together eventually anyway. Why not sooner rather than later?'

Instead of agreeing with him she turned again to her window. The loading had been completed and the support vehicles were accelerating away from the aircraft as if it was about to explode.

'How are you?' Matt asked lamely.

'Fine,' Linda replied. Then, as if reassuring herself that it was true, she turned to him again and said, 'I'm fine. You?'

'Me? I'm fine too.'

'That's nice.'

With Linda looking out of the window again, Matt sank into a dismal reverie. God this is awful, he thought. But he refrained from initiating any further inane exchanges and took out his *Economist* instead. As the plane left the runway, climbed over the grey suburban spread and banked towards the southern Home Counties, he tried to bury himself in one of the articles, but after reading the same paragraph four times he admitted defeat. It was impossible to concentrate. Flicking through *Newsweek*, he stared glumly at the coloured pictures.

A tank was smashing through a barricade. A European crowd was rioting somewhere. A clutch of children were starving in Africa. Guerrillas posed with

Kalashnikovs, and a rock star was sprawled on a sofa as if he had just been shot by one of them. Politicians were making speeches from podiums decorated with slogans and banners, and two heads of government were shaking hands in a tentative tribal encounter as old as the species itself. Lastly, in the science section, a scientist was displaying the latest photographs of the sun, which, he claimed, in a certain number of years would explode and consume all trace of the planet.

So what's the good news? Matt wondered. He tossed the magazine aside and tried to look past Linda. The plane had broken through the layers of cloud and was now purring in a bright-blue sky, the fine pinhead beads of rain having been chased across the window and driven back into vapour.

Eventually the first of the meals was brought and, unable to divert her attention any more to the view outside, Linda resigned herself to conversation.

'I read your report on Chelyabinsk and the rest of the decommissioning programme. How widespread do you really think the racket is?'

Matt took a sip of red wine and winced. 'God, it's freezing. I bet this doesn't happen in First Class.' He smiled at her. 'I would have thought the office would send you Club at least.'

She ignored the comment. Matt shrugged. 'It's very hard to say, but from the general confusion everywhere I'd guess that it's getting worse. The generals have seen their divisions disbanded, in many cases they haven't been paid for months, inflation's rocketing, the economy's in ruins . . .'

'I get the picture.'

'All the new Russian mafia has to do is find one

general in the right place at the right time who'll listen to their offer and bingo! They've got their hands on a supply of plutonium, uranium and, if the Hong Kong report's true, on complete warheads and missile systems.'

'How did you become involved?'

'I could ask the same question,' Matt replied.

'Just another interdepartmental posting. But it's a far cry from the squadron for you, isn't it?'

'All good things eventually come to an end,' Matt said. Linda looked up and caught his eye, acknowledging the double meaning with a glare.

'They reckoned I was getting too old to be running around playing cowboys,' Matt continued.

'Well, that's about time!'

Matt smiled. 'I suppose I deserved that.' He sawed through a particularly tough piece of steak and squashed it into the mushy boiled vegetables. 'Life's been pretty dull since I was posted away from the Marines.'

'Forgive me if I don't sound too sorry for you,' Linda said with more bitterness than she had intended. She started to say something to disguise the strength of her resentment but left her last words hanging in the air.

Matt eased back in his seat and watched her toying with her food. 'You've never forgiven me, have you?'

Linda could feel his eyes on her. 'Why should I? There's nothing to forgive. We were never really compatible. It's as simple as that.'

'That's a load of cock and you know it.'

She turned on him, her eyes alive and burning. 'Then why did you just walk out?'

'It was Ireland, Linda. There was no mucking

around. Our work was being affected and sooner or later someone would have got hurt.'

'And don't you think I was hurt?'

'You know what I mean. Two undercover agents had already been compromised and taken out. If you'd been the next I'd never have forgiven myself.'

'It always seems to come back to you, doesn't it?'

'I didn't mean it like that. I could see the danger you were in and our relationship was only increasing the risks.'

'That's rubbish and you know it. You just wanted me on your own terms. You couldn't stand the idea of a woman competing on what you saw as your own ground. Sure you wanted me, but as some cosy little wife, nicely gift-wrapped in some faceless military quarters. The excitement was fine for you, but any girl of yours had to be locked away out of harm's reach.'

'Am I really such a sod for not wanting the IRA to get hold of you? They were ruthless enough to the blokes they snatched. What do you think they'd have done to you?'

'That was my problem.'

'Yes, but it was mine too and you couldn't see that. And while the gloves are off, if I remember, you weren't so chuffed whenever I was out on patrol or off on a mission. You see, it cuts both ways. OK, perhaps you're right. Perhaps I did want you on my terms. But you wanted me on yours just as much.'

They were both silent, the thoughts and emotions that had boiled inside them for almost two years jostling for expression now but coming out instead as the same overriding pain that still held them firmly in check. The hostess cleared away the trays and left them with coffee. Matt ordered a large brandy and relished the sweet trickle of liquid fire in his throat that burned away the words, driving them back inside where he had rashly believed them dead.

Linda too was confused. How the hell had it happened, this coming together after so great an effort at recovery? She found herself silently cursing the man next to her. Out of the corner of her eye she could see the edge of his jacket, smell the same aftershave, feel the same strong presence. But underneath the curses and the condemnation something else stirred, so far below the angry surface that she almost missed it, but not quite.

Strengthened by the brandy, Matt tried again. 'How's the cottage? I hear you've still got it.'

'Oh?'

'I was briefed on the attack. When they mentioned Llyn Brianne I assumed you were at the cottage.'

'I was.'

I suppose the alterations must be complete by now.'

'Yes,' Linda said stiffly. 'They are.'

Matt chuckled. 'I remember when I first saw it. I thought you were mad taking it on.'

'There you are again,' she said. 'You didn't like the independence of it.'

'Not at all. That was totally different. I thought it was terrific. I just couldn't envisage it the way you could. All I saw was this miserable, windswept shell. But I remember the way you spoke about it with such passion and imagination. So it's all come together?'

Linda relented a little. 'Yes, thank you. It has. It

hasn't been easy. What with the cost of renting a place in London during the week, it's taken me ages to save the money for all the repairs and everything. But I suppose I'm just about there now.' She finished her coffee, adding, 'You'd like it,' before she could stop herself.

Matt looked at his hands in his lap. 'I'm sure I would.' He was going to say that he didn't suppose he'd ever see it, but he finished his brandy instead.

By the time the first of the two in-flight films began Linda had already curled up to sleep. The light had dimmed outside and as the blinds were drawn and the film began, Matt looked at the sleeping form beside him. She had pulled her legs up under her, angling herself away from him defensively. Was it really so long ago that she would have rested her head on his shoulder? Yes, it was. The past was an altogether different country and the time they had spent there seemed as distant as if it had only happened in a story.

Feeling the need to stretch his legs, Matt unfastened his seat-belt and walked to the service area. All the passengers were either asleep or plugged into the film. Two hostesses were chatting in whispers, perched on fold-away stools in the small kitchen. Matt troubled one of them for another brandy and then stepped over to the thick window pane in the adjacent exit door. The sunset had all but deepened into night but on the brim of the horizon a livid swathe of scarlet and orange curved across the earth's distant surface nearly twelve kilometres below. It was impossible to tell whether they were flying over water or some land mass. No lights winked up at the tiny capsule as it droned through the encroaching darkness.

Looking out of the window at the vast emptiness, Matt could feel the same strange thrill that sometimes touched him when roaming on Dartmoor at night, a blend of feelings. There was fear, a sense of his own insignificance, and an almost overpowering sense of the earth's primitiveness. At times like that he knew how little the human animal had changed since its days of cave-dwelling infancy. This very aircraft in which he was travelling at some incredible speed to the other side of the world – it was just one more sophisticated tool, in essence not far removed from the first rickety wheel. Both were just markers on the technological spectrum which people like him had developed to tame everyday life.

But in the heart, he knew, nothing had changed. Nothing had been tamed. Once he would have recoiled at such a thought but not now. He had seen too much to be fooled by the illusion of civilization. The veneer had been stripped away in the Falklands, in the Gulf, on the streets of Belfast and even in the rural beauty of Ulster. His work had connected him with the underlife that most people were able to ignore, pretending it wasn't there. But Matt knew only too well just how close it was. Roaming on Dartmoor at night, or patrolling in the 'bandit country' of South Armagh, he could feel its hot breath on the back of his neck, and here, in the warmth and comfort of this rocketing cylinder, he could sense it all around them, barely inches away on the other side of the aircraft's fragile skin.

He had seen it in all its guises. In the clawing and

stabbing gutter fights amid the snow-covered rocks around Port Stanley, in the high-tech incineration of living flesh on the clogged and hellish Basra road, and in the murders, kneecappings and punishment beatings of the IRA and loyalist terrorists in Ireland. He glanced back at Linda; only the top of her head was visible above the rows of seats. Maybe she had been right to accuse him of being over-protective. But he couldn't help it. No one could ever be shielded from suffering and death. He had just wanted to improve the odds.

So here they were again. He wondered what awaited them in Hong Kong. Hopefully the investigation would be straightforward, but there had already been one attempt on Linda's life and if it was somehow connected to the find of the warhead in Hong Kong they could expect further dangers along the way.

Matt leaned against the back of a seat and took a sip of brandy, tipping his head back and feeling the wonderful burn in his throat. He found his thoughts going back to the cottage at Llyn Brianne. Linda had once driven him there to look at it. All the way she had enthused about the seclusion, the view, the countryside, and he had to admit that she had been right. That night they had slept on the floor, the wind howling in through the numerous cracks in the window frames and rattling the loose tiles on the roof.

He remembered their lovemaking, rolled in a couple of sleeping-bags zipped together and laid on an old mattress. It had been wonderful, and afterwards they lay tightly together in the dark with a storm raging outside and pushing to get in, and the slow morning greyness coming at last under the door and spreading over Linda's bare shoulders. Matt had slipped from the bags and gone outside to wash. When he returned, Linda had been sitting up, blinking and rubbing her eyes. He had tried to coax her out into the cold morning but she had refused, pulling him back instead and laughing and joking until they had ended up making love yet again, only stopping abruptly when the front door swung open and a sheep wandered in, chewing and quite unimpressed by the two glistening bodies, entwined and helpless with laughter on the rumpled sleeping-bags.

Matt finished his brandy and returned to his seat. After settling down as gently as possible so as not to disturb Linda, he leaned back and tried to sleep. But it was no use. There was too much to think about. While he had been away she had turned. The noise of the engines filled the cabin but even so, Matt could imagine the sound and gentle rhythm of Linda's breath, and when he turned his head to look at her before closing his eyes once again in an effort to sleep, she was watching him.

It was raining heavily when Sir Anthony Briggs stepped out of his office and marched briskly down Whitehall. An open-top tour bus drove slowly past, the taped commentary playing to a miserable huddle of soaked visitors on the upper deck, the bottom one already crammed, with small circles rubbed in the misted windows through which the more fortunate tourists were peering at the sights. Sir Anthony smiled wryly and turned into Downing Street. He produced his pass for the policeman at the large cast-iron gates and strode down the wet pavement, studiously avoiding the puddles. At the door to Number 10 another policeman in a rain cape nodded a greeting as the door opened and Sir Anthony stepped into the red-carpeted hallway.

'Morning, George,' he said, shaking the water off his umbrella and slipping out of his overcoat. 'Is the boss ready for me?'

'Good morning, Sir Anthony. I'll go and see.'

'Busy day?'

'Murder. There've been greeting calls from two new ambassadors, a press conference over the Conservative Party funds scandal, the Chancellor's been running through his budget proposals, the PM's dreading Question Time in the House this afternoon, and to cap it all Mrs PM phoned to say the cat's been run over.'

'Nothing out of the ordinary then?'

'You could say that.'

Sir Anthony moved into the ante-room and mopped his brow dry with a handkerchief, stuffing it back into his pocket as the door opened and he was ushered into the presence of the Prime Minister.

'Never let the buggers get you down,' the PM said cheerily as his private secretary bumbled out with his arms piled high with papers. He looked at his watch. 'Right, you've got ten minutes of my undivided attention.' He got up and marched to the door. 'After I've ordered some coffee, that is.' He swung open the door and shouted down the hallway before striding back to the table and sitting down.

'What more have you got for me?'

'Not a great deal yet, sir.'

The PM held up his hand. 'One minute, do we need the Chief of the Defence Staff in on this?'

Sir Anthony shook his head. 'No, Prime Minister. I've already given an update to the CDS and all the service chiefs. CGS has put the SAS on stand-by and GCHQ are getting their latest results to me shortly.'

'Good. Keep me informed.'

Sir Anthony nodded. He took some papers from his briefcase and slid them across to the Prime Minister. 'This is a summary of the decommissioning programme over the last six months. As you can see, there've been quite a few hiccups. Even if we assume that most of them have genuine excuses and that the warheads and missile bodies have indeed been destroyed, it still leaves a sizeable number unaccounted for.'

The Prime Minister scanned the sheets of paper. 'Are you suggesting that all these nuclear warheads could be trolling around the black markets of the world?'

Sir Anthony took a deep breath. 'Yes.' He watched the effect of his answer on the man opposite him. 'That is, I'm painting a worst-case scenario. Hopefully they've all been destroyed, just as the Soviet . . .'

'Russian,' the Prime Minister corrected.

'Sorry, Russian authorities say they have.'

'And what of the Hong Kong find?'

'That's not confirmed yet, sir. One of my operatives will be arriving in the Colony shortly and she's accompanied by someone who should be able to identify the device.'

'Good. What's he from?'

'Oddly enough, the SBS, but he's made nuclear weapon systems his speciality and he was also the person who first alerted us that we had a potential problem.'

The Prime Minister grimaced. 'I'd say it's gone a bit beyond potential, wouldn't you agree?'

'Er . . . yes, perhaps.'

'And what will they do when they get there?'

'They're under strict orders to cooperate with the Royal Hong Kong Police, but I don't doubt they'll do a little digging around of their own.'

'Undoubtedly,' the Prime Minister said with a sly smile. 'Just tell them not to step on any toes. The Governor's been on the phone to me this morning. Needless to say they're all very embarrassed by the whole episode. At least it's been kept out of the press so far.'

'Yes. And I consider it essential that it remains so. We don't yet know where the root problem is, but it may well be that we have to use the SAS boys to go in and do the business somewhere sensitive.'

'Any clues?'

'Not yet. But if the missiles are being transited through any third party we might be able to go in and stop it.'

'What if it's China?'

'Then we've got real problems. We'd have to wait and see where it is, but any operation there would be fraught with danger. With the trouble over the hand-over coming to a head the last thing we need is to get caught with British Special Forces stomping all over the Middle Kingdom.'

'I can tell you now, Sir Anthony, it won't happen. Not while I'm PM. I simply wouldn't authorize it.'

'Russia's much the same. Any covert operation there

would be a similarly high-risk affair. Relations have never been as good as they are now. In both cases we'd have to rely on purely diplomatic means.'

Sir Anthony leaned back in his chair and steepled his fingers. 'However, if we find that nuclear devices are going into Iraq or Iran, for instance, that's another matter altogether.'

'And what if there are other warheads in Hong Kong itself?'

'The SAS will be on stand-by but the RHKP have their own anti-terrorist force already on the ground.'

'Any good?'

'They're SAS-trained.'

'That doesn't answer my question.'

'I'm not a military man myself. I'd have to ask the Chief of the General Staff.'

'Well, let's see what he has to say. If he reckons they can handle whatever comes up I'm happy for the SAS to remain in England. There's no point flying them all the way out until we know whether they'll actually be needed or not.'

'Right, sir.'

'And what about the SBS? Do we need to alert them?'

Sir Anthony thought for a moment. 'That might be an idea, Prime Minister. I hadn't considered it but they could be useful. Especially if we find that warheads are being illegally transported on the high seas. The SBS would be the only ones with the necessary expertise.'

The Prime Minister pushed back his chair. 'Let's hope it doesn't come to that. God willing, this is just a one-off. But I'm afraid your ten minutes is up. Question Time beckons and I haven't run through my briefs yet. Let me know the moment you hear anything.'

'Yes, Prime Minister.'

Hu Fat had been watching the godown all morning and was content that Yip had found just the right place for the next phase of the operation. When the blue Nissan saloon pulled up outside the warehouse's front entrance and a small man in his early forties stepped out, Hu Fat smiled and reached for his briefcase.

'Time to go.'

With Yip at his heel, he sauntered across the street and went up to the man, who looked at him expectantly.

'Mr Lim?' the man asked politely.

Hu Fat smiled and held out his hand. 'Yes. I'm pleased to meet you. My assistant has told me much about your helpfulness.'

The man laughed in embarrassment and wagged a finger at Yip, unrecognizable in an ill-fitting suit. Hu Fat had also dressed for the occasion, but his own suit had been tailored for him by one of the best Indian cutters in the city. The cloth was English and the shoes Italian. He looked every inch the prosperous businessman.

'You'll be wanting to have a look around,' the man said eagerly.

Hu Fat nodded condescendingly. 'Indeed.'

'This way, this way,' the man said, scuttling away sideways like a crab, his two important customers in tow. 'I am sure it will meet your every requirement. But above all it will be very cost-effective. I will give you the best deal anywhere in town.'

'I know you will,' Hu Fat replied.

Entering the warehouse by a small side door, Hu Fat looked up at the ample storage space. Huge cranes hung from overhead beams and rails were laid down the centre of the warehouse to cater for any rolling stock that needed to be transferred straight from ship to rail system.

'You see,' the man said proudly. 'Every modern convenience.'

'Wonderful,' Hu Fat replied, truly impressed. Behind him Yip chuckled and shook his head in wonder.

'And is there an office?'

'This way. I'll show you.'

The man led them up a tall flight of metal steps, to a glass-panelled door, where he fished in his pocket and produced a set of keys.

'Just one minute. We'll have it open in a second.'

As he entered the room Hu Fat looked out of the windows, which gave on to the waterfront. A quay ran parallel to the warehouse and on all sides the other warehouses and jetties were deserted.

'It's very quiet,' he remarked.

'The man's eyes narrowed. 'It's . . . private, if you know what I mean.'

Hu Fat stared at him hard until the man broke into a nervous giggle. 'I mean, it's none of my business what you want it for, but if it's quiet you want, this is certainly the place.'

He was right. Looking out of the windows at the back of the office Hu Fat saw the desolate sandy hills of Castle Peak rising up to meet a clear-blue sky.

'And what guarantee have I got that our deal will stay private?'

'You have my word. In this business I rely on my reputation for discretion. I own this and one other godown in Yaumatei. All I do is hire them out. I don't give a damn what they're used for.'

'Good. I'm very glad to hear that. Not that we'd dream of breaking the law, of course.'

'Of course,' the man replied, his eyes wide with innocence.

Hu Fat thought for a minute. 'Who else knows about this arrangement?'

'No one. Only me, and that's the truth.'

'Good. But surely your wife or secretary knows you're here?'

'Wife? Do I look stupid?' The man roared with laughter. 'When I need a wife I go to the floating brothels in Yaumatei. It's cheaper to row out to the sampans and buy a girl when you feel the need. And as for a secretary, I do all the administration myself.'

'Then you are all alone in the world?'

The man frowned, perturbed for the first time at the line of questioning. 'Yes. I am alone.'

'I will ask you once more,' Hu Fat said coldly, all friendliness gone from his voice. 'Who else knows you are here?'

The man went slowly pale and answered, 'No one, I promise,' before he realized his mistake and frantically tried to backtrack.

'Well, my assistant knows,' he stammered, his tongue tripping over the words. 'And my brothers, of course. In fact they will be coming here to help us with the contract.'

Hu Fat grinned broadly, hugely amused by the pathetic attempt at a lie. 'But didn't you just say you were alone in the world?' he asked wide-eyed in mock puzzlement. 'That no one knew you were here? That no one would come looking for you? Surely you weren't lying to me?'

At his side Yip chuckled, loving the game.

'No! Of course I wouldn't lie to you. I just meant that I . . .'

'That you what? That you didn't want me to think I could slit your scrawny throat without a care in the world?'

The man blubbered, sensing the icy fingers of danger clamping tightly about him. 'I . . . I . . .'

'I . . . I . . .' Hu Fat mimicked, as his hand slid out from his jacket and he pressed down on the fat wooden handle of a switch-blade with his thumb, springing a six-inch steel blade into place.

The man looked desperately about for an avenue of escape but Hu Fat and Yip were between him and the door. He let out a shrill cry like a snared animal and tried to dart round them, but Yip was too quick for him and dropped him to the floor. In an instant Hu Fat stood over him.

'Thank you for the hire of your godown,' he said politely. 'Too bad you won't be enjoying the pleasures of the Yaumatei sampans again.'

Having positioned the blade carefully over the man's heart, he smiled nicely as he drove it in.

7

The news that his stay in Hong Kong was to be extended and that he was to be assigned to the team heading up the inquiry into the find of the nuclear device in Tolo, came as a pleasant surprise to Sergeant Des Cooper. Not so much because it confirmed that he had been right in the first place, but more because Matt Harbin was to be one of the key members of the team.

Des could remember when Matt had been a young lieutenant on his first tour with the SBS. Des had been a corporal then and together the two of them had grown in the organization, each learning from the other as well as developing a hard-won mutual respect. They had been in the same Section for most of their tours and in the course of numerous training exercises had come to know each other's strengths and weaknesses. But it was on real operations that the bond had been cemented.

In the Falklands they had found themselves as one half of a four-man reconnaissance team that was put ashore a good two weeks before the first major landings in San Carlos Water. After landing by raiding craft from a submarine, they had made their way inland and established an OP to monitor

Argentine deployments. The shit had hit the fan when the OP's position had been compromised and they had been obliged to shoot their way out. One of the men had been wounded in the engagement and they had spent a rough four days on the run before rendezvousing with a helicopter and being lifted out. During the evasion phase they had been pursued by up to a company of Argentine marines, helicopters and Pucara fighter aircraft equipped for ground attack. Des had never forgotten Matt's leadership and cool, calm directions throughout. He had the ability to think clearly even under the most extreme pressure, producing reasonable solutions to even the most desperate problems. He was a good guy to have with you if you were in a tight corner.

After that their careers had gone their separate ways. Matt had gone off to do the sort of dull headquarters jobs that fast-track officers got pulled into, and Des had done a stint with the SAS at Hereford. He had come across Matt several times in the intervening years but they hadn't actually been on an operation together until the Gulf War. Then, once again, they had found themselves in the thick of it with only their wits and their M203 assault rifles and grenade launchers between them and half a battalion of Iraqis. They had been conducting a covert recce up the Shatt-al-Arab waterway in the direction of Basra when an Iraqi flotilla had decided to come down it in the opposite direction. They had beached their badly shot-up craft and set off on foot to exfiltrate out of the danger area, the enemy in hot pursuit. However, when the Iraqis had walked into Matt's third devastating ambush, discretion had got the better of their valour and they had withdrawn in some disorder, 40mm grenades from Matt's M203 following hard on their heels.

Once back in safety the patrol had been retasked and in the closing days of the war Des and Matt found themselves with the main body of the land forces in the race towards Basra. By that stage the Iraqi divisions were crumbling and everywhere the enemy were surrendering by the thousand. But there were still pockets of hard resistance and Matt and Des had run foul of one or two of them.

Despite the difficult work of the investigation ahead Des hoped that there would be time for a good long talk over a few beers. The CO had called him in that morning to give him the news about his extension and also to tell him of Matt's impending arrival. Des had gone straight to the transport pool to find the duty driver and stand him down. He would go to the airport himself and collect his ex-boss and the other member of the team from London.

The traffic out to Kai Tak airport was as thick as ever. Over on Lantau Island the construction of the new airport was underway, although it would be several years before it was completed and ready to handle the ever-increasing traffic from all over the world. For now Kai Tak would have to cope. With its single runway jutting perilously out into the eastern end of the harbour it had seen more than one aircraft skid over the edge into the filthy green water. The approach and take-off routes for many of the flights lay over the crowded heart of Kowloon itself. It had always struck Des as a miracle that so far the Colony had never suffered the catastrophe of a fully laden Jumbo ploughing into the crowded tenements.

He remembered coming in to land for the first time some years earlier, looking out of the window and being startled to see himself level with an apartment block. The aircraft had been so low he had almost been able to see what the occupants were watching on TV in their tiny flats.

When he had signed for the black staff car, Des headed off early to the airport to allow plenty of time to park and be ready to meet the incoming flight. However, as usual the combination of roadworks and traffic jams delayed him so that by the time he pushed his way through the bustling crowds thronging the arrival hall, the flight had already landed and the first of the passengers were pushing their trolleys down the steep ramp and into the waiting arms of relatives, friends or taxi drivers eager for a fare.

He didn't have long to wait before he recognized the tall figure of Matt Harbin, but a second later he was stunned to see Linda Kirkdale following close behind. In a flash he realized what had happened. He and Matt had been working together when Matt and Linda had broken up and he had witnessed at first hand the effect on his boss. He couldn't help wondering how long a shadow the past relationship of Matt and Linda would cast over their participation in the inquiry.

'Over here, boss,' Des called above the jostling heads.

Matt turned in his direction and broke into a surprised smile when he saw the familiar face from his SBS days. He pushed through the crowd and shook Des warmly by the hand. Des noticed that Matt looked tired. It was nothing unusual after a fourteen-hour non-stop flight, but he suspected that the weariness had more to do with the confrontation with Linda than with jet lag. But he didn't have time to say anything before Linda herself joined them.

'Hello,' she said, holding out her hand. 'It's Sergeant Cooper, isn't it?'

Des beamed. 'Now that's what I call a memory. Call me Des.'

'It's been a long time. Where was it?'

Des took her trolley and steered it towards the exit. 'Ireland, wasn't it?'

'Oh yes.' The smile on her face stiffened but remained polite, friendly. She threw a sidelong glance at Matt, but he was busy trying to avoid a collision with a family of five Chinese pushing their way into the concourse. Des watched her expression, trying to read her thoughts. How had she taken it? he wondered. Matt had had the support of his mates and another fast-moving mission to help him recover, and even then Des had been surprised by the wound he had carried and concealed. He supposed there had been no such buffer for Linda, returning to the soulless anonymity of London and an office life devoid of helpful distractions.

'So how have you been keeping?' he asked jovially.

'OK, thanks,' she answered, more at ease again. 'I might have guessed it would be you on the Tolo operation.'

'Well, a bloke's got to keep his hand in.'

Matt drew alongside them as they headed for the multi-storey car park. 'What's the programme then?'

Des laughed. 'Ten minutes off the plane and you want to get stuck in.'

'You know me. Never one for hanging around.'

'We're off to see a Chief Inspector Turner tomorrow morning. Until then your time's your own.'

'Where are we staying?'

'They've given you rooms in Gun Club Barracks.'

'Tamar's closed?'

'Yes. It's all part of the rundown for 1997. The government's selling off the military real estate for redevelopment so the Chinese People's Liberation Army doesn't have anywhere to billet their troops.'

'I'm not surprised. The last thing potential investors want is a load of nose-picking PLA squaddies sauntering around Exchange Square, machine-guns at the ready.'

'Yeah,' Des replied. 'It's been bad enough having the arse-scratching Brits for the last century or more.'

Once in the car, Des drove out of the airport and made his way laboriously back through the flyovers, underpasses and roadworks towards the centre of Kowloon. He had diplomatically split up his two charges, shepherding Linda into the front seat and Matt into the back.

'So,' he tried, after a difficult silence. 'How come you two ended up on the same assignment again?'

Might as well go in at the deep end, he thought.

Matt smiled. 'I wrote the original report and Linda works in nuclear non-proliferation.'

'The same organization as in Ireland?' Des asked, glancing across at Linda.

'The same one.'

'Well, there you go. Sounds like fate to me,' Des said, not bothering to disguise the mischief in his voice.

In the rear-view mirror he caught sight of Matt's warning frown.

'Anyway,' he continued quickly. 'Like I was saying,

tomorrow we're off to see Fred Turner. He's the guy who's heading the RHKP side of the inquiry.'

'Nothing in the press yet?' Matt asked.

'Not a whisper.'

'That's one thing to be grateful for. If word got out it could create a mass panic.'

'Where the fuck would people run to though?' Des asked.

'Don't know, but you could bet there'd be mobs on the street and the police would be hard pressed to maintain law and order.'

Linda had been watching the passing crowds and drinking in the unfamiliar sights and sounds. Turning to Des, she asked, 'Have the police any idea what the Triads were up to?'

'Not that I know of. I should think they've got every possible contact and informer working on it round the clock.'

'They're probably hoping we'll sort it out for them,' Matt said.

Des laughed. 'I wouldn't bank on it, boss. You'll probably find they won't give you the time of day. My guess is they've got egg on their faces and they've been ordered to be nice to you, that's all. They'll be going hell for leather to sort it out all by themselves like big boys. The last thing they probably want is a handful of Brits telling them how to do things.'

'You wouldn't do that, would you, Matt?' Linda asked over her shoulder, the sarcasm stinging him.

Des gunned the motor and shot the car into Austin Road. 'Ah, that's what I like to hear. Just like old times. Just like Ireland.'

* * *

The Bund and waterfront of Shanghai had changed little in the years since the foreign colonialists left and the Communist government took over. Impressive majestic buildings vied with more modern ramshackle neighbours for dominance of the scene. Steamers, barges, cargo ships and ferries ploughed through the murky waters of the Huangpu rivalled by an even heavier weight of traffic along the adjacent roadways of the Bund. Trees were in leaf but the rise in prosperity over the past ten years had resulted in a corresponding increase in traffic and pollution, so much so that the greenery was already showing signs of contamination. Here, as elsewhere throughout China, little had been done to protect the environment in the mad and vulgar rush to get rich.

Yet for all its smog, noise and filth, Shanghai held a particular fascination for Yang Zulin. As he strolled along the Bund he enjoyed watching the bustle. It was a vibrant city, China's only real rival to the wealth and power of capitalist Hong Kong, some thirteen hundred kilometres further south along the coast. He turned into a small park and watched the old people going through their tai chi exercises, the gentle movements flowing one into the other. He regretted never having learned it himself but he had always been more concerned with the here and now. The practitioners' eyes held a glazed, far-away look as they concentrated on the exercise pattern of hand and foot movements. It was a sublimely gentle art, combining both mental and physical aspects and Yang sat down on a bench, soaking up their calm like the relaxing waters of a hot bath.

The park had been concreted over, but here and there defiant blades of grass were poking through the cracks, making the most of each narrow opportunity to state their case and remind the city dwellers that nature would have the last word.

A row of old men sat on the other side of the path from Yang, each holding a caged songbird. While their owners talked or played draughts, the birds bounced up and down, stirred by unknown forces that swept through them at the sight, so close in the overhead branches, of their freer brethren.

A siren wailed and, looking round, Yang saw a convoy of police cars weave through the momentarily halted traffic. He checked his watch. Of course, he thought; those would be the prisoners being taken for public execution in the stadium on the outskirts of the city. Found guilty of offences ranging from car theft or political opposition, to murder, they would be forced to kneel in a row, placards hung round their necks emblazoned with their crimes, before being shot in the back of the head with a pistol.

With the sirens fading in the distance, the songbirds started up again. Yang looked up as a thin figure approached and sat down next to him. The man was dressed in a stylish, loose-fitting overcoat and smart hat, and Yang smiled secretly at the incongruity of the vivid orange trainers on his feet. China might well beat the capitalists at their own game, he thought, but a simple thing like a Western appreciation of matching colours would take longer to evolve.

'Everything is going according to plan?' Yang asked, apparently addressing thin air.

'You know about the problems in Hong Kong?' the

man replied, unaware that he was seriously annoying a powerful man by answering one question with another.

'Of course. But I take it you have it in hand.'

The man grunted, looking towards Yang for the first time. Under the broad brim of the hat Yang could see an ugly face, the cheeks hollow and scarred. The man smiled but looked away sharply at the cold expression of rebuke on Yang's face.

'Take care, my friend, take care. We must not be seen together.' Yang looked idly across at a barge labouring up the Huangpu, his eyes doing a professional sweep of everyone in the park as he did so. The barge was laden with bricks for one of the many building sites in the city. With the water lapping hungrily at its gunwales it looked as if a single extra brick would sink it.

In an attempt to appear inconspicuous the man started to explore his uneven teeth, digging enthusiastically between the gaps and stumps for shreds of his last meal, talking at the same time. Listening to his report, Yang couldn't help wishing that this was one of the men shortly to be kneeling in the stadium before the coldly scowling guards and executioners. He wondered what the man's orange trainers would look like on the corpse, but then the guards would probably have stolen them beforehand to save such treasures from getting soiled when the body toppled forwards and the blood dribbled round the sides of the clenched face to pool beneath the startled eyes.

When the man had finished and sat silently watching the caged songbirds, Yang stretched, yawned and folded his arms.

'Good. I'm glad steps have been taken to sort out this mess. I wouldn't want there to be a second compromise. There's too much at stake.'

'That is well understood,' the man replied, foolishly thinking that he had just been praised, oblivious of Yang's deathly imaginings directed at him. 'A lot of money must have been wasted.'

Yang glanced at him, his contempt poorly concealed. 'Money is nothing. Do you understand? Nothing.'

The man blanched, sensing Yang's suppressed anger.

'I only meant . . .'

Yang stood up abruptly. 'It doesn't matter.' He glanced around the park. The tai chi had finished and the elderly people were going through a series of warm-down exercises, holding on to tree trunks and swinging their legs slowly back and forth, circling their heads and waving their arms. Watching them, Yang felt suddenly very stiff and old himself. He turned back to the man, who was moving away in the opposite direction.

'Comrade,' Yang called softly, his voice little more than a hiss of exhaled breath.

The man turned expectantly.

'I will await news of the next phase with anticipation. It will go well.'

Uncertain whether Yang's last words were encouragement or threat, the man nodded solemnly and walked away. Yang waited until he had disappeared before leaving the park and strolling back down the Bund. In the park the game of draughts had finished and the old men were getting to their feet and hobbling away, the songbirds clinging firmly to their perches in the swaying cages.

Chief Inspector Fred Turner sat back behind his desk and surveyed the three people in front of him.

'I wish I'd known about your trip to the Wanchai club earlier, Sergeant Cooper. From now on I must insist that you tell me everything. If the police go in one direction and you lot in another, the whole investigation will go off at half cock.'

Matt glanced at Des, who smiled mischievously like a schoolboy.

'No problem,' Des replied. 'After my experience with Inspector Chan I wasn't sure who I could trust, so I reckoned it would be best if I just went with one of my mates.'

'Well, in future . . .' Fred began.

Des held up his hands in surrender. 'Understood. Don't say another word.'

As Fred outlined the progress of the inquiry so far, Linda jotted down the relevant details in her notebook, pausing every so often to ask a pertinent question.

At a break in the briefing Matt asked, 'When can we see the device?'

'This afternoon. I've got a car standing by to take you all out to Lantau Island, where we're keeping it. It's been made safe now, but when we thought it might still go off we put it as far away as we could while still keeping it in Hong Kong waters.'

Matt smiled. 'I'm afraid there isn't anywhere far enough for a device like that.'

Fred shrugged. 'So I've been told, but it still seemed better than holding it in the middle of Central.'

'What's the next step?' Linda asked.

'When we've got as much information from our informers and other sources as we can gather, I intend to launch coordinated raids on the premises of every Triad that we believe is involved.'

'Won't that arouse some suspicion?'

'We'll do it under the cover of a crack-down on the drug dealers or something,' Fred replied.

'Nice one,' Des remarked. 'And what do you hope to find?'

'Solid information on who's behind it and whether there's any more out there.'

Matt flipped his notebook shut. 'We should plan on the worst case and assume there is. Or at least that they might be planning to get hold of another one.'

'That's my fear,' Fred said. 'Next time we might not be so lucky. And if the Triads get their hands on another nuclear device the government will be at their mercy.'

An hour after leaving his office Fred and the others stepped off the Lantau ferry at Silvermine Bay and got into the two waiting cars that Fred had organized.

'It'll take about half an hour to Tai O,' Fred told Matt as he strapped himself in and the cars set off. In the rear car the driver waited until Des and Linda were settled in the back and then followed his boss out of the car park and on to the long, winding road to the south of the island.

'So,' said Des, taking advantage of his first private chat with Linda. 'I was sorry to hear the way things turned out between you and Matt after Ireland.'

'Thank you,' she said. 'But it seems a long time ago. I think we've both got over it by now.'

Des smiled. 'Well, I know the boss and I can tell you he hasn't.'

Linda looked at him inquiringly, unsure whether or not to resent his intrusion on her past relationship.

'And from what I've seen I'm not so certain you have, either,' Des continued.

Linda felt herself prickling. 'Nonsense. What makes you say that?'

'I may be an old squaddie masquerading as a sergeant but I've been around a bit. It's painful watching the two of you together, both of you trying to pretend everything's fine. Anyone with an ounce of insight can see that it's not.'

'Really?' Linda said smiling. 'And what do you suggest, Professor?'

'What about a bit of honesty for starters?'

'Honesty about what and to whom?' Linda said, getting ever more uncomfortable with the accuracy of Des's perception.

'You could admit to each other that you're still . . .'

'Still what?'

'Concerned about each other?'

Linda looked away, staring out of the window at the steadily rising hills and the thickening woodland around them. Fearing that he had gone too far, Des sighed.

'But perhaps it's none of my business.'

'It's a bit late for that,' said Linda sharply, but instantly regretting it.

The cars drove on, Matt and Fred exchanging theories about the origins of the nuclear device, Des and Linda sitting in silence in the rear car. As they passed through the small seaside village of Pui O,

Des noticed the comfortable holiday villas and little restaurants before the cars sped out of the far side and climbed along the winding coast road towards the Shek Pik reservoir.

They had just rounded a bend when Des noticed the front car slowing to a halt.

'What's up?' Linda asked.

'I'm not sure.'

Craning over the driver's shoulder, Des could just see the tail end of a car protruding from a clump of bushes.

'It looks like an accident,' he said warily. Linda caught his tone immediately and looked behind. The road was empty. In front, Fred had got out of his car and was walking towards the car, which looked as if it had careered off the road and over the side of the slope. However, although Matt had also got out, he had moved off to a flank and seemed to be looking closely at the road's surface itself.

'What's he up to?' Linda asked.

'Checking for skid marks,' Des said, all hesitation gone, his voice cool and calm but different from the way he had spoken until now.

'Let's get out. I'm getting claustrophobic in here.' Reaching over the police driver's shoulder, he undid the flap of the man's holster and whipped out the revolver. 'Don't mind me, mate.'

Before the policeman could protest Des was out of the car, Linda springing out behind him.

'Stay close to me, love,' he said.

'I fully intend to.'

A woman appeared from the lip of the road where the car had gone over the edge. She cradled her arm swathed in a makeshift bandage and was gabbling rapidly in Cantonese.

'What's she saying?' Matt called over to Fred.

Fred spoke to the woman.

'She said there are two casualties down below,' he called back over his shoulder. 'Come and give me a hand.'

'Careful, Fred,' Matt called as the Chief Inspector strode towards the woman, beckoning his driver to join him. But he didn't pay Matt any attention.

When he had closed to within ten metres of the woman the expression on her face changed, the previous wince of pain hardening into a cold stare.

Des noticed it first. 'Hit the deck!'

As Fred stared in disbelief and horror the woman withdrew her hand, which until that moment had been concealed in the improvised bandage. Dwarfing the small clenched fist that brought it into the aim was a 9mm Makarov pistol – levelled straight at him.

'Drop!'

Compelled by the force of Des's shouted command, Fred fell to the ground just as two rounds from Des's police-issue Smith & Wesson .38 clipped past his ear and slammed into the woman before her finger could tighten on the trigger. Toppling back over the sharp drop, her body crumpled out of sight, the snap and slash of branches telling of her fall. Fred's driver had barely stepped from the lead car when there was a tell-tale whoosh from the thickly wooded hillside overlooking the road and his vehicle exploded in an orange ball of flame and flying metal.

'Ambush!' Matt screamed, and darted for the driver,

dragging him clear of the burning wreckage. But it was too late. He was already dead.

Grabbing his pistol and spare ammunition, Matt rushed for Fred and helped him into cover.

'Over here!' Des shouted.

Darting past the inferno, Matt and Fred dived over the far side of the road, landing in a heap beside Des and Linda.

'Nice shooting,' Matt said as he checked the drum of his revolver to ensure it was full.

'It's amazing I even gave her a headache with this fucking peashooter,' Des complained, taking advantage of the pause to slip out the empty cartridges and replace them with two new bullets.

With a loud crash the driver of the second vehicle slid down the bank beside them, his face white with fear. He looked at his revolver in Des's hand and seemed to be thinking about asking for it back but thought better of it.

There was another tremendous explosion and the second police car erupted in a ball of flame.

'Jesus Christ!' Fred shouted. 'This is a bloody battle zone! What the fuck's going on?'

'It's your patch,' Linda snapped, cool and controlled, wishing she had a handgun herself. 'I was hoping you'd tell us.'

Fred opened his mouth but Matt spoke first, instinctively taking command. 'Save it. Right now we've got to get out of here. We're sitting in their killing ground.'

So far all the firing had come from the wooded slope that climbed away from the road on the other side of the ambush site. Behind the position where they had taken cover, Matt saw that the ground dropped away into an area of thick undergrowth before rising gently again and disappearing into thick woods.

'We'll try this way,' he said.

Linda held back. 'How do we know it's not a come-on?'

'They didn't expect us to get out of the cars alive. If we're lucky, they haven't got it covered.'

'Let's just fucking move!' Des shouted, giving Linda a hard shove in the back.

After sliding down to the bottom of the slope, the five of them broke into the bushes and pushed and slashed their way ever deeper into the welcome concealment of the jungle. From behind them a burst of machine-gun fire raked the bushes. There was a shout and Des turned round to see the police driver stumble and fall. He darted back for him.

'Give us a hand!'

Fred gripped the man under one arm while Des took the other, and together they helped him away from the ambush site as a livid patch of blood spread across the pale-green chest of his uniform tunic.

'This man needs help,' Fred panted as they dragged him after Matt, starting up the slope that led into the relative safety of the woods.

'No time now,' Matt called back. 'If we stop here they'll cut us to pieces. We'll all die.'

As if to reinforce his point a second burst of fire riddled the bushes, followed by a series of bursts, each one heavier than the last.

'Sounds like they've brought up the fucking big stuff,' Des gasped as he heaved the policeman over the trunk of a fallen tree, bullets snapping in the air around him. He checked the casualty. 'Fred's right, boss. This guy's a goner if we don't stop soon.'

Matt stopped on the brow of a small rise. They had climbed now to a spot level with the road, separated from the ambush site by a good hundred metres of undergrowth and trees. In front of them the ground rose even more sharply all the way to the first of the big hills that dominated Lantau in a jagged spine running the length of the island.

'OK. We'll make a stand here.'

Easing the wounded man to the ground, Fred went to rip open the man's tunic to get at the wound. Des stopped him.

'Not here. It looks like he's got a sucking chest wound. Blood's light and frothy. Clamp something over it and press hard. Seal the hole front and back. Linda, give him a hand.'

Darting back to where Matt lay behind a rock, Des dropped into position beside him.

'Arcs?'

'You take nine to twelve. I'll cover round to three o'clock.'

'Roger. Wish we had some proper fucking fire-power though.'

'Make the best of what you've got,' Matt replied.

The firing from the road had stopped but below them Matt and Des could hear the sound of several people thrashing around in the bushes.

'Here they come,' Matt said softly.

'Can I help?'

They turned round to see Fred holding a Walther PPK.

'Jesus,' Des grinned, 'it's James fucking Bond. Shaken *and* stirred.'

Lying down beside them, Fred aimed at the approaching sounds. The attackers had fanned out and approached in an extended line. To the extreme left of Des's arc a man emerged from some bushes. Des steadied and fired. The man clutched his stomach and doubled up, dropping a Polish RAK PM-63 machine-pistol to the ground.

'God, what I'd give for that,' Des whistled.

On the right, a second man slumped to his knees and fired a long burst at the flash from Des's muzzle. But Matt was on to him. The earth at the man's side spat once as Matt's first round missed, but the next round found its mark in the centre of his chest. The man coughed hard as if winded, seeming surprised to have been hit, then almost gracefully toppled over on to his side and lay still.

There were shouts deeper in the bushes and a sudden fusillade of shots.

'Either they're about to pull out or they're getting ready to rush us,' Matt said, calmly reloading. 'That's the fun of combat,' he smiled genially at the pallid Chief Inspector next to him. 'You never know which.'

8

With mounting rage Hu Fat had watched the ambush develop on the road below him. Incredibly, apart from the one driver killed in the car, the rest of the intended victims had got clean away. He had given strict orders that as soon as the cars halted, the RPG 7 anti-tank rockets were to be fired, catching all the occupants still inside. That way a nice clean kill would have been achieved with no messing around. But no. Against his better judgement he had handed over command of the operation to a senior soldier of the Black Wolf Triad. It was all part of the new cooperation that had been forced on them by the vast scope of what the boss was calling the Hong Kong Gambit. As far as Hu Fat was concerned it was in danger of becoming a farce. He was convinced that he could have handled the entire venture with just his own resources. However, his boss was the one calling the shots, so if it was cooperation he wanted, cooperation he would have, fuck-ups and all.

He had found himself a nice little spot higher up the wooded hillside than the killing group, and had settled down beside a tree to watch the developments. The moment he had seen the door of the rear car open and a man move quickly away he knew that everything was about to go to rat shit. The way the man moved indicated to Hu Fat that he was dealing with a professional. The old car accident scam was bullshit and he had said so, but the Black Wolves had insisted. It had worked with a bullion robbery, they told him.

'I think you'll find that these fellows aren't quite the same material as the dumb security guards,' he had warned them. And of course he had been right. It was well known that the police-issue handgun was a piece of useless shit and yet the *gweilo* had dropped the woman from a very respectable range. From the noise she made going over the hillside she was obviously out for the count. Not bad shooting for a foreign devil.

By the time the morons had got the first of the RPG 7s into action the target car was empty except for one expendable running-dog policeman. Another of the men had also aroused Hu Fat's interest. After debussing from the first car he had executed similarly impressive combat movement drills. After that it had all become depressingly predictable until finally Hu Fat had made his way down the hillside, floored the commander of the disastrous ambush with a straight-handed finger thrust deep into the solar plexus, and taken command of the follow-up himself.

Having sent half of the force in extended line pursuit after the fleeing targets, he had taken the remainder of the Triad soldiers and led them in a wide arc to establish a cut-off position in the rear of the likely escape route. He knew that time was no longer on his side. He had intended a simple hit and run, not this long-winded cross-country race. It wouldn't be long before reports of the attack reached the police station at Tai O and a heavily armed support group came racing down the road.

Hearing the bursts of fire and the single weak answering cracks of the police Smith & Wessons, he smiled knowingly, imagining the success of his feint. The sacrifice of a few Black Wolves would be well worth it if his ploy worked. After pushing the pace through the dense undergrowth for some ten minutes he arrived at a place which he judged must be above the policemen.

'Shake out in a firing line here. Get down, shut up, and wait till I tell you to fire,' he commanded roughly. The Triad soldiers scowled but having seen the ease with which this unpleasant character had dropped their boss, no one questioned the order.

'Now we wait,' Hu Fat said contemptuously. 'We wait for them to come to us. Only this time we fire when I say so.'

Matt waited until the firing had stopped and the last of the rustling bushes to his front had fallen silent before thinking out his next move.

'They've gone,' Fred said triumphantly.

But Matt wasn't so sure. Des too was hesitant about moving.

'Wasn't much of a follow-up, was it?'

'But they're not trained soldiers,' Fred protested.

'They were good enough to know how to use rocket launchers and sub-machine-guns,' Matt said.

Fred got to his knees. 'Well, I think we should get out of here. We'll have to walk to Tai O and as soon as we're there I'll set up a search. If we can call in the

Marine Police in time we might be able to prevent them leaving the island.'

Des looked around at the overshadowing hill country. 'I reckon we should go across country. Never go back into a killing ground. It's SOP.'

'I know,' Matt said. 'But nothing about this operation's Standard Operating Procedure.'

'What do we do about him?' Des asked, pointing to the policeman.

Linda sat back on her heels beside the body. 'There's not much any of us can do. He's dead.'

Fred glared through the trees in the direction of the road, where the flames from the burning cars had died down, to be replaced by thick black plumes of belching smoke, acrid with the smell of oil and rubber.

'The bastards'll pay for this.'

'Then let's ensure we get out alive to see that they do,' Matt said.

They started away through the trees, climbing steadily. But they had barely gone twenty metres when Des stopped.

'What's the matter?' Matt asked.

Des frowned, sinking on to one knee. 'I don't know.'

'Oh, come on,' Fred said impatiently. 'The longer we delay, the more chance those fuckers have of getting away.'

'No, wait,' Matt said. He had learned over many years to respect Des's intuition.

'There's something familiar about all of this.' He glanced up at the innocent-looking hillside in front of them, the pines swaying gently in the sunlight, inviting them into their welcoming shade. Des nodded slowly.

'I reckon I know who's behind this. It's got the same hallmarks as Tolo.' He turned to Matt. 'Don't you think we fought off that follow-up party a little too easily? If I'm right, that was the decoy.'

'Don't be stupid,' Fred protested. 'At least two of their men were killed.'

'This fucker doesn't give a shit. If he's who I think he is he's up there right now waiting for us. On Tolo we underestimated him and he slipped round the back. I saw what he did to Josh Higgs.'

'Well, what if it isn't him?' Fred answered, becoming more cautious, infected by Des's suspicions.

'Do you want to risk it?' Linda said. 'What do we do, Matt?'

Matt thought for a moment. If Des had a hunch, he for one was not about to ignore it. But there were only two avenues of escape, the hillside or back through the ambush killing ground, a route that under normal circumstances he would never even consider.

'We'll go back down to the road.'

'That's fine by me,' Linda said.

'But we'll keep down in the siding for as long as possible, below the level of the road itself. When we reach the Shek Pik dam we'll contour round below it to the south. I wouldn't like to be caught in the middle of a bare-arsed feature like that with a Triad killing group on either end.'

'How far is it to Tai O from there?' Des asked.

'About an hour's walk,' Fred replied.

After a final check on his revolver Matt led the way back down to the road.

'And when we get there, Fred, you can show us this bomb of yours.'

*   *   *

Two days later the same group of four sat in the operations room of the RHKP headquarters building. Fred stepped up to the briefing map, where a dozen or more coloured pins were stuck in a street plan of Hong Kong and Kowloon.

'I want the raids to happen at exactly the same time,' he said. 'The Triads mustn't be able to get any warning to each other that we're making our move. With luck we'll sweep up the information we're after.'

In the rows of seats before him the officers of the police Special Operations Unit each made notes on their own allotted tasks. At the back of the room Matt, Des and Linda listened carefully. The briefing had gone well and all the points had been covered. The information received from the police informers had been sketchy but just enough to go on. By adding it to what he already knew about the criminal underworld, the Chief Inspector was confident that he had been able to identify the Triads involved and the locations of the majority of their bases in the brothels and bars of the Colony.

Sitting between Matt and Linda, Des was still thinking about the trip to Lantau. When they had finally got to Tai O and seen the device, it had been confirmed. It was one of the integral nuclear mini-warheads from a Soviet SS-18 MIRV missile. Looking at it in stunned surprise, Matt had voiced the concern in all their minds.

'The question I want answered is where are the other nine that sit beside it under the missile nose cap.'

He hoped that the raids now being planned would at least reassure everyone that they weren't in the Colony and that the find had been a one-off. If that was the case then it would become a matter for NATO, the UN and Russia's Minatom. Of course it would still leave the question of how and why the warhead had been smuggled out of Russia from under the noses of the inspectors, and who had arranged to ship it to Hong Kong. He reckoned that the next day or two would prove very interesting.

Des glanced at Linda. He had to admit that he'd been impressed by her in the Lantau ambush. She had been as cool and unruffled as she had been in Ireland. Matt too had proved that he hadn't lost any of his old touch in a tight corner. But something else had happened. Years of experience had honed Des's senses to a fine pitch and he had been particularly pleased to pick up the slightest of changes in the relationship between Matt and Linda. It was so slender that they weren't even aware of it themselves, but to Des that wasn't surprising. They were both still more concerned with concealing their deep feelings for each other. But for Des it was as obvious as it could be.

He settled back in his seat and folded his arms as Fred brought his briefing to an end by running through the numerous coordinating instructions that would pull the many separate raids together into one integrated whole. Des smiled. If things went on like this the only nuclear fission taking place would be between Linda and his old boss. Mind you, he thought, in its own way that could prove equally as explosive.

Oblivious to the noise from the surrounding community of floating sampans, Hu Fat was gasping, his eyes tightly shut. Beneath him, the Yaumatei whore convulsed on the blue and white striped mattress, her legs splayed open to either side of the boat, toes braced against the gunwales for support as her client bore down with an aggression that frightened her. She had never seen him in the area before and sincerely hoped that she wouldn't see him again.

He had drawn alongside the sampan about half an hour earlier and without saying a word had thrown down a handful of ten-dollar notes. She had barely had time to retrieve them from the bottom of the boat before he had clambered aboard and virtually ripped open her *cheongsam*. The narrow-fitting dress was conveniently designed with splits up both sides all the way to the thigh. Normally she would just have hoisted up the flaps and lain back for her customer to do the business. Anyone wanting to open the top would have to pay more.

But this man had instantly taken charge and when she had protested at his roughness he had slapped her once, although not as hard as her ex-husband used to, and pushed her down on to the mattress. The cotton fabric of the *cheongsam* – she reserved the only silk one for just two special customers – had snagged on a nail. The material had torn and she had almost cried out. But one look from the customer had cut her short. Thereafter everything happened in silence.

Tearing at the dress's high-buttoned neckline, Hu Fat yanked it open, buttons popping like firecrackers and tinkling on the wooden floorboards. He slid a hand inside and cupped one breast, then, becoming impatient and drunk with anger and lust, viciously tore the dress all the way open until the girl's breasts lay bare and exposed. Feeling the excitement mounting inside him, he sucked at the dark nipples, opening his trousers and wriggling them down to his knees.

The girl had attempted to help but that wasn't what he wanted. He slapped her hands aside and felt between his legs, arching his buttocks and bringing himself into her. She had tried to kiss him, whispering in his ear, asking him how he would like her to act. Stupid cow, he thought. As if it wasn't bloody obvious. But what could you expect from a Yaumatei whore?

With the girl spread-eagled on the padded floor of the sampan, Hu Fat burned the anger out of his heart. It had consumed him ever since he had lost the *gweilos* on Lantau. He would get even with them for the loss of face they had caused him in front of the Black Wolf soldiers. The men had barely been able to suppress their sniggers when it became obvious that the intended victims had slipped away.

'So we bungled the ambush?' one of the boldest soldiers had said, grinning. 'Thank goodness you took charge when you did.'

Hu Fat had pushed the man against a tree and stuck the barrel of his pistol in his mouth. It was only the realization that he was surrounded by the man's comrades that had prevented him from pulling the trigger.

But how had it happened? How had the *gweilos* known to return the way they had come instead of taking the safer wooded escape route? He thought he knew. And if he was right, he would get even with the man responsible one day, whatever it cost. Even if he had to follow him to Britain and make use of his Triad contacts in London's Chinatown. Such serious loss of face could not go unavenged.

The girl wriggled on the mattress and Hu Fat thrilled at the touch of her skin, moist with a film of perspiration. The sampan smelt of dried fish and on all sides voices carried from the neighbouring boats. Cantonese pop music crackled from a dozen radios, and against the side of the sampan shallow ripples lapped and broke, agitated by the competing rhythm of Hu Fat's thigh muscles.

Feeling the end approach, Hu Fat lowered himself on to the girl's breasts. He had to admit that she was attractive. He could see what had drawn the warehouse manager to her. Too bad the man would never be able to screw her again. He wondered if he would tell her that one of her clients now lay underneath the polluted waters off Black Point.

Running his hands the length of her body, Hu Fat grasped the girl's buttocks, pulling her closer to him in the final moments, anchoring them together as he exploded, his head flung back, white lights sparkling behind his clenched eyelids.

In the same rush and pulse his anger left him. The girl drew up her knees and tried to ease herself free, eager for this unusual client to be gone from her. But still Hu Fat remained on top of her.

'Not yet,' he hissed.

Rebuked, the girl caressed his shoulders, feeling the tension slipping out of the firm muscles.

Hu Fat felt it going as well. He slipped from the girl and rolled on to his side. In a second she had swung her legs away from him, muttering under her breath.

'What are you complaining about?' he snarled.

She gestured to her ruined *cheongsam* as she tried to locate the scattered buttons and gathered the shreds of brightly coloured cloth around her to cover her breasts.

Hu Fat dug into his jacket pocket and tossed a couple of hundred-dollar bills across to her. A smile flitted across her face and she snatched up the money. Taking comfort from this act of generosity, she sidled over to Hu Fat and whispered in his ear.

'Maybe I did, maybe I didn't,' he said gruffly.

When he had straightened his clothes, stepped into the adjoining rowing boat and disappeared into the night, the girl prayed to all the gods that she had long ago accused of deserting her, that this particular client hadn't found their brief liaison enjoyable. She slipped out of her torn and crumpled dress and sat naked in the bobbing sampan, staring into the darkness. The next client would have to see her in ordinary blouse and slacks. If she wasn't careful she would end up looking like the fisherwomen, barely distinguishable from their menfolk, all trace of femininity lost along the trail of hard labour that marked and cursed their lives.

In the early hours of the morning the long row of police vans cruised steadily up Hennessy Road. In the front vehicle Fred Turner spoke urgently into his radio.

'Is everyone in position?' He waited for the responses: police sections reporting in from all over the Colony. When the last was in and ticked off on the clipboard on Fred's knee, he drew a deep breath and again pressed the radio's transmit switch.

'Go, go, go!'

In the back of the van Linda sat squeezed between four heavily armed policemen. She gripped the edge of her seat as the vehicle lurched forward, swinging round the corner into O'Brien Street. A moment later she was almost thrown to the floor as the driver stepped hard on the brake and the van skidded to a halt outside the alley leading to the club that Des and Harry had previously recced.

'Everyone out!' Fred shouted. The doors at the rear of the van swung open and the policemen poured out. Behind them the other vans similarly disgorged their occupants. As a dozen policemen jogged round to the other side of the club to cordon off the entire block, the main part of the force ran down the alley and up the steps. Before anyone inside the club could react the front door had been smashed into matchwood and the policemen were racing up the inner stairs. A single Triad soldier reached into his pocket and was cut down by a savage swipe from a riot baton. Another appeared at the top of the stairs, pistol in hand, and managed to get off a wild shot that snapped past Linda's face. Beside her a policeman in a bulletproof vest fired a quick burst from his Heckler & Koch MP5 sub-machine-gun. The deadly 9mm rounds found their target and flung him back against the far wall, lifeless before he slid to the floor.

'Linda, I told you to stay in the van!' Fred yelled, seeing her reach the top of the stairs with the leading policemen, a Steyr GB pistol firmly in her grip.

'No way. You'd better get used to seeing me at the front,' she shouted back. Immediately after the Lantau ambush she had paid a visit to the police armoury, vowing not to get caught again without a handgun. She had been delighted to see the Steyr. With a magazine capacity of eighteen rounds it was perfect for this type of work, where every second was at a premium and any time spent reloading left you wide open to attack. She racked back the slide and bounced the first round into the breech, then moved down the corridor, following the policemen into the heart of the brothel.

Halfway along, they came to a second corridor, leading away to the left. Fred signalled for one of his men to explore it. He caught Linda's angry frown and nodded his head in exasperation. 'OK. You can go too. But don't get yourself shot.'

'Don't worry about me. London won't mind.'

'It's not London I'm worried about. It's that boyfriend of yours. He'd kill me.'

Linda flushed but before she could answer back, Fred had disappeared into one of the rooms that his men were clearing. She followed behind the young policeman, holding the Steyr GB in a solid, two-handed combat grip, moving with her back to one wall, her eyes wide for trouble, her breathing steady and controlled.

Suddenly everything happened at once. Doors at the end of the corridor burst open and five men broke into the open, three of them carrying knives and one a pistol. But in the split second it took to register, it was the fifth man who most alarmed Linda. In his hands he carried a Franchi Model 12 Special Purpose Automatic Shotgun. The stock of the twelve-bore SPAS was folded shut and for the first few seconds his line of fire was obstructed by his companions. The man screamed at them to get clear as he swung the muzzle of the short-barrelled weapon towards his intended victims.

The policeman fired off a burst from his MP5 and

the lead Triad soldier went down, coughing blood. But before he could engage his next target the man with the SPAS had shouldered his way to the front and fired. His first round impacted on centre chest of the policeman's body-armour vest. Although the solid slug from the twelve-bore cartridge was unable to penetrate the Kevlar vest, the force of the blow smashed the policeman's ribs and flung him back into Linda.

With a grunt then a cry of pain, the man collapsed against her. As he sank to the floor Linda went down with him, keeping the relative protection of his vest and body between herself and her opponents. A second round hit the wall by her head and a shower of plaster sprayed the air. The third round hit the policeman again, avoiding the vest altogether. Powering into the flesh and bone, it shattered the shoulder. Blood splashed on to Linda's face as she sought an angle on the gunman.

Using one hand to hold the unconscious policeman in place, she steadied her pistol hand as best she could and fired continuously, one shot after the other, suppressing her anger and fear as she did so. As bullet after bullet blazed at her enemies she tried to count the rounds. It would be impossible now to reload. The eighteen 9mm rounds in the Steyr would have to suffice. Every one of them had to count.

The SPAS fired again, but the man had lost his aim. Linda's return fire was having the desired suppressive effect. Then her first round hit home. The Triad soldier with the pistol crumpled to the floor. Then another man, his knife clattering on the filthy tiles, spun around and collapsed. Finally, as another solid slug from the

SPAS shattered a tile a hand's width from Linda's knee, a round from her GB found its mark. The man with the shotgun grunted and clutched his stomach. The muzzle of the SPAS dropped and his next round exploded into the floor at his feet. Linda paused, aiming carefully before firing again. The next three rounds all hit home. As each one impacted into the wounded man, he spun, staggered and finally fell to the ground, the lethal SPAS tumbling from his weakening grasp.

Blind with rage, the last man rushed at Linda. With every muscle in her taut forearm aching and screaming for release, she aimed and fired once more. The hammer clicked helplessly on an empty chamber, the last of her eighteen rounds spent. As the man crashed into her they both toppled to the floor, the wounded policeman sliding aside in his own blood. Linda's attacker was short and thin but desperate, a cornered rat with only one avenue of escape, and that blocked by the *gweilo* woman who had killed his friends. In the scramble on the ground he had lost his knife and without the precious seconds to retrieve it, he swung wildly with his balled fists, punching Linda in the mouth and eye.

She tasted blood and fought for self-control. The reflex action was to curl up, clench the eyes shut to protect them, grunt with fear, draw up the knees to cover herself as best she could. But she had been trained long enough to know that in certain circumstances the body's reflex actions meant death. Designed for survival, in a life-or-death battle like this they would result in the exact opposite. Instead of submitting to her instincts, Linda forced herself to keep her eyes open, focusing on her opponent, directing and transmuting her fear into controlled rage.

Seeing the next punch swinging wildly down, she jerked her head aside. The man's fist crashed into the solid tiles of the floor, his full weight and all the power of his shoulders behind the blow. He winced, gasped. Linda knew that she had created her moment, perhaps the only split-second break in the onslaught that she would achieve. In the struggle on the floor the man had got himself on top of her. Now, as pain blinded him to the switch in the fleeting balance of initiative, Linda gathered every ounce of her strength and tore herself from under him in one convulsive movement. The man tipped over to the side, put out his broken hand for support and cried out as his full weight fell on the shattered bones in his fist.

Linda was up in a flash, swinging her knee into the man's side, where the fragile floating ribs marked her target area, and then levelling a series of sharp, accurate, open-hand strikes at a selection of vital points. The man collapsed under the rain of blows but Linda didn't stop until she was sure he was unconscious.

She sank to her knees. Her face bloodied and her hands pounding with the agony of her blows, she crawled to the policeman. He was still breathing but losing blood fast. She screamed over her shoulder for assistance, but deeper in the brothel there were confused shouts and the sound of firing as other engagements took place. She tore off the policeman's beret and stuffed it over the shoulder wound from the SPAS. Then, when she had secured the makeshift bandage in place, she laid him on his side in the three-quarter prone recovery position, retrieved and reloaded her Steyr and went in search of help.

When Hu Fat reached the wharf after his visit to the warehouse manager's whore, he found Yip waiting where he had left him. The small fisherman was squatting on his haunches smoking a cigarette, looking blankly at the bobbing vessels.

'Missing your old life?' Hu Fat asked without interest.

Yip grinned and shook his head. 'Never. I had to work for a living in those days.' He patted the pocket where he kept his knife. 'This is fun.'

Hu Fat grunted. 'Good. A happy workforce is an efficient workforce.'

They set off down Ferry Street, Yip sniffing the night air like a fox in search of garbage. Hu Fat listened intently for something. Yip eyed him cautiously.

'What's up?'

Hu Fat tilted his head to catch the more distant city noises. 'I don't know. There seem to be a lot of sirens tonight.'

'The American fleet's probably in town. You know what the *gweilos* are like. American ships are dry, no alcohol at all. When they hit the shore they go crazy.'

'Maybe,' Hu Fat said carefully. 'Maybe.'

They headed into the northern heart of Kowloon, winding through the network of backstreets towards the club where Hu Fat was staying. It was owned by one of his many relatives who had been happy to ingratiate himself with such a fast-rising star in the Triad underworld. But as they drew close to the street where the club displayed its brightly decorated front entrance, Hu Fat slowed the pace, his senses alert and warning. Instinctively Yip drew in close beside him, one hand reaching into his pocket for the reassuring touch of steel.

'Fuck it,' Hu Fat growled as he poked his head round the corner.

Ranged in front of his relative's club at least four police vans were parked. The sound of shouting and smashing plates came from the club's interior and as he watched, Hu Fat saw a number of waiters and barmen being escorted out by policemen. Handcuffs were fitted and the men and women were loaded into separate vehicles.

Yip clucked like an old woman. 'Was your uncle involved with drugs?'

Hu Fat looked at him as if he was stupid. 'Of course he was. But that doesn't account for the raid. He pays the right people and gets left alone.'

He stared hard at the vans and the policemen surrounding them, noting the uniforms, equipment and weaponry. He nodded knowingly, his lips twisting into a sardonic smile.

'They're from the Special Operations Unit.'

'The what?'

Ignoring the question, Hu Fat drew back into the shadows, deep in thought.

'What's the matter?' Yip persisted.

'We could be seriously fucked, that's all,' Hu Fat said severely. He looked at his watch.

'Shouldn't we go to the Shanghai Street club and warn them?'

'Forget it. They'll have been hit too. If the Special

161

Operations Unit's involved they'll have coordinated the raids right across the territory.'

He turned on his heel and set off into the night. 'Come on. And try not to look so suspicious. If we're stopped and questioned we're just a couple of guys out on the town, right?'

'Right.'

The MTR would be shut by now, the last train having gone some hours ago. If they were to reach Castle Peak in time they would have to steal a car. A taxi might allow them to be traced. Hu Fat checked his watch again, his finely honed mind speeding through the options open to him. The police would undoubtedly come up with valuable information. It might even lead them to the warehouse and to Hu Fat himself.

But such information would be concealed among a mountain of trivia that would also have been lifted in the numerous raids. It would take the police time to sift through it all and sort the wheat from the chaff. And then it would take yet more time for them to organize and mount an operation, and by then, Hu Fat sincerely hoped, it would be too late. If he could only prepare a few things before the police got their hands on the one or two vital pieces of intelligence, he could beat them yet. The only thing that burned him to the core was the bitter intuition that he had again been outmanoeuvred by the *gweilos* from the Lantau ambush. He felt it in his bones, robbing him of the fast-fading residual pleasures of the whore, yet strengthening his resolve to get even with them, and to destroy them utterly.

9

'I just hope the backup's close by, that's all,' Des said as he led the way through the market stalls towards the rear entrance to the sprawling mess of Chungking Mansions.

'Yeah, well,' Matt answered. 'We'll have to do the best we can.' He hadn't been any happier than Des with Fred Turner's decision not to raid the Mansions along with the other clubs and Triad locations around town. It had been judged as inappropriate to stage a major cordon-and-search operation in the centre of the city's tourist area, the main shopping precinct of Nathan Road.

'The last thing I want is a score of Aussies buzzing away with their sodding videocams, broadcasting to their mates back home about the crime capital of Asia. I'd be scalped for it.'

So Des and Matt had been assigned two plain-clothes policemen instead, with a Special Operations Unit task force on stand-by if necessary. But Des wasn't happy and had moaned all the way into town.

When he found the back door that he had last seen when tracing Inspector Chan back to his home, where the killers had been lying in wait for him, Des hunted around until he located the small cross at the foot of the steps. Tucked away behind some burning sticks of incense, it proved that he had led the team back to the right door. As he went inside he sniffed the incense and grinned.

'If it keeps the evil spirits out, let's hope it keeps the fuckers in too.'

Once inside the building he had some trouble finding the next cross. Corridors led off in several directions and it took him a while to locate a familiar turning, hunting around at ground level for the tiny mark he had scored when last there. But once he had done so the trail became ever easier until he rounded the last corner and found himself looking down the approach to the door where he had spotted Inspector Chan.

'Here we are,' he said.

One of the policemen stepped forward. 'Leave it to us now.'

'Not on your life,' Des snapped. The policeman took one look at him and gave way. 'OK. If you insist.'

'I do.'

Moving stealthily down the corridor the four men closed on their objective. While one of the policemen went over to the far side and covered the stairwell to ensure that no one could approach from that angle, the other one covered the way they had just come.

'Seal off the area,' Matt said. 'Nice and tight so no one goes in or out. We'll do the business.'

The policemen smiled. 'Whatever you say.'

'Right then,' Des said, watching Matt closely. 'Officers first, I reckon.'

'Thanks a bunch.'

Matt took a deep breath and braced himself against the wall opposite the door. 'Here we go, ready or not.'

He drew up his knee and with all his strength slammed the sole of his boot into the door immediately beside the lock and handle. With a sickening crash the door flew open and smashed against the inside wall. The next second Matt was diving into the room, executing a forward roll and coming up in a kneeling firing position. His eyes swept the room, the barrel of his pistol following, ready for an opportunity target.

In the hall outside Des heard the cry, 'Room clear!'

Then he too burst in, dropping to his knees a couple of metres from Matt and covering an arc that took in the other half of the room.

He winced as his knees hit the floor. 'Gawd, I reckon I'm getting too old for this.'

'That'll be the day. You'll be doing forward rolls in the old folks' home when you're eighty.'

The sitting-room they had entered was bare of furniture save for a simple table standing empty in the middle.

'Comfy sort of place, isn't it?' Des said.

'Hello, hello. What have we here?' Matt asked, pointing with his pistol barrel to another closed door that led into a side room.

'Your turn, I reckon,' he said.

Des got to his feet and sized up his target. 'OK. Here goes.'

He charged the door, ramming it hard with his shoulder, but rebounded clutching his arm. 'Strike a light!'

Matt grinned. 'Perhaps you were right about being too old. Stand aside, grandad.'

He squared up to the door and levelled his Browning at it. Both he and Des had chosen Browning 9mm High

Power pistols for the job, the standard handgun of the British Armed Forces. Offered Austrian Glocks by the Special Branch, they had declined.

'No thanks, mate,' Des had said. You can keep your synthetic stuff. I'll settle for the metal. If it jams I can still slug the fucker with it. The Glock wouldn't have the bottle.'

The 9mm bullets spat into the lock, shattering the mechanism and jarring the door open, but something was obviously wedged behind it.

'Give it another shove,' Matt shouted.

'Yes, bwana.'

Des powered into it again and this time it slowly juddered open. A scream burst from inside and a moment later they found themselves staring at a naked Chinese girl in the middle of a double bed. She clutched frantically at the sheets, pulling them up to her chin and letting rip with a torrent of abuse.

'How's your Cantonese?' Des asked.

'Non-existent, like yours,' Matt answered. 'But it doesn't take the brains of a rocket scientist to guess what she's saying.'

Des checked under the bed while Matt scanned the room. 'Nice place you've got here,' he said while the girl continued screaming. The two policemen came in and tried to calm her down.

'Quite a pair of lungs she's got on her,' Des joked.

One of the policemen laughed and moved towards yet another door, which was partly obscured by the girl's bathrobe hanging across it. He reached for the handle and turned it.

Standing on the far side of the room, Matt felt the noise explode in his ears as a shotgun round blasted through the thin plywood of the door. Carrying pieces of shattered wood along with its forty-eight lead pellets, the buckshot round drove deep into the policeman's chest and tossed him casually back across the room. He was dead before he hit the bed, where he came to rest lying across the feet of the screaming, blood-spattered girl, driving her to hysteria.

'Get down!' Matt screamed.

Swinging their guns on to the door, Matt and Des each pumped half a dozen rounds through the shattered wood, spreading their shots to maximize their chances of hitting the firer on the other side.

'Go!' Des shouted, and swung his foot at the door. But it took a further two blows before it gave way. Still firing, he ran through the opening, spinning on his heel to check for an opponent. But there was no one to be seen.

'Where'd the fucker go?' Matt asked, following Des into the bathroom.

Des was hunting around frantically. 'Might have been a booby-trap wired to the handle.'

'No. And anyway, how'd the guy who fixed it get out?'

Matt looked up at the ceiling. 'There!'

A skylight swung on its hinges, still moving under its own momentum.

'Give me a leg-up,' Matt said.

'Check it out first. He could be waiting on the other side.'

'I hope the fucker is.'

Des helped Matt up to the skylight. 'Whoever he is he must be a sodding gymnast to have got up there by himself.'

As Matt heaved himself up through the skylight he called down. 'There's a fire-escape out here. I got a glimpse of him. He's a couple of flights up. I'll track him from here. You go up the main stairs and try to cut him off.'

'Roger! Be careful.'

Darting back through the sitting-room, Des barked at the policeman, 'Have you called for the backup yet?'

The man was pale and frightened, looking at his dead colleague. He shook his head.

'Well, bloody well do it! And be quick.'

Out in the hall, he turned right and found the same stairwell from which he had originally spied Inspector Chan some days before.

He launched himself at the stairs, taking them four at a bound. By the time he reached the top he was panting, his leg muscles screaming with agony after the sudden exertion. In front of him a single fire exit stood locked and barred, the only way out. Putting his shoulder to it, he smashed it open and emerged on to the large, open roof of the building. A score of ventilation-shaft covers dotted the roof, low walls running between them in a lattice-work of cover, ideal for any hidden gunman.

'Stone the flaming crows,' Des groaned.

Off to the far side he could make out the railings of the fire-escape, disappearing over the side of the building. Anyone coming up it would have to have climbed up that way, he thought. From down below he could hear the sound of Matt's boots on the metal steps as he cleared upwards from floor to floor.

Suddenly Des caught a movement to his front and

the next moment he was diving to one side as a stream of buckshot blazed at him from across the roof top.

'That you?' Matt called.

'Who the fuck do you think it is?' Des shouted. But his voice drew further fire and lead shot ricocheted off the aluminium ventilation-shaft cover beside him. He rolled out of the way, came up into a firing position and let off a double tap in the direction of his attacker. He knew he would be unlikely to hit the man, but if he was lucky it would have the effect of suppressive fire and put him out of the way long enough for Des to get a fix on him.

Sure enough, he caught a glimpse of the man's shoulder ducking out of sight.

'Gotcha!' he muttered, racking back the slide of his Browning to clear a jammed empty brass case.

Shifting carefully to one side, he prepared to fire again as soon as the man popped up to have another go at him. The next thing he knew was a blast of lead whizzing past his ear from another angle.

'What the . . .?'

He dived to the ground and scrambled behind a ventilation-shaft cover as yet another shotgun round came his way, spitting on the floor of tar and lino.

'Changed your fire position, have you, you cunning fucker?'

He cursed himself for underestimating his opponent. The man had clearly been in gunfights before and knew never to come up in the same position twice, a mistake that had almost cost Des his life.

Spinning round the side of the shaft, Des blazed off another four rounds at the man but his target was already behind one of the low walls and Des could hear him scuttling away. Looking up, Des saw that there was no other way off the roof.

'Matt!'

'Here.'

'About time,' Des called across. Although he couldn't see Matt he could estimate where he was from the direction of his voice.

'Can you get a line on him?'

'Not from here,' Matt answered. 'I'm going to move. Cover me.'

'Wilco.' Des waited for Matt's next warning cry and then popped up and blazed off the remainder of his magazine in the rough direction of the killer. From across the rooftop he heard Matt's sprinting steps and the sound of him diving to the ground. A second later another shotgun blast was let loose in Matt's direction.

'Got you now,' Des muttered to himself as he fumbled in his jacket pocket for a replacement magazine clip. His fingers met nothing. Desperately he hunted through another pocket and then another, but all with the same result.

'Fuck!' It must have bounced out of my pocket on the run up the stairs, he thought.

He looked around, searching for a solution.

'Matt.'

'What?'

'Can you bung us a spare clip?'

'What have you done with your own?'

'Lost the fucker.'

Even from this distance he could hear Matt swearing.

'I'll have to lob it. Ready?'

Des got up to his knees. 'Yes.'

'Here!'

Arcing through the air, the magazine clip sailed across and clattered to the floor. It skidded towards Des but stopped well short and in the open.

'Great,' Des muttered.

'Got it?'

'I will have. Just as soon as I've had my bollocks shot off.'

'Stop whining.'

Des gathered himself ready to spring and when Matt fired off a couple of double taps in the direction of the gunman, he shot forward and snatched up the clip, going straight into a forward roll and diving behind the adjacent ventilation shaft. Still flat on the floor, he popped out his empty clip and snapped in the new one, racking back the slide to load and cock the weapon.

'Back on line!' he shouted.

'About time.'

Des thought for a moment, taking stock of the situation. The best answer would have been for him and Matt to move steadily forward using fire and manoeuvre, each covering the other, movement in the open always being covered by suppressive fire on the gunman's position. That way they would gradually have closed on him until one or other of them had been able to get a clear killing shot.

But ammunition was at a premium. Des had at most thirteen rounds and Matt probably about the same, maybe less. The only way, Des reckoned, was to take a chance. Lure the gunman into the open and kill him. But for that a trick would be needed. It would be impossible for him to call across to Matt and tell him of his idea because in all likelihood it would give the game away. The only way would be to deceive Matt as well.

Popping his head round the ventilation-shaft cover, Des fired off a single round, keeping his head exposed long enough to draw a blast from the shotgun. Lead pellets ricocheted off the cover and stung the air by his face.

'Jesus, that was close,' he muttered quietly. He cried out as if in pain.

'Des!' Matt called urgently.

Des didn't answer.

'Des!'

Des could hear the alarm in Matt's voice and it pained him to leave his boss in agony. But it was essential that the gunman believe that he was dead, and if Matt's tone was anything less than sincere the man could pick it up. Then one of them might really get hurt.

From the other side of the roof Matt shouted, 'You murderous little fucker! I'm going to get you!'

Another shotgun round was fired at Matt, and then another as the gunman switched his full attention to Matt, deciding that his shot at Des had struck home.

Hugging the ground as close as he could, Des crawled out from behind his cover and towards the sound of the gunman's firing. Matt was blazing away now, the noise of his Browning covering the sound of Des's movement across the roof.

'Easy, Des boy, easy,' he whispered to himself.

He passed behind another ventilation shaft and then another, closing inexorably on his target. At last he caught a glimpse of the top of the gunman's head.

A tuft of jet-black hair bobbed up and down behind the low wall a few metres to his front but although Des tried to get a bead on it, it was never in view long enough. He knew that if the man discovered his position now he would be a goner. He was well away from any cover and all the gunman would have to do was swing his shotgun round and let rip. He had to get a little closer still.

Matt fired off another round and the gunman replied. At last Des saw his chance. He edged to the side and slowly manoeuvred into a position behind the gunman. The danger now would be of getting too far to the rear and finding himself in his boss's line of fire. If Matt had really been convinced that he was dead, the last thing he'd be prepared for would be the figure of another man emerging in front of his sights. He was probably so keyed into the fight that he would think it was the gunman and fire an accurate double tap before recognizing his target as Des.

Des waited for his moment. And then it came. Attempting to get a good bead on Matt, the gunman suddenly popped up from behind the wall and fired. In the instant he fired, Des was up and steadying himself on his knees, using the noise of the shotgun blast to cover his own movement. He waited until the split second when the man was starting to go to ground again and then called, picking the precise moment when the gunman was off balance and still mentally focused on the result of his last shot.

At the sound of Des's voice so close by, the gunman spun round in alarm, almost dropping his shotgun. What he saw was the muzzle of Des's Browning aimed straight at his centre chest and the tiny tongue of flame exploding from the barrel's black hole as round after round was fired at him.

The moment Matt realized what had happened he darted forward, moving from cover to cover, calling as he went to identify himself to Des. In a few quick strides he was standing over the body of the gunman, who lay motionless on the floor, face down.

He turned to Des. 'You devious fucker. You gave me the shock of my life.'

Des stood up slowly and moved forward. 'Sorry about that. But it's nice to know I'm wanted.'

'I wouldn't put it that strongly,' Matt replied.

Des put the toe of his boot under the man's chest and tipped him over on to his back.

Matt caught the sign of recognition on Des's face. 'Do you know him?'

'You could say that. He's the guy who tried to knife me outside the Cat's Whiskers.' He looked down at the surprised face of the dead gunman. 'Nice to make your acquaintance at last, mate.'

Fred Turner was exhausted after the raid on the brothel. He sat heavily at his desk and leafed through a pile of papers seized in the search of the offices and rooms. There had been a mountain of stuff but he had sorted out some of the most important while his men examined the rest. The door opened and Linda came in. Her face was bandaged and there was a swelling around one eye. Fred shook his head when he saw her and started to speak, but before he could get the words out she cut him short.

'Don't you dare,' she snapped. 'I've just had a bellyful from Matt. He heard about the fight from one of your men and I had to listen to all the old reasons why a woman shouldn't get involved in a raid.'

She slumped in a chair, wincing at the jarring shock to her head. 'It was like Ireland all over again. Don't do this, don't do that. I won't bloody stand for it.'

Fred closed his mouth and stirred his coffee. The door opened again and Matt and Des came in.

'I hear you boys have been taking Chungking Mansions apart. With casualty lists like this I'm not sure how much longer we can keep the truth from the press.'

Matt glared at him. 'What do you mean by allowing Linda . . .?'

Fred held up his hands in surrender. 'Look, I suggest you sort it out with the young lady herself afterwards. Can we please bury our differences for now and concentrate on the job in hand?'

He looked from one to the other, Linda bloodied and sore, Matt fuming, and Des grinning merrily in the middle.

'Please?' Fred repeated meekly.

Matt sighed. 'All right.' He pulled up a chair. 'What have you got?'

Fred heaved a sigh of relief. 'It's hard to say at the moment but there's one interesting name that's come up from two separate raids. And this too.'

He held up a notebook. 'It's a list of phone numbers from the Chungking Mansions flat you raided.'

'So who's the guy?'

Lenny Fong. He owns a couple of godowns around town.'

'Godowns?' Linda asked.

'Warehouses. We've come across him before but

never been able to pin anything on him. He's less than discerning about what he allows people to put in his godowns. It seems he might be in business with the Triads again.'

'You said he has more than one godown.'

'Yes, but it's the one at Kam Hong that's been mentioned by the blokes under questioning.'

'Where's that?'

Fred got up and walked across to the wall map, sticking his finger on the spot.

Des whistled. 'Castle Peak. Perfect. A ship could get in there and unload its cargo without anyone seeing. Nice and quiet.'

'And out of the way,' Fred continued. 'If we're to look anywhere I reckon that's as good a place as any to start.'

'Then what are we waiting for?' Matt asked.

Fred stared at him. 'What do you mean? The Special Operations Unit's spread across the Colony. It'll take hours to get them together and days to sift through all this shit.'

Matt leaned across the table. 'And do you want to be the one to explain to the Governor, London and the press why it was that the police sat around drinking coffee while the Triads got their nuclear warheads out of the way?'

Linda stood up. 'I'm afraid I agree with Matt on this one,' she said.

'I was afraid you might. OK, give me four hours to get a team together. With the fire-power these guys are using I don't want this to go off at half cock.'

'Make it two,' Matt said sternly.

Fred looked at him. 'Two it is.'

Out in the corridor, Matt went to the drinking fountain and poured himself a cup of water. Des checked that no one was within hearing distance before broaching what was on his mind. 'Boss, I know we're here to cooperate with the police and all that, but don't you think it's time we called in some help. I mean, this thing's getting bigger by the minute.'

'SAS?'

'Don't be daft. SBS. If there's a ship involved it might have put to sea. Only we've got the expertise for that.'

Matt winked at him. 'I've already spoken to London.'

'And?'

'They said to wait out. Sort of, don't call me, I'll call you.'

When Des had gone, Matt made his way down to the canteen. A score of policemen were sitting around in groups eating bowls of noodles or rice, and telling war stories from the various raids. To one side Linda sat over a bowl of fried rice and chicken. Matt went over to join her, sat down and looked at her hard.

'If you're going to say . . .' Linda started.

He held up his hand. 'I've come to say I'm sorry.' He ran his fingers through his hair. 'I was out of line. Just when we meet up again, I don't want us to go through all the old Ireland routine.'

'Really?' she asked.

'Really.'

She sat back and appraised him. 'Do you know, I think you're telling the truth,' she said at last.

He smiled at her. 'Linda, since I met you again on

the plane coming over, I've decided one thing. I want to be with you. At any price.'

'Despite my job?'

'If that's what it takes, yes. Despite your job.'

He leaned across the table and took her hand. 'You can get yourself blown away if that's what you want, but so long as you're in this world I'd like us to spend our time together.'

Linda smiled. 'I never thought I'd hear you say it.' She squeezed his hand. 'But I'm glad you did.'

The traffic out of London had been especially bad, solid on the M25 as usual, but by the time his car was roaring up the A41 towards Aylesbury Sir Anthony had cleared his mind ready for his meeting with the Prime Minister. After turning left beyond Tring and following the signposts for Wendover, the driver at last pulled up at the large gates of the red Tudor mansion. He flashed his pass at the policeman on duty and a minute later the car skidded to a halt on the gravel driveway of Chequers.

Sir Anthony found the Prime Minister in his study, a mass of paper sprawled across his desk. He looked up as Sir Anthony entered, and said, 'And I always thought that Prime Ministers were supposed to come to Chequers for a break.'

Sir Anthony smiled. 'Well, I've worked for a number of them, sir, and I haven't known one to manage it yet.'

The Prime Minister waved him to a chair and sat back. 'What news from the Jewel in the Crown?'

'Hong Kong?'

'Is there any other?'

'I would have thought North Sea oil was a contender.'

'Too messy. Lacks the glamour of the Orient.'

The PM got up and poured some coffee from a jug on the sideboard.

'Not much of a lead so far, I'm afraid. There's some mention of a warehouse that the police are going to raid, but that's not why I asked for this appointment.'

'Oh?'

'My team has requested Special Forces backup.'

'SAS?'

'And SBS. You know, boats and that sort of thing.'

The PM frowned. 'Thank you, I did know that.'

He walked to the window and looked out at the ornamental gardens and lush green lawns. 'I'm not sure I can authorize that.'

'But . . .'

'Let me explain. With the hand-over of the Colony to China in 1997, it's vital that the Hong Kong Government and authorities are seen to be able to cope with every eventuality. China would leap at the slightest excuse to move its own troops in there the minute our flag comes down, and you can imagine that it wouldn't be long before they switched from safeguarding the Colony to suppressing people's freedoms. If the Colony's to maintain the confidence of the international business community on which it depends, it's vital that never happens.'

'I know, but . . .'

'I'm afraid there aren't any buts on this one, Sir Anthony. In fact, if China got to hear that British Special Forces were running around the streets chasing nuclear warheads they could even use it as an excuse to move in early. If they simply marched across the border there's not a damned thing we could do about it.'

'The UN . . .'

'Would protest and then shut up. China's not another Iraq that can be ostracized from the world that easily. It's the largest growing market around. And it's not another Argentina either. There's no way, either diplomatically or militarily, that we could stop them.'

Sir Anthony sank back in his chair. He thought for a moment before trying another tack.

'All right, sir. I accept your decision. I agree with your reasons why we must leave the RHKP to handle all land-based operations. That rules out using the SAS. But if there's a ship involved on the high seas, their Marine Police simply don't have the expertise. The Chinese could hardly complain if any operation conducted by British Special Forces happened outside Hong Kong territorial waters.'

The PM looked at him suspiciously. Detecting an Achilles heel, Sir Anthony went for it like a terrier.

'At least let me put them on stand-by notice to move.'

The PM wagged his finger at him. 'Now I know how you got your job. You could sell oil to the Arabs.'

'Only if it was in our national interests, sir.'

An hour later Sir Anthony was on his way back into London. He sat back in the car, pleased with the outcome of the meeting. He hadn't quite got all that he had hoped for, but he had expected that and had therefore asked for more than he really wanted. He enjoyed the political game. Once you understood the rules it was like any other game.

He peered over the driver's shoulder at the dashboard clock. He would be back in the office in time for his meeting with the commanding officer of the SBS. Thank God he hadn't arranged for the SAS CO to travel all the way up from Hereford, he thought. He wasn't the sort of man that Sir Anthony liked to irritate.

Back in Whitehall, he bounded up the stairs, strode through the outer office, burst into his room and slung his briefcase down on the desk. He was startled to turn round and see the chief of his Far Eastern section standing behind him. The man's face was pale and he held a piece of paper quivering in his hand.

'What have you got there?'

'You'd better read this, sir. It arrived while you were away. From the Americans.'

Sir Anthony took the offering and scanned it, feeling his knees go weak as he worked through the lines. He slumped into a chair and read it a second and then a third time.

'The head of the CIA's going to call you on the secure line in just under half an hour. He wants to know if we've got any ideas about what the devil to do.'

Sir Anthony read the signal yet again, running his finger across the stark names of the countries over which the American reconnaissance satellite had recently passed.

'They must be mad,' he stammered. 'What the devil are they up to? They must be absolutely raving bonkers.'

As the Intelligence officer turned to go, relieved that

the weight had been shifted from his own slender shoulders on to those of his boss, Sir Anthony called after him.

'And if the SBS CO's there, tell him to get in here immediately. And I want the RAF and the Navy too. You can forget the fucking stand-by. We'll have to get the boys moving soonest.'

10

The road out to Castle Peak followed the ragged coastline round the western side of the Colony. Sandy-coloured hills rose on the right-hand side, the rounded tops worn bare by countless summer typhoons that had swept out of the South China Sea over the years. Beyond the high-rise mess of Tuen Mun, the last of the major urban areas was left behind and the New Territories opened up. But even here, what had once been rich agricultural land was now networked with roads and towns that would soon rival the conurbations of Kowloon and Central.

In the back of one of the unmarked trucks that Fred Turner had commandeered at the last minute, Matt, Des and Linda familiarized themselves with the weaponry they had drawn from the armoury of the Special Operations Unit. Matt and Des had each chosen a standard Heckler & Koch MP5. In the close quarter engagements that they expected the German sub-machine-gun's high rate of fire and powerful 9mm bullets would match the situation perfectly. In addition they would both carry a Browning pistol.

Linda, on the other hand, had decided to increase the fire-power of her Steyr GB with a 9mm Micro-UZI, the smallest and lightest version of the UZI family with a twenty-round magazine and a rate of fire nearly double that of the MP5. Being a very short-barrelled weapon, it would be accurate only at very close range, but the rate of fire would amply compensate for Linda's smaller build, giving her a punch equal to that of any of the men.

Among the teams that Fred had assembled, the MP5 generally reigned supreme, but there was a smattering of M16s, tear-gas grenade launchers, and the lethal SPAS semi-automatic shotgun. The policemen allocated the SPASs had been issued with special discarding sabot tungsten-carbide slug rounds, capable of penetrating an armoured personnel carrier.

Eyeing one of the shotguns, Des whistled. 'Fred wasn't kidding when he said he was going into this one prepared.'

'If the Triads know we're coming we'll need to be,' said Matt, looking around at the policemen. 'I only hope these boys are up to it.'

'Just watch out for yourself,' Linda said smiling.

Des caught the undercurrents of the exchange between her and Matt. 'Have I missed something here? The last time I saw you both together you were at each other's throats.'

'Don't worry about it, Des,' Matt laughed. 'Let's just say Miss Kirkdale and I have reached a new understanding.'

Des raised his eyebrows. 'I see, Miss Kirkdale is it now? That sounds sort of possessive.'

'You couldn't be further off the mark. The possessive days are over.' He slammed a full magazine into his MP5. 'You're looking at the liberated man of the nineties.'

'Is that the decade or your age?'

'Ha, bloody ha.'

The truck gave a lurch and sent them sprawling on the floor. Daylight was coming in through a single small window in the rear but it was just enough to enable them to gather up their kit again and settle back in position.

'Luxury transport, that's what I like,' Des said. 'No expense spared.'

They had started to climb a slight hill and Matt got up to peer through the back window. Behind them a further two trucks were similarly winding their way up the rise that heralded the arrival at Castle Peak.

'Won't be long now,' Matt said.

Des squinted along the sights of his MP5. 'And then we breakfast on Triad bollocks.'

The plan that had been devised had been arrived at in a short space of time, speed being the priority. Consequently it was simple in the extreme. Two of the trucks were to pull up short of the gates of the godown complex and the men would debus to form a tight cordon and act as a reserve to be called forward as and when necessary. The lead truck, however, would plough right through the flimsy barrier and the Special Operations policemen inside, including Matt, Des and Linda, would only debus when it had come to a halt immediately outside the godown doors. All being well, the *Atlas Star* would still be at its moorings alongside the adjacent wharf and after clearing the godown they would board the ship and search it from top to bottom.

Bomb-disposal experts and a team of specialists capable of disarming nuclear devices were on call and would be flown in by helicopter once the area had been secured by the ground force.

From the cabin at the front of the truck, where Fred had planted himself in order to navigate, they suddenly heard the Chief Inspector hammering on the intervening wall.

'This is it, boys,' Matt announced, sitting on the floor and bracing his back against the walls of the truck for support. 'Hang on tight!'

A moment later the truck swung round in a huge arc as it veered off the road and headed towards the barrier. They heard the muffled voice of someone outside shouting, the faint crack of a pistol firing and then the splintering of wood and the sound of breaking glass as the truck accelerated past the guard post and into the warehouse complex.

'How far to the godown itself?' Linda asked.

'About two hundred metres,' Matt replied. 'There are a dozen or more godowns on the site. Ours is the furthest.'

'Sod's law,' Des muttered grimly.

The truck had barely gone fifty metres when there was a muffled scream from the cab, followed by a series of explosions. The vehicle slewed violently and crashed into something solid. In the back, bodies flew everywhere. One or two men cried out as they were crushed or hurt. Realizing that they must be within earshot of the Triad soldiers in the godown, Matt was the first to his feet.

'Debus, debus, debus!' he roared. Time was now of the essence and every second counted. Whatever had caused the truck to crash, the men in the godown would have been alerted by the noise and in no time at all they would doubtless be bringing their fire to bear on their attackers.

After kicking his way out of the back of the truck, Matt jumped to the ground and ran round to the side to check that Fred was all right. Close behind him, Des and Linda followed, peeling to left and right.

'Caltrops!' Des shouted, pointing to the rows of savage metal spikes that had been laid across the full width of the road.

'No wonder the tyres exploded!'

The truck had slewed sideways into the wall of one of the godowns near the main entrance, bouncing off and coming to rest at an angle. Matt wrenched open the door to the cab and found Fred rubbing his head. A trickle of blood ran down into his eyes from a small cut in his scalp. Matt quickly checked it.

'Looks worse than it is.'

'I'm fine,' Fred said shakily, stumbling out of the cab and drawing his Walther PPK. In the seat next to him, the driver lay slumped over the steering wheel. Matt found a healthy pulse in his neck, yanked him across both seats into a recovery position and left him.

'He'll be OK.'

The man who had fired as the truck had rammed the gate was crouched behind the guard post, potting off rounds at the debussing policemen. Retribution came in the form of a barrage of SPAS rounds, a mixture of solid slug, buckshot and tungsten-carbide penetrators. As the guard post disintegrated around him, the man screamed, flung away his pistol and stood up with his arms high enough in the air to dislocate the joints.

'One down, about a hundred to go,' Des shouted across to Matt as the two of them joined the policemen racing for the godown. But when they had gone only a few metres all hell was suddenly let loose. From windows in the upper floors of the large godown to their front a stream of automatic fire poured down on them and the assault came to a swift halt. Policemen scrambled for any available cover or were hit and wounded, falling in the open where others then tried to reach them.

'Get some suppressive fire down!' Des screamed over the noise of the battle. He dived behind a wall and with his MP5 blazed away at one of the windows where he had caught sight of the muzzle flash from one of the Triad weapons. He saw his rounds impact on the red-brick wall and adjusted his fire accordingly, aiming off until he brought his rounds on to his target. Designed for short-range anti-terrorist engagements, the MP5 was outclassed at this distance by the longer-range weapons being deployed by the Triads.

'These devils have got Kalashnikovs,' Fred stammered next to Matt.

'They certainly sound like them, though they could be the Chinese variant. If they've got Soviet weaponry it ties in with the warhead. They've got a deal going somewhere.'

'Bloody Russians threw in a job lot. It's like dealing in washing machines. This week's special offer . . .'

His words were cut short by a spray of automatic fire that swept across the top of the wall, showering him and Matt with splinters of plaster, cement and brick dust.

Des saw the remaining glass of the window shatter and a man toppled forward, smashing through the frame and cartwheeling to the ground below, to land with a thud on the concrete.

'Cover me!' Des shouted, and doubled forward as soon as Matt let rip with a burst of MP5 rounds. He went a full twenty metres before finding suitable cover behind a pile of sacks of cement. They had already taken a number of hits but absorbed the full power of the bullets as well as sand.

This'll do nicely, Des thought. A man could get seriously happy just sitting here, watching the world go by. He checked his magazine, popped it out and slammed a new one home, cocking the handle on the front left-hand side of the weapon and releasing it to spring back to the foresight, a new round ready in the breach. He looked back at Matt and caught his eye.

'Give me an indicator,' he shouted. He got the thumbs up from Matt and the moment Matt fired at one of the Triad fire positions Des swung round the corner of the sacks. In a split second he identified Matt's fall of shot, the tell-tale spray of impacting bullets revealing the Triad soldier in one of the windows. He took aim and loosed off a series of short, three-round bursts until, once again, the man had been silenced.

Ducking back behind cover, he breathed rapidly, filling his lungs with oxygen and calming himself. But the Triad firers had got his position now, the foremost of any in the attacking teams. Bullets whined and snapped all around him and he felt the wall of sacks shift. These aren't going to last much longer, he thought, desperately hunting around for his next piece of cover.

Fred had seen Des's predicament and waved one

of his teams forward. With suppressive fire from the longer-range M16s and the powerful SPASs, the policemen were up and running. Matt followed them. As he hit the ground beside a building, he saw Linda sprinting towards him, the ground at her feet alive with bullets. She hurtled past him in a forward roll and break-fall. Matt felt the anger rise within him but clenched his teeth, biting back the abuse that masked his fear for her safety. She wriggled on her stomach beside him and grinned, though the paleness of her face told the true story of her feelings.

'Do you come here often?' she said.

Matt forced a quick smile and poured his anger into his next burst of fire at the Triad soldiers holding the godown. The rounds arced across the ground-floor entrance, where big green double doors were tightly shut. A man was firing through a small hatch and Matt watched with satisfaction as the wood tore and shattered around the eyepiece. But a second later another firer was using the same firing port.

'Jesus, how many of these guys are there?' Linda asked.

'I don't know, but they certainly mean business. This is a regular war zone.'

Fred fell into position beside them. 'I've called for the other two squads. This one's almost spent. We'll pass the other one through to clear the actual godown, and use the third and final one to tackle the ship.'

'You've seen it?'

'Yes. It's further along the quay.'

'Bingo!' Matt said.

'I'd save the celebrations until we've seen what's on board,' Fred cautioned, pulling a fresh clip from

his pocket and stubbing it into the butt of his
PPK.

'Why do you bother with that peashooter?' Linda
asked.

'We go back a long way. It's sort of sentimental.'

'Sod that,' Matt said. 'Give me a Browning any
day.'

Off to one flank they saw the next police squad
approaching the godown from an angle.

'The Triads haven't seen them yet,' Fred said. 'If they
can just breach the main entrance we'll be away.'

As they watched, one of the policemen edged along
the wall of the godown itself, his colleagues being
careful to direct their fire well away from him.
Slipping right underneath the firing port from which a
Kalashnikov was blazing, he fastened a shaped charge
of plastic explosives against the centre of the double
door and lit a short fuse, then darted back round the
corner of the godown just in time.

An enormous explosion shook the air and the doors
vanished in a cloud of acrid black smoke. When it
cleared they saw a gaping hole where the doors had
been, and no sign of the firer who had been concealed
immediately behind them.

'Go!' the police squad commander shouted, and his
men ran forward and in through the breach, firing as
they went.

'Let's go!' Matt said, getting to his feet. Every
instinct in him ordered him to tell Linda to stay where
she was, but he resisted the temptation, though it tore
him apart. This is how it's got to be, he thought. It's
this or nothing. But as he ran towards the hole in
the front of the godown, he wondered whether the

risk to Linda's life was a price worth paying for his selfish pleasure of winning her affection again. As he approached the entrance, Des came up beside him and read his thoughts.

'Don't even think about it, boss. She wouldn't pay any attention even if you ordered her to keep back.'

Swirling smoke obscured the cavernous interior of the warehouse, but as their eyes became adjusted to the gloom, they were able to make out a series of balconies running round the upper levels, ringing the vast central well that presently stood empty.

'You could fit a regiment of bloody tanks in here if you wanted to,' Des said.

The policemen were working their way steadily forward, moving from sparse cover to sparse cover, firing at anything that moved. When Fred came through the doors, Matt shouted back to him.

'Most of the fuckers have bugged out. These are just the small fry they've sacrificed as a rearguard. We mustn't let them delay us. Get the last squad to the ship now. Send them round the back.'

Fred took in the situation inside the godown at a glance and nodded. 'Wilco.'

Des grinned. 'Got him eating out of your hand.'

'Don't knock him. Our Fred's a good man.'

Matt looked around at the warehouse battle. 'Come on. Let's leave the cops to finish off here. Let's get to the ship.'

Round the side of the godown, they found Fred directing the commander of the last squad towards his task. The first men were already fighting their way up one of the three gangplanks, and it seemed that the Triad soldiers had pulled back altogether.

'Do you think they've had enough?' Fred shouted.

Suddenly there was a whoosh, followed by an explosion as an anti-tank rocket detonated among a group of policemen huddled together in preparation for their own part in the assault.

'Does that answer your question?' Matt said.

'Sounds like an RPG 7,' Des said.

'Where is he?'

'I saw him,' Linda called. 'Beside the red lifeboat!'

'Got it.'

Both Matt and Des aimed their MP5s at the spot and sure enough, as soon as he had reloaded his RPG 7 with a fresh rocket, the firer reappeared in the same place. But this time he had barely got his head and shoulders above the gunwale when he was raked with 9mm fire from the two MP5s. He spun back out of sight, the rocket launcher tumbling from his grasp over the side of the ship and splashing harmlessly into the dark-green water below.

'Nice shooting,' Fred shouted. But he was worried about his casualties. The engagements had been more ferocious than even he had expected, so he sent one of his inspectors to arrange for further backup and medical support.

'I think it's time we went up,' Matt said, jabbing the muzzle of his MP5 towards the nearest gangplank.

Des stared hard at the exposed ground between them and the side of the ship. 'Well, don't expect to be piped aboard.'

The moment he heard the sound of the crashing truck and the pistol shots from the main gatehouse, Hu Fat prepared to make his escape, but not before he had organized the defence of the godown and the ship. Triad soldiers had been pulled in from all parts of the Colony for the operation, although a number had fallen foul of the raids in the night and were now under interrogation in various police cells throughout Kowloon and Hong Kong island. Hu Fat shouted out commands to his men and sent them scurrying to their prearranged positions. Firing slits had been made in the walls and doors, and any window that gave on to the approach road was reinforced with sandbags and taped up to minimize the hazard from flying glass.

Each man had been allocated his position and at Hu Fat's signal they set to with a will. Nevertheless, despite the careful preparation, Hu Fat realized that any resistance would be only temporary. Eventually the police would be able to bring superior fire-power to bear to outgun them, but by then, Hu Fat sincerely hoped, he himself would be far away.

The battle developed pretty much as he had anticipated, so that by the time the second police squad was called in, Hu Fat was ready to pull out. Naturally he had not informed anyone else of his imminent departure. He fully expected most of the Triad soldiers to die or be captured where they stood. His ulterior motive in this, and one that he was particularly proud of, was that with so many of the other Triads' men slaughtered or rotting in jail, the Hong Kong underworld would be left wide open for any new man to move in and fill the power vacuum. Hu Fat would be that man.

The only other person to whom he had confided his intentions was Yip. The little former fisherman had at first been puzzled by it all.

'But what about the cargo? Don't we have to safeguard it?' he had asked, wide-eyed.

Hu Fat had smiled indulgently, relishing the sweet taste of exclusive knowledge. 'That's for the others to do. Believe me, it'll be all right.'

Yip had accepted Hu Fat's assurances and grinned with delight at the prospect of becoming a big operator in the Hong Kong criminal fraternity.

When the shaped charge blasted a hole in the front door of the godown, Hu Fat and Yip were busy in one of the ground-floor offices. They had barricaded the door with two filing cabinets and as the battle raged on the other side, they heaved aside the desk and lifted a metal trapdoor concealed underneath. Yip clucked in admiration of Hu Fat's foresight when he saw the lapping water below and the small, slender boat bobbing gently on the wash that swept up the subterranean tunnel from the bay.

Before dropping down into the boat, Hu Fat picked up a canvas satchel and gingerly lifted out a claymore anti-personnel mine. Fixing it on the far side of the room, he aimed it at the door. He adjusted the normal trip-wire to act as a booby-trap, attaching one end to the door handle and the other end to the detonator lodged in the matrix of plastic explosive and steel ball-bearings.

'That should do it,' he said.

Then, having jumped down into the boat where Yip was waiting, his hand ready on the outboard motor, Hu Fat pulled the trapdoor shut on top of him and fastened a hand-grenade to the underside with black masking tape. After twisting a fine piece of wire around the loosened pin, he tied the other end to a nail in the roof of the tunnel. Whoever opened the trapdoor would unwittingly lift the grenade up into the room as well, but by the time they saw it fastened on the underside, the wire would have tugged the pin free, exploding the detonator in the high-explosive core.

'After those little surprises they'll think twice before they follow us.'

Yip chuckled, but before he could start the motor, Hu Fat stopped him. 'No. We won't use the motor until we're out of earshot.'

He passed him a paddle. 'Use this. I'll cover us.'

Crouching in the prow of the boat, Hu Fat picked up the Kalashnikov he had placed there in readiness for the escape. During the early stages of the battle he had walked brazenly around armed only with a pistol, enjoying the glances of the Triad soldiers, who had admired his courage at facing the massive police onslaught with so inadequate a weapon.

'What about the cordon?' Yip asked, putting the full power of his thin shoulders into the paddling.

'By now the police will have called them in to reinforce the main assault. They will have had to, if our fire-power was as I intended.'

'And the Marine Police? Won't they have a launch watching the coast?'

Hu Fat shrugged. 'It's possible. That's a chance we'll have to take. But we only have to slip along the shoreline a few hundred metres to get clear of the godown complex. Then we'll hit the beach and pick up the van I've hidden down the road. We'll be having lunch in Kowloon before the battle here's even finished.'

Yip nosed the boat carefully down the tunnel that

led under the quay. Overhead they could hear the sounds of heavy fighting, muffled by the layers of concrete and timber. They emerged on to the open water some way beyond the *Atlas Star*. The men on the ship were too preoccupied with the battle on the landward side to notice the small craft sneaking away to safety, their boss lying in the prow, Kalashnikov at the ready.

When Hu Fat judged that they were out of earshot, he gave the signal to start the outboard motor, and with a tug at the cord Yip kicked it into action. Making little more than a gentle purring sound, the tiny engine sped them quickly down the coast. As they looked back they could see huge spouts of black smoke erupting from the godown as the police Special Operation squads stormed it. Then an RPG 7 fired, the rocket-propelled grenade exploding on the quayside, to be followed a moment later by screams and shouts.

'They're going for the ship,' Hu Fat observed without emotion. 'Unless the resistance caves in it'll be ages before they realize their mistake.'

He waited until the boat had rounded a headland before directing Yip towards the shore. Reacting to a soft pressure on the throttle, the nose swung round and made straight for a spit of sand, before sliding up on to it and coming smoothly to a halt.

'Quick,' Hu Fat said as he hopped out of the boat. 'Follow me.'

'What about the boat?'

'Leave it!'

Yip looked back at the craft, still sufficiently a man of the sea to abandon the boat only with reluctance.

But a final order from Hu Fat tugged him away. However, they had just cleared the sandy beach and were starting towards the road, when Hu Fat darted aside into a clump of bushes, pulling Yip in after him. He cursed under his breath. Barely thirty metres in front, a policeman on a motor cycle had stopped a car in the lay-by next to which Hu Fat had parked his van. They were well outside the original police cordon and it seemed likely that the traffic policeman had stopped here purely by chance, his duties unconnected with the raid on the godown. Presumably, while he had been waiting there, listening to the noise of his more exotic colleagues involved in the raid, he had exercised his own meagre authority by stopping a passing car on some speeding pretext or the like.

'Shall I kill him?' Yip asked eagerly.

'Wait,' Hu Fat replied. 'We'll see if he clears off first. We don't want them to know that anyone's got away if we can avoid it.'

They settled down and watched. But the traffic cop was obviously in no mood to hurry. He was enjoying the morning and the exercise of his power over the unfortunate occupants of the car. He asked for the driver's licence and ID card, and checked them both line by line. Then he inspected the vehicle, checking the tyres, lights, indicators and bodywork.

Finally he returned the driver's documents to him and waved him away. But the driver neither left, nor did the policeman get on his motor bike and go. Instead, the car doors opened and an entire family got out. Two boys ran to the roadside to urinate, the mother stretched her legs, and her husband seemed to be consulting a road map. But of greater concern to

Hu Fat was the policeman. He had almost got to his motor bike when he noticed the bonnet of Hu Fat's van protruding from the bushes. Hu Fat cursed as he saw the policeman switch direction and saunter across to it.

With agonizing slowness the policeman undid his top pocket and took out a notebook. Then came the pencil. He licked the tip, balanced himself on his feet, squinted at the number-plate and started to write.

'Fuck! The arsehole!' Hu Fat muttered. He looked at the Kalashnikov in his hands and considered shooting the lot of them from his position in the bushes. But it was just possible that the noise of the firing would be heard by the police in the godown. Hu Fat thought it unlikely, but it was a chance he was not prepared to take at this stage in his escape.

He laid the weapon on the ground, then cocked his pistol and stuck it in his belt under his jacket.

'Come on,' he said to Yip, and together the two of them strode out into the lay-by.

The policeman looked up with a start. 'Is this your vehicle?' he asked.

Hu Fat smiled warmly, every inch the innocent motorist.

'Yes, officer. I hope I'm not illegally parked?'

'What's it doing here?'

'I was driving past and heard the noise of shooting. My friend and I went down to the beach to see if we could see anything.'

The policeman sighed like a teacher who has caught a truant.

'Let's see your ID.'

'Sure,' Hu Fat said. 'Sure. It's right here.'

He put his hand in his pocket and pulled out the pistol. The policeman stared at it stupidly for a moment, as if frozen in time. As the pieces of the jigsaw fell into place in his reluctant brain – the concealed van, the nearby gun battle between his colleagues and the Triads – his face paled visibly and he backed away.

'I wouldn't do that if I were you,' Yip warned, seeing the policeman start to reach for his holster. But amazingly the policeman's hand kept on moving. It seemed to have a will of its own. The man even looked down at it, as if willing it to stop but no longer able to control his own muscles. He looked up again at Hu Fat, almost with embarrassment.

'Stop!' Hu Fat commanded.

But the policeman no longer knew what he was doing. Panic had fogged his reason and, galvanizing himself into action, he fumbled with the holster flap and got his Smith & Wesson .38 halfway out before the first of Hu Fat's bullets knocked him flying across the tarmac.

At the first report of the pistol, the mother of the family screamed. The two boys raced back towards the car and as they all dived into it, the father struggled to start the engine. Yip was beside him in a flash, but the man's spare hand had started to close his window.

With his knife in his hand, Yip tried to get at the driver, slashing through the closing window. Hu Fat looked on with disgust, unmoved by the spectacle except for being struck by the unseemliness of it all. Aiming casually at the car, he fired a single shot which shattered the windscreen and wounded the man behind the wheel.

Having got the door open, Yip dragged the driver out and put his knife to the man's throat. The woman screamed.

'Shall I kill him?' Yip asked.

Hu Fat considered a moment, then walked up and crouched beside the wounded driver. He took out the man's wallet and removed the ID card and driving licence. He appraised it carefully, noting the name and address. Ignoring the screams from inside the car, he stared coldly into the terrified man's eyes.

'Do you know who I am?' he asked.

The man coughed, stammering.

'Answer me!'

'No. I've never seen you before. How could I know you?'

'Good,' Hu Fat smiled. He wagged the licence in front of the man's eyes. 'But I know who you are.' He looked into the car. 'And judging by where you live I can guess where your kids go to school too.'

The man swallowed hard, glancing across the lay-by to the prone, motionless body of the policeman.

Hu Fat motioned Yip out of the way. He stuffed the documents back in the man's pocket. 'Get in the car and clear off. If I hear you've said anything to the police about what you've seen, then I'll find you again. And your wife, and your kids. Is that understood?' The man nodded rapidly.

As they went towards the van and got in, Yip looked uncertainly at his boss.

'Shouldn't we kill them?'

'We've killed their will to resist. That's far better.' He smiled warmly at his companion. 'If you're going to help me build a truly powerful Triad you've got

201

to learn how to instil fear in people. It's our whole power base. A pile of bodies is unproductive. But live ones with the will knocked out of them, that's another matter.'

11

Although the ship was small for a cargo vessel, Matt estimated that it was nevertheless large enough to accommodate a thirty-metre-long SS-18 missile in its main hold, especially if the missile body and warheads were broken down into their constituent parts. He got hold of Fred Turner and told him to pass an order to his men to warn them to avoid, if at all possible, setting the ship alight. The last thing they needed when they were so close to a possible missile find was for a fire to consume the ship and create a radioactive leak or worse.

'If there is a missile on board and the propellant explodes it could spray radioactive material all over the Colony,' he said as he and Des jogged towards the nearest gangplank.

Although the upper decks were now safely in police hands, firing from the bowels of the ship indicated that the Triad soldiers throughout the vessel were far from subdued.

'Watch out!' Des shouted.

Matt swerved just in time to avoid a burst of machine-gun fire from one of the portholes that raked the gangplank. Des returned the fire with his MP5, the rounds snaking their way across the hull and into the shattered cabin. A man screamed and the firing stopped.

Once on deck, Matt checked with the police commander to ensure he was not going to run into the middle of the clearance operation and then made his way forward.

'If there is anything on board I reckon it'll be in the forward hold,' he said, as Des located a hatch cover and gingerly opened it, checking for booby-traps before easing himself down into the ship. Glancing to left and right, he found that he had entered a narrow passageway, the cream-coloured bulkheads darkened with the grime of years.

'All clear,' he called up, and the next moment Matt dropped down beside him.

'Which way, boss?'

Matt shrugged. 'Let's try over there. We've got to get deeper down. There's got to be a way into the hold somewhere around here.'

They made their way along the narrow passageway, and had almost reached the end when they heard footsteps running in their direction. Matt beckoned for Des to take cover behind one of the heavy watertight doors before ducking out of sight himself. A moment later two Triad soldiers in jeans and T-shirts came round the corner. They were talking hurriedly and clearly didn't expect any police or security forces to be in this part of the ship. The next thing they knew two figures emerged from nowhere. Matt grabbed the lead man by the shirt and swung him out of the way to give Des a clear line at the other.

'Don't kill them!' Matt shouted as he pulled his man to the ground. Des cursed under his breath, reversed his MP5 and stabbed the butt into the midriff of the second Triad man. Carried forward by his own momentum, the man was winded by the hard butt, doubling over and collapsing to the floor. Meanwhile Matt's opponent had jerked free and was wrestling his way on top. Des looked at them bemused. 'Having trouble, boss?'

Matt pulled one hand free, made a fist and shot it at the side of his opponent's head. The man felt the blow but in the rush of the fight, shook it off, returning a telling punch of his own. Finally Matt managed to bring his greater weight to bear, swinging the man heavily into the bulkhead and while he was stunned, rabbit-punched him on the side of the neck.

'Took your time,' Des mused as he used the sling of the man's Kalashnikov to fasten his hands behind his back.

Matt stood up breathing hard. 'I must be more out of condition than I'd figured.'

They were just about to continue their exploration of the ship when a police inspector appeared, freezing on the spot when he saw Matt and Des's two MP5s levelled at him.

'Don't shoot! I've been looking for you,' he said. 'We've secured the ship. There's just one or two hostiles in the stern accommodation area that we're clearing out now, but otherwise it's all over.'

'And the search?'

'Chief Inspector Turner wants you to join him down below. This way.'

As they followed the policeman back down the corridor, Des grinned at Matt. 'So Fred beats us to it again.'

They found him in the central hold. It was empty. He looked at them and pointed to the open space, bare except for a few cardboard boxes and packing material.

'Nothing!' he bellowed. 'All this for nothing. Do you know how many casualties we've had? Thirteen, and five of them dead.'

Matt picked up a piece of packing material and examined it.

'I wouldn't waste your time,' Fred said. 'We've already checked it out. Household electrical appliances. And we've searched the cabins up top. Nothing.'

Matt flung the piece of casing into a corner and thought furiously. 'But why would the Triads make such a stand over nothing? It had to be a cover for something.'

'Matt's right,' Des said. 'They wouldn't engage us in a full-scale battle for an empty ship.'

'Not unless they'd been duped as well.'

They turned at the sound of Linda's voice.

'What do you mean?' Fred asked.

'I've just been speaking to one of the junior soldiers in the godown. He'd been wounded and was almost incoherent. But he kept on repeating something about the missile. He said that they had to protect the missile.'

'Then where the fuck is it?' Fred asked.

Instead of replying, Linda handed a piece of paper to Matt. 'This has just arrived from London. It's from Sir Anthony.'

Fred waited until his impatience got the better of him. 'Well? What does it say?'

Matt passed it across to him. 'The Americans have been speaking to Sir Anthony. It's a report from one of their satellites over eastern China and the Yellow Sea. The good news is that it's no longer your problem, Fred. The Colony's quite safe.'

He turned to Des. 'The bad news is that the *Atlas Star* was a decoy all along. There *is* an SS-18 missile on the loose, but the ship that's really carrying it docked this morning at a place called Chongpo.'

Des stared at him blankly. 'Sorry, boss. You'll have to translate. Where the hell's that?'

Linda took up the thread. 'It's a small port north of Pyongyang. The missile's in North Korea.'

Around the conference table in the command bunker at Northwood, Sir Anthony counted more military top brass and leading politicians than he had ever had to brief at any one time in his life. He had just concluded his report on the situation and the time for decisions had come.

'The question is, gentlemen, what military action, if any, can be taken? And by whom?'

'Surely it's an American problem?' one officer remarked. 'If anyone can do anything it should be them.'

Sir Anthony shook his head. 'Unfortunately they don't see it that way. It's not simply a question of launching air strikes. North Korea will obviously deny all knowledge of the missile and the UN will have to condemn such an overt attack upon a sovereign state.'

'Then what about a covert operation? Why can't they use their Navy SEALs?'

'I agree with the General,' Sir Anthony said. 'However, I've already been in touch with the Pentagon and their only units with the required expertise are already fully committed to current operations in the Caribbean. By the time they could redeploy sufficient men it is likely that the missile would have been moved ashore. With every day that passes the security round the missile will become tighter, and once it is moved up-country it will be almost impossible to detect. But at this moment we know exactly where it is.'

The Prime Minister looked up. 'Thank you, Sir Anthony. Gentlemen, I have spoken with the President and he has requested that we ourselves mount a covert operation to destroy the missile before it leaves the ship.'

A murmur ran round the table.

'But what about the North Koreans? We can't just send troops into one of their ports and blow up a ship like that.'

'As Sir Anthony said, the North Koreans will want to deny any involvement in this illegal acquisition of nuclear weaponry. Well, that can work both ways. If we can manage to destroy it and get clean away, in all likelihood they won't dare say a word to anyone. They'll just bite the bullet and be forced to go without.'

An admiral leaned forward. 'But are we really to believe that they want to launch a nuclear strike against South Korea?'

'We can't afford to take any chances. With the collapse of the Communist world they've become ever more isolated. They know that some sort of spectacular success is vital if their regime is to survive at all. It's a gamble they just might be prepared to take.'

'And the targets?'

'As you know, the SS-18's a MIRV missile, capable of dividing after launch and hitting up to ten or more separate targets simultaneously. The one missile could destroy the entire industrial capacity and infrastructure of South Korea, not to mention the massive loss of life.'

The Prime Minister spoke again. 'The Americans have put their forces in South Korea on full alert and the Korean government is staging a full-scale civil defence exercise. They're playing the whole thing as just another dry run. Washington's also deploying extra Patriot anti-missile batteries to protect Seoul and other likely targets. If things ever went as far as a launch they might be able to shoot down most of the incoming MIRV warheads. But some would be bound to get through.'

There was a stunned silence round the table. After letting the facts sink in, Sir Anthony summed up. 'In the event of any such attack by the North on the South, America would be forced to counter-attack. That could bring in China, and who knows where it could end. The only option open to us is to destroy the ship before it can offload its cargo.' He paused before continuing. 'It is recommended that the job be given to the SBS. They're the only organization with the expertise. In the event that the missile is offloaded before we can destroy it, our options then shift to either a ground operation by the SAS in cooperation with the Americans, or else to an air attack by American Stealth fighter-bombers.'

'Why can't the Stealth bombers be used right now?' someone asked.

'Because we have to be sure that the job is done. We can't risk even a single warhead going missing. An air attack couldn't guarantee the destruction. We need eyes on the ground who can verify that nothing escapes the attack. Putting it simply, gentlemen, we need the SBS.'

As everyone filed out of the room at the end of the meeting, the Prime Minister drew Sir Anthony aside. 'How soon can the SBS be got moving?'

Sir Anthony smiled shyly. 'They're already on their way, sir.'

'Where are we to rendezvous with the American submarine?'

'Inchon, just west of Seoul. The SBS Sections will land there shortly and we'll join them on board,' Matt said. He looked at Linda and decided to risk it. 'Do you really have to come along?'

'You know I do. I'll be Sir Anthony's only representative. He'll want detailed reports virtually by the minute. If anything goes wrong the Stealth bombers will have to be called in immediately.'

Fred Turner came into the room. Since he had arrived back at the police operational headquarters his feet had hardly touched the ground. 'Right, a plane's been laid on and there's a car outside to take you directly to the airport – outrider escort, the works.'

He smiled at them. 'I almost wish I could come too,' but as Des opened his mouth to speak, Fred quickly added, 'I said almost!'

As he led them down to the waiting car, Fred assured

them that he and his men would continue to track down the remaining Triad links in the chain.

'I don't think they'll give you too much trouble,' Matt said. 'I reckon they've had the stuffing knocked out of them.'

'Do you think they were just middlemen all along?'

'I'm sure of it. The find of the warhead in Tolo was a stroke of luck for us. It put us on to the trail, but we were wrong to assume they wanted it for their own ends. They were just doing what they've always done: a spot of smuggling.'

'Well, they were certainly moving into an altogether different league,' Des added.

'Yes,' Fred said. 'And somehow we've still got to find who's at the back of it all. Personally I'd put my money on China. Since Deng's departure from the scene it's been a hotbed of conspiracy.'

'I'm not so sure. It's hard to see what they'd stand to gain by inciting a war between the two Koreas. They've got far more to gain by continuing with their economic reforms and trade with the West. Why risk the lot over such a stupid gamble?'

'That remains for someone to find out,' Linda said, kissing Fred goodbye.

He grinned. 'Watch out for yourselves, you lot. When it's all over come back to Hong Kong and I'll show you the town properly. And you can leave your MP5s in the armoury!'

Ted Wilcox and Dave Hunt were first on to the submarine. Ted wrinkled his nose at the smell of diesel.

'How old did you say this tub was?'

'Take it or leave it, pal,' the American lieutenant said.

'The least I'd expected was a nuclear-powered job – not this antique rust-bucket.'

'It's the commies you should be worrying about. Our job's just to get you there. But I don't know why we bother. They're only going to cut you to ribbons anyway.'

Ted jabbed a thumb at him. 'Cheery bloke, isn't he, Dave?'

'Big mistake, relying on the Yanks to do the insert,' replied Dave, glaring at the smiling officer. 'Bound to fuck it up.'

The lieutenant went off down the passageway laughing. 'Who's in charge of you jokers? Mickey Mouse?'

The two SBS troopers stared at each other in consternation. 'How'd he know? Fuck, they've blown our cover!'

Major Jerry Lane ducked round the corner, narrowly missing his head on a pipe. 'Someone call me?'

'Just baiting the Yanks, boss.'

'That's all right then. Pass the word that I'm having an Orders Group at 1700 hours in the galley.' Before he disappeared he added, 'Oh, and by the way, Major Harbin and Sergent Cooper will be joining us on this one.'

'Des? He'd better have my Rolex,' Ted warned.

When the men were all assembled in the galley Major Lane outlined once again the scope of the operation. He had already given a detailed briefing before they had left Eastney but now they were aboard the submarine he was able to provide the most up-to-date information on the objective.

'Our intelligence sources inform us that security around the ship is surprisingly light. I suppose the last thing they're expecting is an attack from the sea or the land. The air defence cover has been considerably increased to cater for the most likely option of air bombardment, although how they expect to cope with Stealth bombers is beyond me. They obviously haven't any idea what they're capable of. Anyway, the plan will be for us to mount a sabotage raid by night. The sub will take us to within a few kilometres of the coastline and from there we'll go in by canoe and inflatable. Satellite photographs have pinpointed the target ship for us.'

'So we sink it with limpet mines, right?'

'Not quite, Ted. That way the commies would be able to recover the plutonium from the sunken ship and perhaps use it again in a missile of their own design. It would slow them up but we can't afford to let them get their hands on any weapons-grade plutonium at all. We've got to board the ship and blow up the missile itself. Then we'll sink the ship. With the missile casing blown wide open and the nuclear core disrupted, any North Korean divers going near the wreck will get fried by the leaking radiation.'

'How long will the radiation last, boss?'

'About two hundred and fifty million years.'

Ted whistled. 'That ought to see out the present crisis.'

'The extraction will again be by sub. An RV will be arranged out at sea, where we'll be picked up. However, because our cover will probably have been blown by then there'll be Stealth bombers on stand-by ready to provide diversionary raids if necessary.'

'What'll their objectives be?'

'The first wave will take out the air defence systems and airfields, which'll open the door for the second wave. They'll hit the port and dock facilities, concentrating on the moorings of the North Korean patrol vessels which would be used to pursue us. The third wave will be held on call for any opportunity targets that arise. They'll be our reserve, for use as and when we need them.'

'Who'll control them?'

'Des Cooper will act as Forward Air Controller. He's FAC-trained.'

'God help us,' Ted murmured.

Major Lane went on to cover the mass of coordinating instructions necessary to pull the entire operation together and concluded the O Group an hour later after the men had had a chance to ask a battery of questions. He was sitting in his tiny cabin afterwards when there was a knock at the door and Matt Harbin walked in.

'Matt! We hadn't expected to see you for a few hours yet.'

'The Hong Kong end laid on a special plane to get us here early. How are things?'

'As well as can be expected considering we're just about to launch the squadron virtually unaided against the most hard-line communist regime in the world.'

'What's the problem? You've got me and Des. Oh, and there's one other.'

He peered out into the corridor and called someone. A moment later Linda poked her head around the door.

'Jerry, this is Linda Kirkdale. She's from Intelligence.'

Jerry Lane stared in disbelief at the attractive woman before him. 'You don't intend coming with us on this, I hope?'

Matt held up his hand. 'Before you say anything else I might as well tell you that it's been ordered by London. Sir Anthony wants her to keep an eye on us.'

Jerry shook his head. 'Well, you might be from Intelligence but you could do with a bit more of your own.'

Linda bristled. 'Just get me to the target area and concentrate on your own job, Major Lane.'

'Anything you say, Miss Kirkdale.'

Matt laughed. 'I can see you two are going to get along like a house on fire. Now, where are our quarters?'

Jerry led them down the narrow passageway to a couple of doors at the end.

'The one good thing about the Yanks is their style of doing things. If this was a Brit sub we'd all be in hammocks. Here they've allocated us cabins.'

Matt looked inside. 'Hm, not bad. Bit cramped, but otherwise I think it'll do.'

He hoisted Linda's kitbag on to his shoulder and stowed it in the adjoining cabin for her. When Jerry had gone, Matt looked at her and caught her warning glance.

'Don't worry,' he said. 'I'm not going to try

and persuade you to stay behind. I've learned my lesson.'

She smiled. 'How long do we have aboard?'

'Not long,' Matt answered. 'It's not a very long trip up the coast. But I expect the captain will take the boat quite a way out to sea before coming in again towards the target area. If we were to creep straight along the coastline we could be detected by the North Korean sonar buoys.'

Linda took him by the hand. 'Why don't you show me around the sub. I've never been on one before.'

'OK. Then we can meet up with Des in the galley and run over some details. I could handle a coffee as well.'

'Or something stronger.'

Matt shook his head. 'Not on an American sub. They're all dry. Navy policy.'

'Then you should have taken advantage of the duty-free on the aeroplane,' Linda said smiling, unzipping a small holdall and revealing the neck of a whisky bottle.

Driving through the centre of Pyongyang, Yang Zulin had to admit that it was one of the most dismal cities he had ever had the misfortune to visit. Of course it wasn't entirely the fault of the North Koreans. The city had been flattened during the Korean War, like almost every other city on the rugged peninsula. But when it had been rebuilt afterwards the soul had been omitted. Lifeless and identical barrack-like buildings stood in rank upon rank and the few monuments were of uniform predictability.

There was the Revolution Museum, the Victorious

Fatherland Liberation War Museum, the Friendship
Tower, the Monument to Martyrs of the People's
Army, the Party Founding History Museum, and,
inevitably, the edifices and sites named after the late
President: Kim Il Sung Square, Kim Il Sung Street,
Kim Il Sung University, among countless others. The
whole thing stank of the worst excesses of a Maoist
personality cult. It was little wonder that no one in the
West saw the North Koreans as anything but a threat.
They certainly couldn't be taken as a serious member
of the community of nations when they named everything so robotically and when the people exhibited the
charm and grace of mindless automata. However, the
more he thought about it the more Yang realized the
incongruity of such sentiments. Perhaps what he was
secretly regretting was the loss of such characteristics
in his own people.

Feeling uncomfortable with the notion, he looked
anew out of the car window and noted the grim
façade of yet another government office block. Surely
he wasn't starting to get used to the intrusion in Beijing
of colourful Western hotels and restaurant chains? He
smiled to himself. No. After the success of his mission
those would be the first things he would get rid of.

As the car left the outskirts of Pyongyang and started
on the long drive north towards the port town of
Chongpo, Yang watched the changing scenery. Here
at last he could see something of the original Korea that
had fostered an ancient civilization, although always
in the shadow of its mighty Chinese neighbour to the
north. Rice paddies and rolling farm land disappeared
into wooded hills and distant mountains. Peasants
worked in the fields and here and there a village lay

sleepily in the afternoon haze. But every so often the country idyll was punctuated by the stark face of an army barracks, ever-present reminders of the martial nature of the North Korean regime. Whenever the car came to a crossroads or roundabout, a towering statue of the late President Kim Il Sung would invariably dominate the scene.

Yang smiled to himself. The good thing about such obedient and organized nations was that, in the right hands, they were the easiest to dupe. Alert and even paranoid to the slightest outside threat, they were as blind as moles to the threat from inside. If one could only gain entry to the inner sanctum, one could bypass all the usual structures that kept the average Western state annoyingly free of serious subversion. But here in North Korea that was still possible. Once accepted and given credence by a handful of the ruling elite, a wily infiltrator would find the entire nation at his mercy. And to Yang Zulin mercy was a commodity in short supply.

When the car finally pulled up outside a modest hotel in Chongpo, Yang started awake. He had been enjoying a snooze for the past couple of hours but now found himself looking at a bleak and featureless town. It would not really be so very serious, he reflected, if the whole place was levelled by the West in retaliation for what he was about to do.

Three men got up to greet him as he entered the lobby. The first one, stocky and strong, held out his hand and spoke in passable Mandarin.

'I am very pleased to meet you, Comrade. My name is Hu Fat.'

Yang smiled. 'Hello. I've heard much about you. You have been doing a good job in Hong Kong.'

Hu Fat returned the smile, a little embarrassed. 'I am sorry that we couldn't get the warheads through covertly.'

'Yes, the police success at Tolo was unfortunate but all's well that ends well. The missile is here?'

Hu Fat's smile broadened. 'Yes, Comrade. The Hong Kong police fell for our decoy and by the time they'd discovered their mistake it was too late for their marine arm or the Royal Navy to prevent the real shipment entering North Korean waters and arriving at Chongpo.'

'I would like to have been a fly on the wall of their operation headquarters when they found out the truth.'

Hu Fat looked suddenly concerned. 'Then you think they know where it is?'

'I'd be very surprised if they didn't,' Yang said. 'But what can they do? This isn't a British colony and they'd never dare attack a sovereign state, especially one that has been so close to China.'

Hu Fat nodded. Beside him a man in uniform coughed politely. Hu Fat introduced him. 'Forgive me. This is General Suchi, the local garrison commander.'

The general bowed curtly and took Yang's offered hand. 'You are most welcome here, Comrade Yang. I have been fully briefed by Pyongyang and you will be accorded every assistance.'

Yang measured him carefully. 'How much have you been told by your government?'

'I know about the missile and that it is to be guarded with all my resources.' He grinned unpleasantly. 'I was too young to fight in the last war with the regime in the south. This time when we attack them we will use the missile's multiple warheads to destroy their military capability first.'

Yang's initial concern turned slowly into a smile of relief. Suchi was obviously a simple fool who could be used.

'Thank you, General,' he said, turning to the last man expectantly. But Hu Fat simply spoke to him in Cantonese and the man went scurrying for the luggage.

'Don't bother about him, Comrade,' Hu Fat said apologetically. 'That is Yip. A good man, but simple.'

'Good?'

Hu Fat sniggered. 'Efficient. He knows how to obey orders.'

'Ah! That *is* good.'

As they walked towards the hotel bar, General Suchi asked Yang how long he would be staying.

'Just long enough to finalize some details with your government.'

The general's eyes brightened. 'The time and place of the strike?'

'Exactly.'

'There will be enough warheads in the missile to wipe out the enemy's forces utterly?'

Yang smiled happily. 'You can rely on it.'

'We will owe you a great debt, Comrade,' the general said, his voice breaking with emotion.

'Nonsense. You will owe me nothing at all.'

The drone of the engines in the heart of the submarine was surprisingly quiet, pervading the vessel with a quiet, hypnotic hum. At first there had been a gentle swaying as it had got underway but now, out at sea, the boat had submerged and glided smoothly through the deep, cold waters of the Yellow Sea. Perched on the edge of her bunk, Linda sat with a glass of whisky cupped in her hands. Beside her, Matt had just poured himself another. With all the preparations complete there was nothing to do now but wait.

'When I think about the last two years,' Matt said, 'I feel angry with myself.'

'Why's that? It was both our faults.'

'No, I mean the waste. Here we are, about to launch into another mission, more dangerous than anything either of us has ever done before, certainly more so than Ireland, and we've just wasted twenty-four precious months when we could have been together.'

Linda smiled. 'Yes, I know. I feel it too. The cottage was never the same after you left. It was meant for both of us.'

'Why are people so stupid?'

'Not everyone is,' Linda replied. 'The trick is to learn from your mistakes, I suppose. Not to repeat them again.'

Matt put his glass on the table and then took Linda's gently from her. 'Leaving you was one mistake I certainly don't intend to repeat.'

She reached up and stroked his cheek. 'Let's just hope we live through this to enjoy our new resolution.'

When his lips touched hers, Matt felt the release of two years of loneliness and pain. All the anger was gone, dissipated into thin air. He felt her ease back on the narrow cot, shifting her weight on the coarse grey blankets to allow him room to join her.

She turned her mouth away from his. 'Did you lock the door?'

Matt smiled down into her eyes. 'Yes. And there's no reason for anyone to disturb us for a full two hours or more.'

Kissing Linda for the first time in two years was like a rediscovery of feeling for Matt. He thrilled at the touch and scent of her, aware of her own rising excitement. With one hand she struggled to free the buttons of his shirt and once it was off, lying in a heap on the floor, she gently reached between them, searching for the buckle to Matt's combat trousers.

Barely able to contain himself, Matt pulled Linda's blouse over her head. They were both hurrying now, not from a shortage of time, but as if the intensity of their passion would in some way compensate for all the missed lovemaking of their separation.

'Linda,' Matt gasped, as she slipped from the last of her clothes and her flesh stroked him the full length of his naked body, both of them alive with the joy of being together and in each other's arms again. In response, she shifted beneath him, drawing him into her, wriggling a moment and then suddenly still, frozen in time, clinging to the wonder of the instant. Matt pulled back to look at her, one hand stroking the soft skin of her shoulders and arms, working towards her breasts. And then a shudder announced the end of restraint as their joined bodies demanded and won the release they had awaited for so long.

12

'Why do you have to go in before the others?'

Matt lay back, his arms around Linda, holding her to him. 'Because we've got to establish an OP ashore before the main assault comes in, just in case Des needs to guide in the Stealth bombers for support. Someone's also got to silence the sentries.'

Linda stroked his chest, feeling an overwhelming sense of apprehension swamp her. 'Be careful.'

Matt smiled at her. 'You know I will. In fact, Des and I'll be safer than the rest of them. As soon as we're ashore we'll hide the canoes and lie-up, as cosy as . . .'

'Rats in a trap,' Linda said solemnly.

'That wasn't exactly what I had in mind. It'll all be over before you know it. Straight in, do the job, and out again.'

There was a light knock at the door and they heard Des's lowered voice. 'Time to move, boss.'

Matt swung his legs off the bunk and slipped into his combat trousers as Linda watched him.

'How long after you do we come ashore?' she asked.

'A couple of hours. Once the way's been cleared for the Rigid Raiders to bring in the main assault force. You'll come in with Jerry.'

223

When Matt and Linda had dressed and checked their kit, they made their way to the rear of the submarine, where the Klepper canoes were being loaded ready for disembarkation.

'Are we going out through the airlock?' Matt asked.

The American lieutenant shook his head. 'No. The captain said it's all clear up top. He's going to surface for all of five minutes to get you out nice and dry.'

'Thank fuck for that,' Des said. 'At least we won't freeze our bollocks off before we even get into the canoes.'

After wriggling into their wetsuits, Matt, Des and the other six canoeists who were to accompany them stood ready to climb out through the hatches as soon as ordered. Major Lane slapped Matt on the back and wished him well. 'We'll be right behind you, mate. Leave the throat-slitting to my lads. You and Des just get the laser target marker set up and once we hit the beach we'll do the rest.'

The lieutenant spoke into the intercom and turned to them. 'Here we go. Surfacing now. Lights on red.'

As the submarine lurched upwards, they held on to each other for balance. A few moments later seamen scrambled up the ladders and opened the overhead hatches. Water cascaded down on to them, but once the hatches were thrown back they found themselves looking up at a sky full of stars. The Kleppers were manhandled out of the submarine and secured alongside the hull as Matt, Des and their men cross-loaded their kit and clambered aboard.

With a final look back at Linda, Matt pushed away from the hull, dipping his paddle in time with Des and taking the canoe away into the darkness. Standing on the outer deck of the submarine, Linda waved after them before turning away and disappearing back into the black, shiny vessel. The next time Matt looked, the submarine had vanished from sight, the dark, swirling waters of Korea Bay closing over it as if it had never been there. Up front, Des took a fix from his compass and steered the nose of the canoe towards it. In the other three canoes strung out in line behind them, the remainder of the advance party dug their paddles into the water and followed the lead that Des had set.

Matt leaned forward and spoke quietly into Des's ear. 'Now you've seen the current, what do you reckon? About an hour?'

'Probably.'

'That's fine. That'll give us at least an hour before the others follow us. In the Rigid Raiders the trip'll only take them about thirty minutes so we've got an hour and a half to do the business and be ready to receive them.'

Apart from a gentle swell, the sea was calm and placid. Powering ahead, the four canoes made good time and at last a thin black line separated itself on the horizon from the deep velvet of the star-studded sky and the luminescent surface of the sea.

'The coast,' Des whispered over his shoulder. Matt turned round to the canoe behind, and signalled to them to pass the message back. He took out his binoculars and studied the target area until he found a patch of lights that winked in the darkness, giving away the exact location of the small port. The closer they paddled, the more lights became visible, until by the time they were only fifteen minutes out the entire waterfront of the port town lay before them.

Des waved his hand to the left. 'The actual wharf's off to the left.'

'Got it,' Matt acknowledged. He remembered the map briefing and how the satellite photographs had shown the target ship to be some distance from the built-up area. The intelligence boffins had assumed that this was for security reasons. The North Koreans had been anxious to keep the missile's arrival secret from all but a small elite and the guard force that would be protecting it. Well, secrecy could work both ways, Matt thought. He didn't doubt that there would be some sort of local garrison that would be able to assist the guards once the main assault began, but they would have to travel out to the wharf first. Hopefully, by the time they discovered that something was wrong, the charges would have been laid, the limpet mines put in place and the raid would be all but over.

Thereafter, once the charges had been blown, the SBS assault force would ditch the Kleppers and use the Rigid Raiders to get quickly out of sight and RV with the submarine out at sea at the prearranged pick-up point. The Kleppers were fine for a silent covert insertion but for a rapid getaway the powerful outboard motor of the Rigid Raider was a safer bet. Especially as by that time they could expect to have North Korean coast guard and naval patrol launches after them.

They eventually came so close to the shoreline that they could see white foam breaking on the rocks and sandy coves. Des had guided them to a point two hundred metres north of the small harbour where the ship lay tied up alongside the quay. In line with the plan that Jerry Lane and Matt had devised, working from satellite photographs and intelligence reports on the layout of the port facilities, the four canoes worked their way steadily down the coast, parallel to the shore but a hundred metres out. A searchlight beam swept across the water, but its operator was concentrating on the landward side, believing the road approaches to be the most dangerous area. It was well known that underwater mines had been laid to protect the ship and prevent any other large vessel from entering the harbour after it. He obviously hasn't heard of the Rigid Raider, Matt thought, imagining the flat-bottomed craft that would shortly come streaking in from the dead of night, spitting fire and death at the enemy.

Des slowed his pace and allowed the other three canoes to slip ahead. These contained the men who would do the silent killing. Then, with the sentries dealt with, the way would be open for the rest of the lads. As the canoes disappeared to various parts of the small harbour, Matt and Des pulled alongside the quay, keeping as silent as they could, listening for the tell-tale footsteps of any guard that might come their way. The tide was out and their canoe was safely well below the level of the wharf. To be seen, a sentry would have to lean right over and stare directly at them. Even then, with their carefully prepared camouflage and the natural darkness of the shadow in which they were sheltering, it was probable that they would remain undetected.

It was a good thirty minutes before they heard the soft padding of running feet and one of the SBS commandos leaned over the quayside and hissed down at them that the coast was clear. Clambering up on to the quay, they saw two of the commandos tipping the dead bodies of the sentries into the water.

'How many were there?' Matt asked.

'Half a dozen. There could be others in the ship. From the noise and lights in the town I'd say that's where their whole force is.'

In the dark Matt saw the flash of teeth as the commando grinned with satisfaction.

'Stupid fuckers,' Des muttered. 'Obviously reckon they're safe in their own country. Overconfidence is the biggest killer.'

'Come on,' Matt urged. 'Set up the laser target marker on the top of that building.'

Unlike the manned laser target markers that could only be operated from a safe distance away, the device Des had brought was remote-controlled. Once set up, it could be left to operate by itself, directing a series of pre-aimed beams at a selection of targets. Once the Stealth bombers were called in, their weapons would home in on the beams, flying down the radar signatures directly on to the prearranged targets. In the event that an opportunity target needed to be engaged, Des could either guide the bomber in manually or use the hand-held device that he had brought for the purpose.

While Des set off to find a way up on to the building, taking one commando with him as an escort, Matt and the others slipped out of their wetsuits and unpacked their gear, clipping on web belts of ammunition and grenades, and unwrapping their MP5s from their waterproof covers. When this was done, Matt led his little force on to the ship.

At the top of the gangplank the first thing he came across was the body of the dead guard, his eyes open and staring, the terror that had momentarily registered as his throat was cut still frozen on his face. Everything appeared to be deserted but from down in the depths of the ship they suddenly heard a roar of laughter followed by the breaking of glass.

'Having a bit of a piss-up, by the sounds of it,' Matt said. 'Let's give them something to celebrate.'

Hu Fat was not happy. After an initial display of enthusiasm the Korean general had revealed his true colours as a complete incompetent. Yang Zulin had stayed only long enough to conduct several meetings with various North Korean officials, all in strict secrecy, and had then departed for the airport and his return flight to Beijing. Before doing so he had left Hu Fat in charge of the operation.

'The Koreans know exactly what to do with the missile,' Yang had said as he stepped into his car. 'Keep an eye on the garrison commander and once the mission is complete you can return to Hong Kong, where you will be a rich man.'

He had gone on to say that he had enjoyed working with Hu Fat and that the two of them would undoubtedly be doing business in the future. He had seemed to be on the point of elaborating when he had suddenly become reticent, as if afraid of giving too much away. Hu Fat had been left wondering what complex strategies were being worked out in the mind of Yang Zulin. Somehow he was certain that Yang was right. They most definitely would be seeing more of each other in due course.

But for now the missile had to be kept safe and delivered to the North Koreans for whatever purpose Yang had agreed with them. Hu Fat and Yip had eaten early, but instead of turning in, had gone for a walk around the town. Everywhere the bars seemed to be full of drinking soldiers and it wasn't long before Hu Fat felt a mounting unease with the overall security situation. He had gone to see General Suchi, but now that Yang Zulin himself had departed, the general had become a different person, cocky and self-satisfied, and had treated Hu Fat as some inconsequential lackey.

'Tomorrow the missile will be taken away. The convoy arrives at midday. Tonight it is in my charge and you can rest assured that it is safe,' he had said, his eyes blurring with the effects of alcohol.

Hu Fat had struggled to keep his temper. He had to remember that he was in the middle of North Korea. This wasn't the Hong Kong underworld, where he was known and feared. He had to tread carefully.

'I have every confidence in your soldiers, General. But should they not be quartered closer to the ship?'

The general had become angry and Hu Fat had been dismissed for making him lose face in front of his subordinates.

Having walked through the town and seen the poor state of the garrison troops, Hu Fat and Yip turned towards the port. After leaving the last of the houses behind them, they headed for the harbour, striding out along the unlit road. In the distance they could see the ship, illuminated by a handful of lights. But as he got closer, Hu Fat stopped.

'The searchlight,' he said bluntly.

Yip looked at him puzzled. 'What about it?'

'A searchlight is supposed to fucking well search. The beam's directed straight along the beach. It hasn't moved for the last ten minutes.'

Yip shrugged. 'The sentry's probably having a crap or something.'

A group of soldiers was coming in the opposite direction. Hu Fat grabbed the nearest of them. 'Have you just come from the harbour?'

The soldier shook himself free. 'Get your hands off me, Chinaman.'

Hu Fat steadied his voice and smiled pleasantly. 'Forgive me.' He repeated his question politely.

'About a quarter of an hour ago. We were on duty but were relieved by the new watch.'

'How many of them?' Hu Fat asked.

'Same as us. Six.'

Hu Fat's eyes popped almost out of his head. 'Six? Do you mean to tell me that there are only six soldiers on duty to guard the ship?'

The soldier scratched his head, a little less certain of himself when faced with Hu Fat's mounting anger. 'Well, there were another four in the ship's signal room. We left them playing cards.'

Yip looked at his boss. 'Should we go and ask the general to reinforce the guard?'

'No. That useless arsehole's well on his way to getting pissed. I'll see he's dealt with later. He'll be lucky to be alive this time tomorrow.' He turned on the six sentries. 'You lot, come with us.'

The soldiers scowled. 'But we've just come off duty. We obey our general's orders, not yours.'

Hu Fat glared at them icily, his eyes boring into them one by one. 'I promise you that if you refuse, each and

231

every one of you will spend the rest of his military career in a labour camp. Believe me, I know what I'm saying. The cargo aboard that ship is a matter of the most direct concern to your government. It's safety is paramount.'

The soldiers looked helplessly at one another, but with no officer to countermand the orders of this overpowering Chinaman, they turned meekly to follow him. But as they approached the harbour and the twin barbed-wire gates that guarded the entrance, Hu Fat heard a noise that chilled his blood. It was a sound that was familiar to him from a dozen high-speed chases in the waters of Hong Kong. It was the deep-throated roar of a British Rigid Raider. But after it came another, and then another, the numbers increasing until the powerful hum seemed to fill the night and sent him sprinting towards the gates and the silhouette of the ship that lay naked and unprotected in the harbour.

Crouching in the prow of one of the assault craft, Linda cradled an MP5 and brushed the salt water from her face. Her black combats were already covered with a fine sheen of moisture as the Rigid Raider bounced and skimmed across the water's surface towards the harbour lights. Around her half a dozen SBS commandos clung to the sides of the speeding boat, heavy with weaponry and ammunition. Major Lane tapped her on the shoulder and pointed to the ship, where a light flashed out at them.

'Morse,' he shouted above the noise of the engines.

'What's it say?'

'It's the all-clear from Matt.'

He grinned at her. 'So far so good.'

As they approached the harbour mouth, the Rigid Raiders tightened their formation until they burst through the narrow opening like a clenched fist. In every vessel the commandos braced themselves ready to return fire should it be necessary. But the advance party had done their job and the sentries had been silenced.

Lane's craft took the lead and swung ahead of the rest, pulling up at a long jetty on to which the commandos scrambled, securing the boat alongside as the remaining craft came in one by one. Matt strode down to meet them.

'We've got it!' he called. The missile's in the hold. The lads are preparing it for demolition now.'

Lane whirled to the explosives experts, who had just landed and were manhandling their cumbersome packs ashore. 'Follow that man, lads.'

A commando ran up to him. 'Where do you want my men, boss?'

'Got the mines?'

The marine nodded.

'There's the ship. Get ready to sink the fucker. Detail the rest of your section to booby-trap the whole dock area with claymores. We want to slow them up as much as possible.'

'Wilco!'

With the demolition, mining and booby-trapping parties set to work, Lane positioned the rest of his men to provide all-round defensive protection in case the enemy discovered them before their business was done. Then, when the deployment had been completed and checked, he made his way on board and went to find Matt in the hold. The missile was disappointing to look at, broken down into its main components, each one packed and crated for the journey.

'Not much to look at, is it?' Lane said as he knelt beside Matt and the demolitions sergeant.

'Depends whether it's screaming right at you or not. Here, give us a hand.'

Together they ripped open the lids of the packing cases, exposing the gleaming metal of the missile body.

'The warheads are over there in those long boxes.'

'Jesus,' Lane whistled. 'How many of the sods are there?'

'I've counted ten. It's a MIRV all right.'

'With that lot they could wipe out a whole sodding country.'

'I expect that's pretty much what they intended to do.'

The sergeant looked up. 'Bit of overkill, isn't it?'

'What do you mean?' Lane asked.

'Well, they should have got their hands on a smaller MIRV. If all they need is something to hop over the border, why go for a fucking great intercontinental sod like this?'

Linda came up behind them. 'I suppose they had to take whatever they could get their hands on.'

But Matt was thinking. 'The sergeant's got a point.' He sat back on his heels. 'Why the hell didn't that occur to me?'

'I'd worry about it afterwards if I were you,' Linda said. 'The fact is the missile's an SS-18. Let's just blow it and get out of here.'

'I'll drink to that,' the sergeant mumbled as he

taped a wad of explosives on to the side of the missile's body.

Matt and the others went from crate to crate, levering open the lids and laying bare the lethal contents for the attentions of the demolitions team. Meanwhile, beneath the ship, frogmen were placing limpet mines on the hull both fore and aft, well below the water-line, checking that the harbour where the ship was berthed was deep enough for the ruptured vessel to sink completely.

'I've got men placing incendiary charges all over the ship. We'll make sure she's burnt out before she goes down,' Lane said.

Matt flung down the lid of the last of the crates. 'Good. Now we know what to look for we can make sure they don't get their hands on any more.'

'Someone's going to pay for this lack of security,' Lane called across. 'The least we expected was a decent fire-fight.'

But at that moment the muffled sound of gunfire reached them. Matt winced and glared at Lane. 'You had to open your big mouth, didn't you?'

Lane dropped the crowbar he had been using on one of the crates and bolted for the exit. 'Get the job finished here, Sarge,' he called over his shoulder. 'I'm going up top to take charge. If the gooks are on to us we'll have to get a shift on.'

After his meeting with General Suchi, Hu Fat had known that the only thing that would rouse him from his complacency would be the unmistakable sounds of battle. So the moment he had guessed what was going on he ordered the Korean guards to fire their Kalashnikovs. At first the guards had refused. 'What at? Everything's fine,' they had said as they approached the gates.

'Then where's the gate sentry?' Hu Fat had asked, exasperated. They had finally only believed him when they had glimpsed the shadowy figure of a man in unfamiliar combat kit darting across the compound on the other side of the locked gates.

'There!' Hu Fat shouted at them triumphantly. 'Who the hell do you suppose that is? Lenin?'

Fumbling for their weapons, the guards jostled forwards. One of them fired at the huge chain and padlock, shattering it and enabling the others to open the gates. But they had barely entered the harbour compound when they were fired at by unseen gunmen.

'Take cover!' one of the guards cried, but Hu Fat kicked him in the buttocks and screamed for them all to go forward.

'Get in there, you cowards! If you stop here you won't move again!'

A burst of fire from the nearest of the enemy's fire positions cut down the guard beside Hu Fat, throwing him back into the Chinaman. Hu Fat used the lifeless body as a shield, edging towards the side of a building, struggling to get the dead man's Kalashnikov from him. Yip crouched at his side, returning the fire with his pistol, but, realizing that they were outgunned and that the Korean guards were doing little to suppress the enemy's fire, he tore the Kalashnikov from the nearest guard, clubbing him with the butt of his pistol when he protested.

The muzzle flash from an MP5 gave away the fire

position of one of the SBS commandos and in an instant Hu Fat had reacted, blazing out a long burst with his Kalashnikov. But the marine had ducked out of sight immediately after firing and the Kalashnikov bullets chewed harmlessly through the stack of boxes and crates to find only empty space behind. Then the man fired again, popping out from behind a low wall – only this time Hu Fat and Yip were ready for him. Yip had watched the first time and caught the direction of the marine's roll, indicating to his boss the next likely fire position. Sure enough, when the man put his head and shoulders round the wall to fire he was met by a fusillade of Kalashnikov fire, the high-velocity bullets raking across his chest and tumbling him across the tarmac, dead before his body came to rest.

Deciding that it was time to move forward and bring greater pressure to bear on the saboteurs, Hu Fat herded the Koreans out of the cover into which they had eagerly retreated.

'Move, you fuckers!' he screamed at the top of his voice, levelling the muzzle of his weapon at them, his finger resting lightly on the trigger in case anyone tried to flee. Reluctantly they got up and jogged after Yip, who was already crossing an open area towards the ship.

It was at that moment that Hu Fat caught sight of some movement on the adjacent rooftop. The building was the tallest in the compound and he realized that a firer on the top of it would be able to dominate the battle. He would also be able to get a better idea of how many of the attackers there were. Tugging at the shoulder of Yip's jacket, he pulled him along after him.

'Stay where you are and keep them pinned down with suppressive fire,' he ordered the senior of the guards. When he caught the glint of relief in the man's eye he added, 'And if you move from here or try to bug out before I tell you to, I will kill you myself.'

The man took one look at Hu Fat and knew that he meant it. He grunted and urged his men to put down a blanket of fire in the general direction of the enemy positions. For a second or two it worked, the incoming bursts from the MP5s lessening sufficiently for Hu Fat and Yip to dart across the open space and reach the cover of a fire-escape, hidden from the marines' view at the rear of the building.

They climbed rapidly to the top, doubling up the iron steps and stopping only when they approached the last flight. Hu Fat signalled for Yip to be silent and peered over the top. In front of him the flat roof was empty except for two figures on the far side. Fortunately neither of them was looking towards the fire escape. One of them was bending over some sort of device and the other one was pointing in the direction of the town and saying something. They were too far away for Hu Fat to make out the words but it seemed likely that the general was at last reacting and that the marine was pointing out the reinforcements that were on their way towards the harbour.

Now we'll see how brave you are, he thought as he eased himself silently over the last step and on to the rooftop. When Yip was standing beside him they started across the open space, their Kalashnikovs side by side, each muzzle aimed at one of the two unsuspecting men, ready to fire in an instant but holding their fire until the last moment, when they would close to point-blank range and be certain of a kill.

General Suchi was enjoying the company of a bottle of whisky and a whore when the sounds of gunfire erupted from the direction of the harbour. He froze in his chair, the whore balanced on his lap. With one hand holding a brimming glass of whisky and the other inside the girl's blouse massaging her breasts, his scope for immediate reaction was severely limited. However, when the ferocity of the engagements mounted in the next few seconds he simply stood up, toppling the whore to the ground, where she scrabbled to replace her breasts in the blouse from which they had exploded. After placing his glass carefully on the table, the general went quickly to the door and shouted for his officer of the guard.

'What the hell's going on?'

'There's firing at the harbour.'

'I'm not fucking deaf, you cretin! Find out who it is!'

He was going for his pistol belt and helmet when he thought again. 'No, just call out the full guard.'

'Where shall I deploy them, Comrade General?'

The general felt his anger rising to crisis point. 'Where the devil do you think?'

He was about to be clever and make some sarcastic suggestion but thought better of it. Results would be quicker if he spoke directly. These were not front-line troops like those down on the border along the 38th Parallel. These were the dross, local garrison troops, and their officers had been selected to match. It did not occur to the general to take the next small logical step in the thought process and question the reasons for his own presence in the garrison. The mechanisms of self-delusion swung into place to save his pride.

Out in the street soldiers were scurrying half-dressed and half-equipped for their vehicles. Engines coughed into life, headlights came on, and an overeager driver promptly backed his truck smack into a parked jeep. Instead of concentrating on the main problem, ignoring the damage and taking his load of soldiers towards the battle, he got out of his cab and went round to the back of the vehicle to argue with the jeep's driver. To his surprise he was met by one of the officers waving a pistol in his face, apoplectic with rage.

When the mess was sorted out and the road was cleared, five truckloads of troops bounced out of the town and hurtled towards the harbour.

'Ram straight through the gates!' the officer in the front truck shouted at his driver, who pressed his foot flat on the accelerator and hunched over the wheel, pressing his buttocks into the seat, ready for the impact. However, when they were some seventy or eighty metres short, the officer caught the movement of two black-clad figures to his left. He never had time to shout a warning, nor to leap from the cab, before a ball of orange flame exploded from the muzzle of the thin tube over the shoulder of one of the figures and the M72 anti-tank rocket blazed straight into the side of the truck. The resulting detonation thrust the vehicle clean off the road, toppling it into the ditch on its side. The few surviving soldiers crawled from the flaming wreckage only to be met by a withering fire from the assembled MP5s of a complete four-man SBS ambush team.

In his jeep at the rear, General Suchi clung to the dashboard as his driver screeched to a halt behind the other swerving trucks.

'Get out, you fools!' the general screamed, stumbling into the road and waving his pistol, more at his own men than at the enemy, who, their delaying action done, had already disappeared to prepare the next surprise.

13

Hu Fat and Yip were halfway across the roof when the SBS commando turned and saw them. Before even uttering a cry of warning to Des he was throwing himself on to his stomach and rolling aside. But his two assailants had been prepared for such a move and their fingers tightened in unison on their triggers, squeezing out two streams of bullets that converged on him with lethal accuracy.

Without even looking to see who the attackers were, Des was also moving, but in the opposite direction, half rolling and half scrabbling towards the door that led down into the warehouse. He was almost there when Hu Fat and Yip swung their weapons on to him, his escort now dead in a pool of blood.

Should have split your fire, Des thought with satisfaction as he reached the open door, the first of the Kalashnikov bullets snapping at the ground behind him. Safely in cover, he knew that he had only seconds to act. Reaching for the smoke grenade on his webbing, he tugged it free, ripped out the pin and hurled it round the door and out on to the roof. With the delicate laser homing equipment exposed in the open he didn't dare use either HE or white phosphorus. The smallest grenade splinter or incendiary fragment would render it useless and without the Stealth bombers the SBS options would be severely curtailed. Somehow he had to hang on and keep the device in operation. If his attackers realized what it was they could put it out of commission with a single burst of fire. Hopefully they had been too intent on their human targets to notice and now the screen of harmless smoke might serve to keep its purpose concealed long enough for Des to neutralize them.

He waited for the pop and hiss of the bursting grenade, counted to three to give the smoke time to build into a screen, and then rolled his head and shoulders out of the door at ground level, his MP5 aimed along his line of sight. But in doing its job the screen had also prevented Des from getting a good shot at his targets. With a series of short bursts into the smoke, he covered all the angles where he estimated his attackers might be, pulling back into cover to spring out the empty magazine and snap in a refill.

A moment later the walls around him erupted with showers of chipped plaster and brick as a hail of Kalashnikov bullets tore into it from the outside, raked from side to side by Hu Fat and Yip, who were like two predatory birds trying to pierce a shell and get at the vulnerable creature within. Des knew that the 7.62mm bullets would soon be able to chew right through both brick and concrete and that he had to move. His cover was good for only a few more seconds before one of the lethal bullets would find him. He reckoned he had two choices. He could either go back out on to the roof and take his chances in a shoot-out there, or he could make his way down into the warehouse and hope that his attackers would pursue him rather than investigate the device he had left up above. On the roof the smoke would give him a momentary advantage, but there were two of them and he was now alone. Even if he accounted for one of the enemy, the chances were that the other one would get him. Once in the warehouse, however, he might be able to lure them in after him and deal with them on ground of his own choosing. He would have to hope that in their eagerness to achieve a kill they would be blinded to the homing device, thinking only of hunting down their quarry.

In one convulsive movement, Des launched himself down the stairs as the spray of Kalashnikov bullets tore right through the brick wall where, only a moment ago, he had been crouching. The homing device would have to go it alone for now. Des had a trap to set.

'Wait till they close inside the killing area,' Matt whispered to the man beside him, a firing trigger for a claymore in each hand. To either side of them, half a dozen marines lay in wait, their MP5s trained on the open ground in front of them into which the first of the North Korean soldiers were furtively advancing.

'Come on, come on,' Matt hissed. 'We haven't got all day.'

Alerted by the ambush on the approach road from the town and by the destruction of one of their trucks, the soldiers were reluctant to get to grips with their unseen enemies. But from behind them came the screams and shouts of their officers, urging them on with drawn pistols, and behind the officers, still in his jeep, General Suchi cajoled and threatened, telling everyone where they would end up if they failed to do his bidding.

'Now!' Matt said aloud, clapping the firer on the shoulder when he estimated that a full platoon of soldiers were before him. Squeezing the triggers tightly, the marine completed the firing circuits, sending an electrical pulse down each of the wires to the two detonators in the heart of the mines. Matt and Linda hugged the ground, their faces averted from the ground-shaking blasts as the matrix of high explosives shattered in a flash of light and the hail of steel ball-bearings rocketed into the dumbstruck soldiers.

Before the smoke had cleared the marines were firing, conserving their ammunition as best they could with controlled bursts, directing their fire with a precision gained from hard training and ruthless battle discipline. In the killing area before them all was chaos as the smoke cleared, revealing the carnage that the detonating mines had caused. Among the dead and the wounded, soldiers staggered back out of the compound, pressing back towards the gates where their own officers met them with single aimed pistol shots when they saw it was obvious that mere encouragement would no longer suffice. Trapped between a well-prepared enemy and a ruthless code of military discipline, the soldiers went to ground wherever cover could be found. Some of them returned a desultory fire at the marines, but most simply cowered behind walls or huddled in the monsoon drains that ringed the harbour.

'That's done it,' one of the marines said to Matt. 'Looks like they've had enough.'

'Don't believe it. They'll regroup and come at us again. We've got to get out of here soon.'

'How's the ammo doing?' Linda asked.

Matt checked his pouches. 'I'm down to my last couple of mags.'

'It's the same everywhere. The lads'll be running dry soon.'

Matt thought frantically. Somehow they had to save their fire for the next big engagement, which he knew would not be long in coming. He turned to the SBS sergeant further along the row of firers.

'We've got to fall back.'

The sergeant stared at him in amazement. 'What the hell for? We've got them licked.'

'Just do as I say. Pull your men back to the line of the warehouses and set up some more claymores. We'll reorganize there and then hit them with the same again when they advance.'

Still the sergeant hesitated, looking anxiously around for Major Lane, his own commander.

'Move!' Matt shouted at him. 'Now! Before the gooks regroup.'

With his jaw set tight, the sergeant reluctantly signalled to the men of his fire teams and, after a quick check on the enemy, led them back to the new fire positions that Matt had pointed out.

'Are you sure, Matt?' Linda asked as she followed him across the open ground.

'It's the only way. We've got the Koreans off balance for now, but it won't last. Next time they'll come forward with their full force and if we're still sitting in the same positions that we've already given away we'll be done for.'

Pausing halfway back to the new position, Linda looked round at the cargo ship. The demolitions team had drawn up the gangplanks and as she watched she could see them busying themselves on the upper decks.

'What are they up to?'

'They're laying booby-traps just in case the Koreans get on board before the main charges and limpet mines go off. The booby-traps'll slow them up until it's too late,' Matt explained.

He looked at her in the ghostly light of the battle. Her face was streaked with soot and dirt and the upper sleeve of her combat jacket had been ripped in the turmoil.

'Are you OK?' he asked.

She forced a smile, concealing her fear. 'Yes,' she answered. 'Worry about your men.'

'We'll soon be out of here,' Matt said, trying to make it sound convincing but hearing the hollow ring in his own voice.

'Come on.'

He pulled her by the hand and together they crossed the last open space before the new delaying position, where the sergeant and his fire teams were already laying out the wire to the claymores and dropping into carefully selected hideouts.

'Got any more M72s?' Matt called across.

The sergeant grinned in response and patted a large canvas holdall at his side. 'Just a couple I was saving for a rainy day.'

'Can you spare one?' Matt asked. 'I've just spotted something that might make a nice little target.'

The sergeant followed Matt's gaze and saw the

grouping of large round fuel tanks towering some two hundred metres away. 'Give me a shout before you fire, boss. I want to get my head down before that lot goes up.'

He tossed one of the short khaki canisters across and then rummaged around for another, which he placed beside him on the ground, in readiness for a target of his own.

There was a shout from the direction of the main gate, accompanied by a further bout of firing, and another wave of Korean infantry surged into view. But unlike their predecessors these men were fired with anger. They had been brought forward by their officers and looked with scorn on the cowering figures of the first wave.

'Here they come, ready or not,' the SBS sergeant shouted, dropping into position and checking that the man beside him had completed setting up the claymores.

'Hang on to those clackers, lad. We'll give them another taste of steel in a minute.'

Matt glanced over his shoulder at the ship. 'I hope Jerry's ready over there. This time I reckon they mean business. We won't be able to hold them much longer.'

After the nasty surprise on the approach road to the harbour gates, General Suchi had stayed in the background, preferring to work through his officers in order to persuade his men to keep up the pressure of the attack. But as time went by he became seriously concerned, not so much with the fierceness of the enemy resistance but with the consequences for himself of the whole raid. He considered that he had worked hard to win his present command position. OK, so it wasn't at the head of a crack border division but he was proud of his command even if it was in a backwater garrison with second-rate troops and conscripts.

But these were troubled times. With the Soviet Union in ruins and China on a road that seemed to be leading inexorably towards capitalism, his own country stood in ever-increasing isolation in a reshaped world. It was not too hard to imagine a future society which would no longer have a place for ex-Cold War warriors like himself. At first he had doubted if the reforms would take hold on the Communist world, but then one by one the old regimes had toppled until North Korea stood virtually alone, the last bastion of truth and freedom.

The plan of that devious Chinaman Yang Zulin had seemed a stroke of brilliance to the general, even though he had only been apprised of the barest of facts. But he knew enough to deduce that the very upper tiers of the governing hierarchy in Pyongyang were behind it, all convinced that in it lay the party's last hope of survival and of triumph over the hated American-backed regime in the South. In one swoop they would be able to close the technological gap and defeat the Seoul regime, the Soviet-built missile raining death from the skies on to all the major South Korean military installations on the peninsula.

But if, because of his own lack of caution, the missile were now to be lost to this band of saboteurs, what mercy could he expect from Pyongyang or from the military intelligence officers who were even now converging on Chongpo to inspect their newly acquired treasure?

Galvanized into action by this powerful combination of self-interest and survival instinct, the general launched himself out of his jeep and strode towards the harbour gates.

'Where's the reserve?' he barked authoritatively.

An officer paled at the sight of his commander and led him to the fresh truckloads of soldiers.

'Out!' the general screamed. 'Come on. You're going to attack!' He looked at the staring faces and rephrased his command. 'We're going to attack!' he announced proudly.

As they tumbled out of the trucks the soldiers were rapidly formed into assault teams by their officers, and once this had been done the general walked calmly to the front.

'Right. Follow me,' he said, and led the way towards the harbour compound.

The inside of the warehouse was very different from the one of the Castle Peak raid. Instead of being spacious and open, it consisted of several floors, each one closely packed with various cargoes, everything from crates of engineering machinery to sacks of rice and flour. As Des moved quickly down the steps he could hear the sound of someone above him, clearing the stairwell he had just left. Having chewed through the brick wall, the Kalashnikov bullets had stopped and there had been a short pause before the two men decided how best to winkle out their quarry.

The moment he heard the familiar rumble of a grenade being rolled through the upper door, Des flung himself behind a wall of sacks. The explosion echoed through the warehouse, the sound amplified in the enclosed space. A shower of dust and debris came down the stairs and Des knew that it would not be long before his pursuers followed. He sprang to his feet and ran away from the staircase, weaving his way through the piles of stores.

You'll never find me in this lot, he thought. In fact it was the perfect place for an ambush. If he could only lure the two of them inside he might be able to split them up and deal with them one by one. He did a rapid check of his resources. Apart from his spare ammunition for the MP5 he had his Browning pistol with its four spare mags, a couple of HE grenades, a white-phosphorus smoke and incendiary grenade, and his combat knife.

'That should do the trick,' he said under his breath, calming himself in readiness for the close quarter battle about to erupt. He considered making his way down to the ground floor and out of the warehouse altogether. But he had to be sure that the laser homing device had been left in operation, and to do that he had to take out these two arseholes who were after him.

Footsteps were coming slowly down the stairway. Behind his wall of sacks, Des could make out the steady tread of someone tensed for instant contact and knew that to reveal himself now would only invite a torrent of fire. Slowly, measuring each step and looking carefully before he placed his feet, he crept further away from the stairs, going deeper into the heaped cargo that towered around him.

A second man was now coming down on to the floor and Des could hear them conversing in muffled voices. That's it, he thought. Split up, you buggers. Divide and rule. Listening intently, he half opened his mouth and popped his ears to catch the slightest sound, cocking his head in the direction of the men. From outside the noise of the battle made it difficult to filter out the sounds he needed to hear, but eventually he was certain that he had achieved his aim and that the two men were no longer working as a team but as two individuals.

Straining his every sense to keep hold of the whereabouts of his pursuers, Des moved on, his MP5 cradled in the ready position, finger on the trigger and safety-catch off. The slightest stimulus could send him straight into action.

When it came, it was from an unexpected direction. A barely perceptible movement from behind sent Des spinning, his finger tightening even as he turned and dropped to one knee, the final pressure awaiting the vital eye contact that would confirm his target as hostile and not another commando who had strayed into the middle of their lethal stalk. He found himself looking at a small Chinese man, wiry and alert, staring back at him with an expression halfway between surprise and deadly concentration. Des squeezed off a burst and felt the MP5 judder in his grasp, the mild shock waves absorbed by his stance and grip, rolling into his tensed body as the rounds fired across the open space between him and his target.

But his target had also moved, a smooth and deceptively fast sidestep taking the Chinaman out of harm's way and out of sight behind a pile of packing crates. Des tracked his muzzle left, following the approximate line of the man's withdrawal, his bullets splintering straight through the thin wood of the cases. Only as an afterthought did he drop his point of aim towards the ground in case the man had hit the deck. But by then it was already too late. He could hear the shuffling and scuttling as his target slithered away on his belly as easily as a snake.

'Shit!'

Des knew that he too had to move. He had now given his position away to the other man, who would undoubtedly have moved to cut him off. He swung around in a standard drill, side-shuffling as he did so and rising into a half crouch, advancing to the end of the narrow passageway, ready for anything.

'Time to up the stakes,' he muttered softly. Holding the MP5 in one hand, his finger still on the trigger, he reached with his free hand for one of his HE grenades, using his teeth to pull out the pin that he had uncrimped and loosened before the battle. It was time for some rapid movement to force his opponents into revealing where they were.

In a sudden spurt of action Des burst across the passageway, turned left and hurtled down the centre of the warehouse floor. As he passed one of the openings between two piles of cargo, he caught a glimpse of the other man, larger and older than the first one. The man swung his Kalashnikov on to Des and fired, but he had been caught off balance by Des's manoeuvre and his bullets spat harmlessly into thin air. With an overarm throw Des lobbed the grenade high over the crates in the man's direction, covering the clatter of it's landing with a short burst from his MP5 in the hope that the grenade might go undetected until detonating and killing his enemy.

It seemed to work because in the second before the explosion, instead of running feet he heard only the sound of the man reloading with a fresh magazine. Once again the crump was magnified, leaving Des's ears ringing and temporarily numbed.

'One down, one to go,' he said to himself, stalking back round towards the side wall, where he estimated the second man to be hiding.

He was almost at the furthest extremity of the large room when his peripheral vision flashed with a dark shape. The next thing Des knew he was sprawling on the ground with the smaller of the two Chinese men on top of him. He had lost his MP5 in the fall, and as he struggled to reach a hand to the hilt of his combat knife he was punched hard in the mouth. Lights flashed before his eyes and he felt his head swim. He fought to keep a hold on his thought processes. Fuck the knife, he thought; you'll be dead before you get it out. Instead he jerked his right knee up into the man's flank and heard the breath rasp out of him. Good, he thought; that one struck home.

The man was small but fast. Another two punches had landed with telling effect before Des got in one of his own. Because he was still pinned with his back to the floor he didn't have the room for a good swing. So, jackknifing his one free arm at the elbow, he struck at the side of his opponent's neck, using a ridge hand blow, the opposite upper edge to the open knife hand. Though the blow was not as powerful as the knife hand, the base of the forefinger drove into the soft muscle and nerve between the man's shoulder and head, and Des knew that he had created a vital opening. Seizing the man by the shoulders, he swung him off, toppling him on to the floor and scrabbling up on to his knees. Before the Chinaman could recover, Des had struck again, this time with a powerful clenched-fist blow to the point of the chin.

But he was suddenly aware of a flash of light beneath him. In tumbling to the ground, the Chinaman had sunk his hand in his pocket and produced a lethal stabbing knife, the point of which was now aiming at Des's stomach. Des jerked himself free as the blade arced upwards in a gutting motion, ripping the front of his combat jacket. As he fell back, landing opposite his stunned opponent, Des grappled his Browning from its holster and before the Chinaman could lash out again, pumped four 9mm bullets into his chest.

The body collapsed to the floor, the lifeblood seeping from it with the last of the breath, as the eyes rolled in their sockets, glazing and fixing in death. Des was getting to his feet when the Browning was savagely chopped from his hand with the butt of a Kalashnikov.

'Not so fast.'

Des grasped his throbbing wrist and turned to see the other man, whom he thought he had killed with the grenade. A thin trickle of blood seeped from beneath his hairline and there was a bruise on one cheek.

'Hope I didn't hurt you,' Des said bitterly.

Hu Fat smiled, but it froze on his lips as he studied Des's face. 'So,' he said at last. 'I might have guessed.'

Des frowned, puzzled. 'Do I know you? You're not from the takeaway in Sidmouth, are you?'

The man snarled and drove the muzzle of his Kalashnikov into Des's stomach, winding him and doubling him over.

'You don't know it, but I've been looking forward to meeting you ever since our Tolo escapade.'

Des felt his blood run cold as the memory of that night came back to him and he saw again the manner in which Josh Higgs had been butchered.

'You!' he hissed, starting towards Hu Fat.

But Hu Fat simply drew back and levelled his Kalashnikov at him. 'Go on, brave marine. Walk into my bullets. You're going to sooner or later. But I thought the Koreans might like a word with you first. I'm sure they'd like you to explain what you're doing in their country. And they've got all sorts of means of making you say what they want.'

Des grinned. 'Oh no. Not the "We've got ways of making you talk" routine! Don't you fuckers ever learn any new lines?'

Hu Fat smiled. 'You can't anger me, my friend. I've got you exactly where I want you at last. Move!'

Out in the compound the battle had entered a new and dangerous stage. The next wave of Korean soldiers had first gained a foothold inside the gates and then surged forward when General Suchi had committed his reserve. Instead of directing the main effort of their attack straight at the marines in a frontal assault, the Koreans had begun to work their way around the sides of Matt's stop line. With his claymores ineffective, Matt and his fire teams had been forced to rely on the fire-power of their small arms, augmented by HE grenades when a sufficiently concentrated target merited it.

Matt finally saw his chance to use his M72 rocket launcher when he noticed a group of soldiers gathering in the area of the fuel tanks in preparation for a fresh assault.

'Here goes,' he said to Linda. He snapped open the canister and pulled the arming clip. With the weapon balanced on his shoulder he sighted down the eyepiece, steadied his breath and waited for Linda to tap him on the shoulder, signalling that the backblast area behind him was clear of friendly forces.

'Firing now.'

Matt squeezed down on the pressure switch, firing the rocket. The blast from the rear of the tube and the explosion of the rocket motor beside his ear were deafening, but the main shock came at the moment of impact. Blazing across the two hundred metres that separated him from the fuel tanks, the rocket arced gracefully, a vapour trail unravelling behind it. The nose of the 66mm rocket struck the nearest of the tanks dead centre and the molten-copper core powered through the tank's skin and exploded in the heart of the fuel.

A gigantic geezer of flame shot up into the night sky like a small atomic explosion, mushrooming above the harbour complex. People in the town who had been listening to the noise of the battle and who had heard the stories of the Soviet missile flung themselves to the floor, thinking that the nuclear warhead itself had just been detonated. A wall of heat shot back across to where Matt and Linda lay, hugging the wharf.

'Jesus, there she blows!' the sergeant next to them shouted.

Matt quickly looked around. The shock of the blast had created a moment's stunned silence all around the harbour. This is it, he thought. Time to seize the moment and run.

'Come on,' he shouted at Linda, grabbing her by the wrist and pulling her after him. 'Sarge, get your men back to the boats. Fire and manoeuvre by teams.'

'Right you are, boss,' the sergeant barked in response, doubling along his line of men to pass the word.

Matt and Linda sprinted towards the water's edge, then ducked behind a wall to get their breath. From where he was Matt could see the Rigid Raiders bobbing below him about fifty metres away. To one side, the ship was now deserted, the charges set, the limpet mines armed, all the timers ticking off the seconds. He was just about to move again when Lane dropped down beside him.

'All set, Jerry?' Matt asked.

'Yes. But look what I found,' Lane replied, handing Matt and Linda a large wallet of papers.

'What is it?' Linda asked, her nose for a good piece of intelligence overcoming her desire to be in the Rigid Raider and screaming away from the battle zone.

'Looks like the missile's targeting instructions. I found them on the bridge. They were chained to the wrist of some dead Chinese guy.'

'Chinese?'

'Yeah. Had his passport and ID docs on him, the lot.'

One glance at the first couple of sheets was enough for Linda's trained eye. 'But this can't be right.'

Matt scowled at the two of them. 'Look, can't this

wait until we're on the sub? The gooks'll be all over us in a minute.'

Lane nodded. 'OK. But London'll have to hear about this pronto.'

The sergeant was doubling back past them when he stopped in mid-step and pointed out into the harbour with horror. 'Oh shit. Look!'

Matt turned to see the low, grey bulk of a Korean patrol launch side on, its hull almost completely blocking the harbour mouth and its guns trained on the wharf, where the lead SBS fire teams were scrambling down into their Rigid Raiders. 'Stop them,' he shouted to Lane. 'Get the lads . . .'

Before the words were out, the gun fired and the shell screamed straight into the cluster of boats and men, detonating against the side of the wharf and sending a shower of oily water into the air.

'No!' Lane shouted. The sergeant snapped open his M72 launcher, swung round to aim it at the launch and fired. But the rocket drove into the adjacent jetty, sending only a few fragments of splintered stone into the launch, which had already reloaded and was preparing to fire again.

'What do we do now?' Linda said, a trace of fear creeping into her voice.

Matt looked at his watch and then at Lane. 'What time did you set the charges for?'

Lane checked the time. He shrugged resignedly. 'Looks like we're all fucked. Anyone for tennis?'

'They're falling back!' General Suchi shouted once he recovered from the detonation of the fuel tanks. 'Kill them! Kill every one of them!'

A moment later one of his officers rushed up to him and in his excitement shook the general by the arm. 'Look, Comrade General, sir! Look!'

The general saw the patrol launch and smiled with grim satisfaction. 'Now we have them. The Party will thank me yet.'

A hundred metres away one of his men stepped into the centre of the SBS's second killing area and stumbled over a claymore trip-wire. But even the rocketing anti-personnel mine couldn't shake the general's confidence. Deaf to the screams and groans of his own men, he focused his full attention on the tight little huddle of saboteurs cornered like rats on the furthest part of the wharf. The launch fired once. A futile attempt from the saboteurs to sink it failed, and then it fired again.

The general watched as his enemies' fragile raiding craft were blown out of the water. He threw back his head and laughed, then urged his men forward yet again, driving them around the sides of the cowering enemy force who had suddenly thrown themselves flat on the tarmac. They were scrabbling for cover. He could see their officers clearly, waving frantically to their men, and he could see the men as well, flinging themselves behind walls in response to the orders, into the deep concrete storm drains, anywhere to escape from his own Koreans, anywhere to escape from him, the commanding general of the garrison force that had defended their ground and protected the missile, the SS-18 MIRV that was to save his party, his nation, his people.

14

In the seconds before the explosion Matt jumped down into the monsoon drain, catching Linda in his arms as she followed after him. Lane joined them and together they huddled in a tight ball against the solid concrete walls.

'Listen, everyone,' Lane said. 'May I just say what a pleasure it's been knowing you all.'

'Wipe that silly grin off your face,' Matt replied. 'I just hope we don't get allocated the same sodding cloud once we're through the pearly gates.'

'What do you mean? You'll be stoking the fires of hell for the rest of eternity, I reckon,' Lane said.

Linda looked at them sullenly. 'Of all the famous last words I have to listen to, it's got to be this male-bonding crap.'

Matt hugged her to him. 'Don't worry, dear. If Jerry's lads have fixed the charges right, the warhead itself won't go off. It should just split open and be disrupted, contaminating the ship.'

'Just!' Lane sniggered. 'I like that!'

The next moment the earth seemed to heave and shudder. As if in a dream Linda could see Lane's lips still moving but his words were drowned out by the roar of high explosives and the secondary detonations that were triggered throughout the ship. Huge spouts of water rose in the air as the limpet mines exploded beneath the surface, the cold spray showering down across the complete harbour complex and soaking everyone to the skin. As yet more charges went off, uniting into a continuous series of explosions, the ship's fuel tanks ruptured and caught fire, the blazing liquid spreading in a scarlet sheet across the water's surface towards the patrol launch blocking the harbour's mouth.

On the bridge of the launch the Korean captain stared in horror at the approaching wall of flame, screaming at the helmsman to get the vessel out of harm's way. But it was too late. As some of the sailors fought to get the launch moving, others jumped over the far side into the sea, swimming frantically for the shore. A moment later the flames lapped at the vessel's grey hull, ringing it until it resembled a grim phoenix, but instead of rising from the burning nest it was set alight and within seconds the relentless prying flames had burrowed their way into the ammunition magazines below deck. The forward gun turret was blown clean into the air as the stacks of shells went up, spinning the gun barrel high overhead like a drum major's baton. Small-arms ammunition rocketed in all directions, skywards like an enormous fireworks display and towards the harbour buildings and wharf, which were peppered and sprayed from end to end.

Soldiers ran in all directions, some mown down where they stood in shocked horror, others making it through the crammed gates, now wrenched off their hinges and swinging wildly. From there they bolted for the town or threw themselves into ditches, wriggling for cover from the continuing onslaught.

In the midst of the wreckage, flames and destruction, the blazing ship, its back broken in three places, tilted on to its side, rolling and sinking, slipping under the tumbling waters of the glowing harbour. As it went, the flames that had engulfed it turned to steam, hissing and rending the metal, groaning and twisting it into gnarled, grotesque shapes, the eerie sounds still audible when it was far below the surface like the hideous threats of a wounded sea monster, sinking and sliding ever deeper, ever further out of reach.

Matt was the first one to peer over the top of the monsoon drain, standing up on tiptoe to see over the edge. On all sides of him, other faces, pale and gaunt, popped up like rabbits from their burrows after a bad storm as the SBS commandos surveyed their handiwork.

'Fuck a stoat,' the demolitions sergeant said. He turned to Lane. 'Is that Endex, boss?'

Lane hauled himself out of the deep drain. 'Not if the gooks get hold of us. After this lot I doubt they'd even read us our rights.'

He looked across at the far side of the harbour. 'Sarge, go and see how many boats we can salvage. And step on it!'

Matt helped Linda out of the drain and together they watched the patrol launch disappear below the water. 'Well, that takes care of the blockade. Now all we need's a boat.'

When the surviving marines had gathered and reformed into their fire teams under the NCOs, Lane and Matt led the way back through the harbour complex. Here and there individual Korean soldiers clung to their pieces of cover, but the shock of the explosions had knocked the fight out of them and they threw away their weapons the moment they saw the marines moving tactically towards them, jogging from bound to bound, each fire team covering the other forward before moving itself.

They were almost across the wharf when Linda pointed to one of the buildings. 'Look, it's Des!'

Pushing a bloodied man in front of him, Des staggered from the doorway. One fist tightly gripped the back of the man's collar, propelling him forward, while the other hand balanced a Kalashnikov, the muzzle firmly in the small of his prisoner's back.

'Where the hell have you been?' Matt called across. 'You were supposed to rig up the kit not sit out the battle indoors.'

Des glared at him and thrust his prisoner over. 'I thought you'd like to meet my new mate here. This is the fucker from Tolo, the guy who slit Josh Higgs.'

Matt stared at Hu Fat. 'Nice work, Des.'

'And he was behind the Lantau ambush, and the smuggling op. We've been having a nice little chat, haven't we?'

He shook his prisoner by the scruff of his neck. 'He got the drop on me but when the fuel tanks went up the stupid sod blinked and almost shat himself.'

'Bring him along. He's got a lot of explaining to do,' Linda said. 'He can start with the targeting instructions.'

'Save it till we're out of here,' Lane shouted back.

Dragging and shoving Hu Fat between them, they made their way down the steps and on to a floating jetty where the remaining Rigid Raiders had been collected.

'It's going to be a bit of a squeeze but it's either that or swim.'

Small explosions were still going off around the harbour complex and here and there sudden bursts of automatic fire erupted into the night as fleeing soldiers ran headlong into others who had been re-formed by their officers and were attempting to retake the harbour. Assuming the dark, fleeting shapes to be the SBS commandos, soldier fired on soldier, each clash developing into a fire-fight until either the true identities were discovered or the superior party had eliminated the other.

Lane crouched in the prow of the lead boat and signalled for his sergeant to cast off. 'Follow behind me in line,' he called to the others. 'I'll steer a way through the harbour mouth.'

The fire on the patrol launch had been extinguished by the sea water until only a filthy black smoke rose from the tip of the prow, which was all that remained visible, sticking vertically into the sky. But pieces of wreckage, some of them alight, were strewn across a wide area and as well as steering through them, Lane leaned over the prow looking down into the water for anything immediately below the surface that could hole the boats. With so few left they could not afford to lose a single one.

Only when the daisy-chain of Rigid Raiders was clear of the harbour mouth did they pull out into an extended-line formation, open the throttles and head for the open sea at full speed. They still had to make the rendezvous with the submarine and there was always the chance of a brush with another patrol vessel.

But huddled in one of the Rigid Raiders Matt and Linda looked back at the harbour, which was glowing with fires, a pall of black smoke crowning the night's work and, best of all, the ship nowhere to be seen. Beside them, Des kept a firm hold on Hu Fat. He had bound his wrists and ankles but maintained a grip on his collar just in case.

'Not a very pretty sight, is it?' Matt said.

Des looked at his watch. 'No. And the show's not even over yet.'

General Suchi stumbled over pieces of debris as he hammered at his ears in a vain attempt to stop the ringing. A soldier came up to him and said something.

'What?'

Again he saw the man's lips move but heard nothing.

'Shout, you arsehole!' he said, pointing wildly at the place where the ship had once been. 'I was next to the bastard when it went up!'

The soldier put his mouth next to the general's ear and shouted. 'There's a call for you from Headquarters.'

The general went pale. 'Which Headquarters?'

'Military Intelligence in Pyongyang.'

The general swallowed hard. 'I can't talk to them right now. I can hardly hear. Tell them I'll call them back, or ask them what they want.'

'They want to know what's going on,' the man shouted. 'They've heard reports of a sabotage attempt on the missile and they want assurance that everything's under control.'

On all sides buildings were ablaze, flames spouting from the shattered windows and lapping at the stacked goods inside. In the harbour there was an almost peaceful emptiness save for the lone shape of the patrol launch's prow protruding from the water like an accusatory finger. Exhausted, the general stumbled away through the ruins, past the ruptured entrance gates, and collapsed into the jeep that he had left a relatively short while before. But that had been in a different era. Then he had been the Garrison Commander and a man of substance. Now? He sank back into his seat and waved a hand vaguely towards the town indicating to his driver that he had had enough of the harbour. Now he would have to face a wrath that would make the saboteur commandos seem like guardian angels by comparison.

He stared blankly out of the window, somehow absurdly comforted that at least the battle was over and that there was nothing more that could go wrong. He watched the ambling lines of soldiers walking miserably home to their barracks, wondering why they turned their faces skywards, tuning in to sounds that were beyond the reach of his deaf ears. Unable to detect the first warning shriek of the Stealth fighter-bombers, the general never saw the sharp black angles of the aircraft homing in on the signals from Des's box of tricks, which was remotely directing them to their targets.

*   *   *

'Japan?'

The Prime Minister turned from the window overlooking the garden at Chequers and stared thunderstruck at Sir Anthony. 'Are you sure?'

Sir Anthony handed over his transcript of the targeting instructions recovered from the ship. 'It appears so. They never intended using the missile against South Korea at all, which explains why they had to acquire the longer-range SS-18 instead of a simple Scud or something that would have been easier to get hold of and would have done the job. When they failed to smuggle it in bit by bit via Hong Kong with the help of the Triads, they attempted to get their hands on the complete thing.'

'And they bloody nearly did!'

'Yes. Mind you, they didn't reckon on a good piece of intelligence work backed up by the best commando unit in the world.'

The Prime Minister pulled a face. 'And a particularly large dose of old-fashioned luck.'

Sir Anthony smiled and helped himself to more coffee from the silver tray, stirring the steaming liquid and enjoying the feel of the crisp morning sunlight pouring through the windows.

'And what about the missile?'

'Completely destroyed.'

'And the plutonium? Couldn't they recover it with divers and use it in one of their own missiles?'

'Impossible. It will have been blown into a thousand pieces which will be scattered throughout the harbour. The whole site of the wreck will be contaminated for centuries and any diver who goes near it will be fried. Even if they could recover some of it they'd never be able to get enough together to make up a complete warhead. Hopefully we've taken care of that particular SS-18 for good.'

'Until they get their hands on the next one.'

Sir Anthony frowned. 'They might try, but at least we now know what to look for. We've contacted Russian Intelligence and persuaded them that they really ought to tighten up their controls.'

'And the Chinese? They were the ones behind it, weren't they? What the devil were they up to?'

'That's the odd thing, Prime Minister. We simply don't know. None of our sources has picked up a thing. It seems the Chinese themselves don't know anything about it. One possibility is that it's a rogue operator.'

'That sounds very nasty.'

'It could be. Particularly as we haven't a clue who he is or why he did it.'

The Prime Minister sat down, leafing through the file, stopping when he came to the map of Japan. 'Why the hell would the North Koreans want to hit Japan? There'd be nothing in it for them except the most monumental retaliation from America and the West. It would have been an act of suicide. Apart from which they don't have any particular gripe against the Japanese.'

Sir Anthony finished his coffee and got up to leave. 'Well, anyway, we'll be continuing to work on it.'

'Using Linda Kirkdale, I trust?'

'Of course. Just as soon as she's returned from a spot of leave.'

When his car had turned on to the A41 and was hurtling back down the dual carriageway towards Tring, Sir Anthony closed his eyes and ran through the numerous questions that crowded his mind. If there was a rogue operator attempting to stir up trouble, how on earth could they find him before he did any more damage? The Prime Minister was right. This time they had been lucky. The problem was, he didn't even know where to start looking.

The drive out of Beijing had not been an enjoyable experience. Usually Yang Zulin was delighted to escape the urban sprawl and polluted air of the capital city, but this morning he was apprehensive about the approaching meeting. It had come as little more than a summons for him to attend the villa and he had to admit to himself that he didn't like the tone of it one little bit. It was the sort of curt message that used to be sent out in the old days of only a few weeks ago before the death of the all-powerful Deng Xiaoping. What had happened, Yang wondered, to encourage the new interim leadership to adopt so combative a tone with him? It was extremely out of character for the shady grey-suits who had been elected to exercise power until the struggles within the party were completed.

It was not that he was afraid. Despite the bungling by the North Koreans of his master-stroke, he did not regret his emergence into the open as the most powerful contender in the battle for succession. He had kept his powder dry all right! No one had known of his grandiose scheme or of the secret intelligence organization that he had set up behind Deng's back in the final months of the leader's life. If one plan had failed, Yang reasoned, at least they all knew that he was now a man to be reckoned with. His succession might not be guaranteed but with the new

THE HONG KONG GAMBIT

organization to back him he was unlikely to encounter
any opponents that could better him.

As soon as the car pulled up outside the villa, Yang
jumped out and marched up the steps, past the guards
and into the main hallway in readiness for whatever
awaited. The trick now, he knew, was to brazen it
out. Of course there would be accusations from the
faint-hearts. There were always obstructionists and
cowards in any great manoeuvre. But he had the
power to overcome them.

He was somewhat surprised to find the meeting
already in progress but with a smile of recognition to
some of the others around the long committee table,
he moved casually to his seat.

'Comrade Yang,' the Chairman began coldly.
'Thank you for attending so promptly. I am sorry
we were unable to give you more warning.'

Yang nodded politely. 'I am always at the disposal
of the Interim Governing Council.'

'I am glad to hear that.' The Chairman was an old
veteran of the Revolutionary days, a close friend of the
late Deng Xiaoping, but a man devoid of real power.
Yang was pleased to see him in the chair. He was
confident that, after an explanation of his plan, he
would be able to win the committee over to his side.

'We have heard of course of the recent happenings
in Korea and are disconcerted to also hear your name
being linked with them.'

Although he had not asked Yang a direct question,
the Chairman looked expectantly at Yang, inviting
him to speak. Yang pushed back his chair and stood
up. This is it, he thought. My moment has come. I
entered this room as a middle-ranking official of the

Security Bureau. I will leave it as the supreme head of the Party.

'Comrades. Many of you have watched with anxiety, as I, the changes taking place in our society. We all agree that we can never go back to the old ways, but economic growth has brought corruption and links with the West that get stronger every day. Much benefit has come from these links but we know that America and the capitalist West are using their businesses to infiltrate our society. None of us can really believe that all they want is trade.'

He paused and looked around the table, dwelling for a moment on each face but receiving only mute stares in return.

'We cannot believe that they will ever let us take an equal place in the international market as an equal member of the world community. No,' he stressed, holding up his finger for dramatic effect. 'All they want is to exploit us as they did with their missionaries and trading ports from the end of the last century until our victorious Communist victory in 1949 when we threw them all out. Well, I for one am not prepared to see that happen. I . . . we will stop them by seizing that central place in the world!'

He stood back and surveyed the scene, impressed with his own oratory.

The Chairman coughed politely. 'Yes, Comrade. Perhaps you will tell us exactly what you intended by this ploy.'

Yang leaned forward, both fists on the table. 'Expansion of our trade throughout the world has to proceed in easy stages. Where do we start? In Asia and the countries around the Pacific rim. But at every turn we encounter rivalry and opposition from the Japanese. They have been our bitterest enemies from the beginning. Only sixty years ago they virtually destroyed our country and enslaved our people. Of course I accept that a direct attack on Japan would invite disaster for China, so I devised a plan whereby the attack would be launched by proxy.'

He strode to the window and looked out, letting the audience absorb his words before continuing.

Turning again to the table, he went on. 'The SS-18 missile I arranged to be smuggled out of Russia and sent via Hong Kong was a MIRV containing ten independently targeted warheads. The North Koreans were told that it was for the destruction of the military capacity of the American-backed southern regime. Of course they were delighted to accept it, especially as I promised full Chinese support. However, I ensured that the missile targeting system would be programmed by my own Chinese experts. Instead of directing it towards South Korea, they would programme it to strike Japan. The American Patriot anti-missile defence batteries that were rushed in to protect Seoul would have been useless. The missile would have gone nowhere near them. Instead it would have crossed the Sea of Japan and as it began its descent it would have MIRVed. Each of the ten warheads would have peeled away from the mother to strike at all the main cities and industrial centres.'

He looked around, pleased at last to see the desired response on the shocked faces of the assembled.

'At one stroke the industrial capacity of Japan would have been destroyed. We would of course have denied any connection with the attack and North Korea would have faced the repercussions alone. World markets would have collapsed as the ruined Japanese withdrew their capital investments from international banks and institutions to rebuild their country. We would have been able to step unopposed into the economic vacuum.'

Yang stood erect, arms folded across his chest, awaiting the Chairman's reply. To his surprise the voice that spoke to him came not from the Chairman but from a diminutive figure entering the room from behind the speaker.

'Thank you for your explanation, Comrade Yang. It has been most enlightening.'

Yang felt his blood run cold. The hair on the back of his neck bristled and a shudder trembled the length of his spine.

'Your plan was ingenious. Quite insane of course, but certainly imaginative. I am only grateful that British commandos were able to halt your scheme before you brought ruin upon us all, destroying everything we have laboured so long to build.'

Yang turned and felt his knees give way. He sank back into his chair just as everyone else around the table stood in respect at the entry to the committee room of Comrade Deng Xiaoping.

Yang stammered, his mouth suddenly as dry as flint. He tried again. 'But . . . but Comrade Deng! You . . .'

Deng smiled. 'Is this the first time you've seen a ghost? Oh dear. I am sorry. Still, where you're going you'll be seeing lots of ghosts.'

Four armed guards moved swiftly round the sides of the table to flank Yang.

'You should have known better than to play games with an old card-player.'

Two attendants supporting Deng by both elbows eased him gently into an armchair. 'We had wind of your scheme but were unable to know exactly what you intended. I knew that you wouldn't make your move until I was dead so I had to hasten nature on its way a little.' He grinned, delighted with his trickery.

'You youngsters think you are the only ones who understand the world. In truth you understand nothing. On the Long March I saw and experienced things you cannot even guess at. We endured hardships that would make you weep just to listen to. Did you think I would let a power-hungry fool like you destroy all we have built?'

He leaned back, tired by the effort and the emotion.

'You see, Comrade Yang. The Hong Kong gambit was mine, not yours. The last great gambit of an old card-player.' With an immense effort he pushed himself forward and held out a small clenched fist, which he waved at Yang.

'And I won!'

The guards pulled Yang Zulin to his feet. He was too shocked even to muster a reply. When he had gone and the members of the committee had been dismissed, the Chairman walked over and looked down at his leader.

Deng sat back to catch his breath. 'You know what to do, old friend?'

'Yes, Comrade Deng. Everyone has been sworn to secrecy. As far as the outside world is concerned you are dead.' He smiled warmly and put a hand on Deng's shoulder. 'You can observe the succession without anyone knowing.'

'The succession?' Deng chuckled. 'I'm going to be too busy improving my game of bridge.'

'So when are you leaving?' Fred Turner asked.

'Tomorrow night, worst luck. Isn't it always the way? Come back from saving the world only to find a signal waiting telling me I'm wanted to run the next selection for another sodding intake.'

Des leaned round in his chair and called for Mimi to bring a couple of San Migs.

'Here, what about me, Sarge?' Corporal Leach said.

'Sorry, lad.' Des turned and called again. 'And a Seven-Up for the nipper.'

He patted Harry warmly on the arm. 'Better start drying out if you intend going for selection. And don't expect any favours from me.'

'Thanks, Sarge. You're a real fucking pal.'

When the beers arrived Mimi slapped them down in front of the three men.

'On the tab?' Des asked. Mimi was just about to give him a mouthful when Fred reached across and dropped a hundred-dollar note on the tray. 'This one's on me.'

'Well, thanks!' Des raised his glass. 'Let's drink to the Royal Hong Kong Police. God bless 'em.'

'And all who sail in 'em,' Harry added with a wink. 'Mustn't forget MARPOL.'

'Are you out on patrol again tonight?' Fred asked.

'Same as ever. Bumming round Tolo, Starling Inlet, Mirs Bay. See if I can pick up any smugglers. I just hope to Christ I don't find any more sodding nukes. Scared the life out of me, that did.'

Des gave Fred a nudge. 'Hey, talking of Tolo, what's happened to Hu Fat?'

'Hu? Bit of a shame really. He was singing like a canary, dropping his old mates in it, left, right and centre. Before they got to him, that is.'

'How do you mean?'

'The Triads don't much like being set up. They lost too many soldiers in the Castle Peak fiasco and Hu Fat took the blame. A couple of their men on the inside slit his throat while he was in the exercise yard.'

Des snorted. 'Killing's too good for him.'

'Yeah, but you should have seen what they did to him before he died.' Fred shook his head and shivered. 'Nasty. Very nasty.'

He took a sip of his beer. 'So. How are you going to spend your last few hours in the Colony?'

'I've got a little visit to pay to Chungking Mansions.'

'Oh? I'm not sure I like the sound of that.'

'Yes. Ted Wilcox is complaining that the Rolex I bought him's not working. So we're going to see the salesman with some of the lads.'

Fred smiled. 'I haven't heard that. Just don't take any hardware with you, that's all I ask. I don't want a shoot-out in the middle of Nathan Road. The press had a field day over the so-called drugs gunfight at Castle Peak. They still don't believe my version of events. If you start something now they'll be convinced the government's about to fall or something.'

'Don't worry,' Des confided. 'Nothing more than a

SPAS and a couple of grenades.' He crossed his heart. 'I promise.'

Black clouds were scudding across the sky, seeming to brush the tops of the soft hills, their reflections drifting on the grey waters of Llyn Brianne.

'We'd better get back to the cottage,' Matt said, panting hard from the run.

Beside him, Linda set an easy pace. 'You're not out of condition, are you? Dearie me. Whatever will the SBS think when you return?'

'I don't know and right now I don't care.' He looked up at the clouds, feeling the first spots of rain on his face.

'You certainly chose a wild spot.'

'We chose it, remember?'

'Sorry. Of course we did. Still, it's great for getting away from everything.'

As they turned for the cottage and set off up the hillside, Matt tried to keep level with Linda but by the time they reached the gate at the end of the cottage lane he had fallen a good fifty metres behind. He staggered to a halt to find her leaning on the gate and laughing.

'You're going to have to get some serious practice in over the next two weeks,' she said.

'Sod that. This is supposed to be a rest.'

They went inside just as the storm broke and within minutes a savage wind was rattling at the roof tiles as rain lashed into the window panes. They wrapped themselves in warm, dry track suits and Matt put a log on the fire, stirring the embers until bright-orange flames reared up to lap at the wood with thirsty tongues. Linda busied herself in the kitchen and returned after a while with a tray laden with a large, steaming teapot, cups, plates and a cake from which she cut two thick slices.

Cradling his mug in his hands, Matt drew his knees up to his chest and stared into the mounting flames as the log began to crackle and spit.

'Two whole weeks,' he said, closing his eyes and relishing the thought. 'Two whole weeks.'

Linda smiled. 'Yes. It's almost too good to be true, isn't it?'

She looked up from her mug as a belt of rain flung itself against the window. 'Oh shit.'

'What?'

She nodded towards the small flashing green light on the answerphone. 'Someone left a message while we were out.'

'Leave it.'

Linda got up. Matt bit his tongue, forcing himself to remain silent. She pressed the button and a moment later the voice of Sir Anthony Briggs was chatting merrily from the speaker.

'Linda! Hello, dear. Listen, I know I'm a bastard of an employer, and you're on leave, and you deserve to be left alone, and . . . well, the thing is, we've received this message from our man in the Gulf. It seems that Iraq's been making overtures to the Russians about getting their hands on . . .'

Matt looked up in surprise when the voice suddenly went dead. Linda stood smiling, her finger on the Stop button.

'I think I've had quite enough of Sir Anthony for a while.'

She came across and sat down beside Matt, moving closer to him as he reached out and drew her into the growing circle of warmth in front of the blazing fire.

'In fact, I think I've had enough of him for a very long while. Tell me, is Devon still as I remember it?'

'What do you mean?' Matt asked, scarcely able to believe his ears.

'Well, what are the married quarters like in the SBS?'

OTHER TITLES IN SERIES FROM 22 BOOKS

Available now at newsagents and booksellers
or use the order form provided

continued overleaf . . .

All at £4.99 net

All 22 Books are available at your bookshop, or can be ordered from:

22 Books
Mail Order Department
Little, Brown and Company
Brettenham House
Lancaster Place
London WC2E 7EN

Please enclose a cheque or postal order made payable to Little, Brown and Company (UK) for the amount due, allowing for postage and packing.

UK, BFPO & EIRE CUSTOMERS: Please allow 75p per item, to a maximum of £7.50.
OVERSEAS CUSTOMERS: Please allow £1 per item.

While every effort is made to keep prices low, it is sometimes necessary to increase cover prices at short notice. 22 Books reserves the right to show new retail prices on covers which may differ from those previously advertised in the books or elsewhere.

NAME ....

ADDRESS ....

....

....

I enclose my remittance for £...............................